Praise for the Callie Parrish Mysteries

"... all 'I's' dotted and 'T's' crossed, Rizer proves her mettle by presenting us with such a gripping story of personal loss, as a loved one fades slowly away, yet she never lets this overpower or derail the mystery or humor. A difficult feat, but one she handles with a hand so deft that I sometimes found myself laughing through misty eyes."
—Dixon Hill, *Sleuthsayer* Mystery Author

"What a wonderfully realized set of characters in an authentic and welcoming sense of place. Callie is wonderful! It's such fun following her and very moving as well."
—David Dean, Author of *The Thirteenth Child.*

"Callie Parrish is a hoot! I laughed so hard I dropped my book in the bathtub."
—Gwen Hunter, Author of the Rhea Lynch, M.D. Suspense Mysteries, the Delande Saga, and more.

"Fran Rizer's Callie Parrish and St. Mary, S.C., are as Southern as fried chicken and sweet tea—and just as delightful."
—Walter Edgar, *Walter Edgar's Journal,* SCETV Radio.

"A lively sleuth who manages to make funeral homes funny."
—Maggie Sefton, Author of the Molly Mallone Suspense Mysteries and the Kelly Flinn Knitting Mystery Series.

The Callie Parrish Mysteries by Fran Rizer

A Tisket, a Tasket, a **Fancy Stolen Casket**

Hey Diddle, Diddle, the **Corpse and the Fiddle**

Rub-a-Dub, Dub, There's a **Dead Man in the Tub**
(published as **Casket Case**)

Twinkle, Twinkle, Little Star, **There's a Body in the Car**

Mother Hubbard Has **A Corpse in the Cupboard**

A Corpse Under The Christmas Tree

★
ON
THE
FIRST
DAY OF
CHRISTMAS MY
TRUE LOVE GAVE
TO
ME

A CORPSE UNDER THE CHRISTMAS TREE

A Callie Parrish Mystery

A Corpse Under The Christmas Tree
ISBN 978-1-62268-050-4

First Print Edition December 2013

Library of Congress Control Number: 2013953499

Also available in e-book form: ISBN 978-1-62268-051-1

Cover design by: David Smoak Graphic Design

10 9 8 7 6 5 4 3 2 1

Dedicated to my grandson
Nathaniel Aeden Rizer
and my sons
Nathan Randolph Rizer
and
Adam Everett Rizer
in appreciation for their
ideas, inspiration, and encouragement

On the First Day of Christmas My True Love Gave to Me A Corpse Under the Christmas Tree

"You don't have to be Santa to come on Christmas Eve."

My brother Mike sang those words as Daddy and my brothers played the melody to an old Ernest Tubb country song, "You Don't Have to Be a Baby to Cry." Daddy had been singing it when Mike butted in with, "Keep pickin' but let me sing. I've got a Christmas version of that tune."

I confess I whapped Mike across his bottom with *Mortuary Cosmetology News,* the magazine I'd been reading while Daddy played my banjo. Hardly an adult action, though I'd been trying really hard to behave like a true Southern lady recently, even with my brothers. The music stopped.

"Why'd you do that?" Mike whined and rubbed his behind. "I was referring to relatives visiting on Christmas Eve."

"Oh, no, you weren't. You were making up one of those smutty little songs you love to sing. It's Christmas night. I've had a wonderful day without anyone being a total redneck, and now you sing something like that! Why do you always have to do something trashy when we get together?" I began gathering up the presents my family gave to Jane and me.

"What are we doing?" Jane asked. She's blind and couldn't see me.

"Going home. I've had enough family for one day." I stuffed my last package into a big Santa Claus gift bag.

"Calamine, will you leave your banjo here for me to play?" Daddy asked.

"Of course," I agreed. After all, the valuable pristine prewar Gibson had been a birthday surprise from him.

"Or I can make these boys behave if you want to stay," he offered while he tuned the banjo again. "Michael was out of line to sing that in front of you."

The Boys are all older than I am, and those capital letters aren't a typo. I refer to my brothers collectively as The Boys because I don't think there's any hope they'll ever grow up.

I'm thirty-three years old, been married and divorced one time each, and Daddy still thinks I'm his little girl. He forbids my brothers to tell risqué jokes in front of me and won't let me drink beer in his presence either. He's the only person in the world who calls me by my given name—Calamine. Everyone else calls me "Callie" or sometimes "Calaparash" all smushed together into one word the way folks here on the coast of South Carolina do double names.

"Jane and I need to head out anyway."

I claim I never take nor give guilt trips, but I realized my reaction to Mike's song had been kind of strong. "I'm probably extra touchy because I'm tired. This has been one of the best Christmas Days ever—even if my family does act a little redneck at times."

"We aren't as bad as 'Merry Christmas from the Family' by Robert Earl Keen." My brother Bill has been argumentative as long as I can remember. He picked up the magazine I'd dropped when I swatted Mike. "And we might be redneck, but we aren't always stuck in a mystery book or a magazine about dead people. This stuff is gross to the rest of us." His wife Molly headed to the kitchen, which fits her routine of leaving the room whenever any of my brothers disagree with anyone.

"I'll have you know that's a professional magazine. I could lose my job if I don't keep up with current trends." I glared at him. "I'd rather be expert at what I do than act like one of you."

"Who's got lights all over the outside of her building as well as a monster decorated tree on the front porch? That's a little redneck," Frankie broke in. He'd been relatively quiet since Jane and I arrived that morning. Today was the first time he'd seen Jane since she broke off their engagement.

"Don't you dare insult that tree!" I scolded him. "It's beautiful, and it didn't look half as big when I found it in the woods. One of you could have told me it wasn't going to fit through my front door."

"You wouldn't have believed us if we'd told you," Mike snapped. Daddy ignored all of us and began picking out a tune on the banjo.

I didn't bother to argue, just went to the kitchen, told Molly good night, and grabbed a bottled Diet Coke for me and a can of Dr Pepper for Jane from the refrigerator. Daddy had a dish of shelled peanuts on the table, so I took a handful of those and dropped them into my drink bottle.

As Jane and I left Daddy's house, I heard Mike singing "Grandma Got Run Over by a Reindeer."

Driving my vintage 1966 Mustang toward home, I glanced over at Jane. She had her waist-length red hair tied in a ponytail she'd draped across her left shoulder and over her dark green sweater. Her more than ample bosom made the embroidered Santa Claus into an even chubbier jolly old elf than usual.

"Are you working tonight?" I asked her.

"Not until late. Why?"

"Big Boy's still at the vet's, and I missed him something awful last night. I thought we might visit for a while."

"You and that dog! When can you pick him up from the vet?"

"Tomorrow."

"Well," Jane acquiesced, "come on in, but you can't stay late. Tonight will be a good night for Roxanne. Holidays always are."

Jane claims Roxanne is her stage name. She also refers to her job as being a fantasy actress. To call a spade a flipping shovel, Jane's a telephone sex operator. She pays her own bills and doesn't have to rely on anyone for transportation to and from work. She just answers the second landline, which is designated as Roxanne's, in her apartment and assumes a low, sexy voice.

"Did you take all those cookies you made to Daddy's?" I asked.

"No, I kept some. I don't know how you can still be hungry after that feast your family called Christmas dinner, but you can have all the cookies you want." She laughed. "So long as you don't put them in your drink."

I drove and drank my Coke while Jane sang, "Jingle Bell Rock." Suddenly she quit singing.

"You've got peanuts in your Coke again, haven't you?" she asked. I don't know how she knew that, but she did. I didn't think I was smacking, and even if I was, she shouldn't have heard me over her loud singing. "Don't you remember almost choking on a peanut in your drink that time? I think you should make a New Year's resolution to give it up."

"I've been putting peanuts in Cokes all my life and I only choked once."

"Once is enough. If you'd died that night, I would have been left with a dead body until 911 came."

Jane has a morbid fear of anything deceased. I work in a mortuary, and death is not so traumatic to me. "I gave up my bad habits," she continued. "When will you give up yours?"

"I don't consider liking peanuts in Coke a bad habit," I protested. "You gave up breaking the law when you quit shop-lifting and scamming stores out of free merchandise, but how can you compare that to something innocent like putting peanuts in Coke?"

"How many times have I told you that putting those peanuts in your drink isn't just a Southern custom like you claim. It's redneck—pure tee redneck. I swear, they ought to call you Callie Boo Boo. I've given up my bad habits. You need to give up a few of yours." She laughed. "My bad habits. Your bad habits. Who's to say which is worse? Shoplifting didn't almost kill me. Maybe we should both make some resolutions. Give up our bad habits, eat better, and get healthier this year."

Jane and I have been friends since ninth grade, and like all BFFs, sometimes we disagree, but I didn't feel like fussing with her right then. Besides, how can anyone argue against getting healthy?

"It's Christmas. We've had a wonderful day, and I refuse to discuss stealing versus eating peanuts with you." I giggled. Okay, I know that sounds like a thirteen-year-old, but I still giggle sometimes. We rode in silence until we were almost home.

"Callie," Jane said. "Tell me when you can see our tree, okay?"

Three of my five brothers had cut down a tree I picked out in the woods near Daddy's house and brought it to my apartment for me. It wouldn't fit into my place, so they stood it on the wide porch that stretches across both front doors of the duplex where Jane and I live beside each other. We'd put so many lights and decorations on it that hardly any green showed through.

"I see it," I said when I turned onto Oak Street. "The timer worked. The lights are on, and it's beautiful!"

Jane's voice became pensive. "You know, Callie, I've never felt sorry for myself for not being sighted, but right now I wish I could see our tree."

"I do, too, but you 'see' more with your ears and heart and brain than most sighted people do with their eyes." I opened my mouth to begin describing the tree to her for what felt like the hundredth time but closed it again when Jane began belting "Rocking Around the Christmas Tree" at a deafening volume.

I pulled into my side of our circular drive, parked, and gathered up several large gift bags of presents. No need to guide Jane to the steps and into her apartment. She had her mobility cane and knew the way.

Glancing up at the porch, I saw a red and white bundle pushed up beside the tree.

"Hey, Jane," I shouted, loud enough to be heard over her singing. "Someone left us a big present on the porch."

I took the gifts into Jane's apartment, planning to separate mine from hers before I went next door to my place. I piled everything on her couch and then went back out to get the package. Wondering if it was for me or Jane or for us together, I reached down to lift it and realized the red and white thing appeared to be a mannequin dressed in a Santa Claus suit.

"Bad news, Jane," I began, but she interrupted from her open doorway.

"Do *not* tell me you see a body somewhere. I am sick and tired of you finding dead people every time we're having a good time. Today was too perfect for me to deal with that again." She trembled. "I don't even want to think about it." She headed toward the kitchen, calling, "I'm going to make fresh coffee, or would you rather have hot chocolate?"

"Coffee," I called and turned my attention to the bundle under our tree. "The package doesn't appear to be a present for us," I called back to her. "I think it's a Santa Claus dummy, probably meant to be dropped off down the street for that man who runs the costume shop in town."

I nudged the red and white cloth with my toe. It didn't feel right. I leaned over and pulled the fake white beard away from the face. I work at Middleton's Mortuary as a cosmetician/girl Friday. I know dead when I see it. The "present" on our front porch was a real person—a man with a very effeminate face or a woman with no makeup—a lifeless human in rigor mortis with a bluish purple complexion which might be bruises or livor mortis where the body had lain face-down after death.

"Change that coffee to hot chocolate," I told Jane and closed the door to her apartment. Standing on the porch, I shivered as I pulled my cell phone from my bra. I keep it there because I've found it's the only way I could stop losing it.

"911. What's your emergency?" the dispatcher asked.

"There's a body on my front porch," I answered.

"What kind of body?"

"A human corpse."

"Is this Callie Parrish?"

"Yes, it is." *Dalmation!* I silently said my favorite kindergarten cuss word at the thought that a report of finding someone deceased made the sheriff's department think of me.

If I'd been on a landline, the dispatch equipment would have shown my name and address, but calling from my cell meant I had to give him all that info. When I'd finished, he said, "I have someone on the way. I'd like for you to stay on the line until authorities reach you."

"Listen, I'm on the front porch. I'm cold, and my friend Jane is in her apartment wondering what's going on," I complained.

"Can't I hang up and wait inside? Tell Sheriff Harmon to knock on Jane's door when he gets here."

"You're on a cell phone. Take it into your friend's place."

"She'll freak out if she hears me and knows there's a body on the porch. Just tell the sheriff to knock on Jane's door."

"It won't be Sheriff Harmon. He's off duty, and if there's a body on your friend's porch, how long do you think you can keep it a secret from her?"

"This is a murder. Don't you think you'd better call him?" I ignored the dispatcher's question.

"How do you know it's murder? Is there a knife or gun wound?"

"Not that I know of, but why would there be a corpse on my porch if it's not a murder?"

"Come to think of it, Callie, if you found a body on your porch, it probably will turn out to be homicide. It's policy for me to keep you on the phone. Can't you just wait there with this line open?"

I was prepared to argue my case, but the discussion ended abruptly when the wailing of a siren announced a patrol car that wheeled into my drive. I disconnected the phone, and James Brown burst out singing "I Feel Good" immediately. I'd been planning to change my ringtone for weeks.

In answer to my "hello," my brother Mike said, "Pa wants me to let you know John and his family are headed up here from Georgia. They should arrive in a couple of hours. Pa wants you and Jane to come for supper tomorrow night while they're here."

"I thought they were spending the holidays with Miriam's family this year."

"They were there when John got a call from Miss Lettie, Jeff Morgan's mom. Jeff's been killed in a car wreck, and she's having him brought back to St. Mary for the services."

"Good grief!" No, not "good" grief. Horrible news and grief are seldom good in any way. And on Christmas! Working at Middleton's Mortuary, I know that people die every day of the year, but this struck home.

Jeff Morgan, a businessman in Charlotte, North Carolina, had been a close childhood friend of my oldest brother John. The two of them and Sheriff Wayne Harmon had been like the Three Musketeers—the ones in the story, not the candy bar. Those three weren't sweet. They were usually in trouble through high school, but Wayne had become an honorable law man and John a financially successful family man in Atlanta, Georgia.

"I'll plan to be there for supper," I told Mike. "Gotta go now."

Since I know a lot of Sheriff Harmon's deputies, I was surprised when the tall, lean man who stepped out of the cruiser was a stranger to me. He was handsome in a striking, but stern, way with chiseled features, and blue eyes. I couldn't see his hair color because he was in a Sheriff's Department uniform, including the hat.

"Hello, are you Callie Parrish?" he asked.

"Yes, who are you?"

"I'm Detective Dean Robinson, Homicide, Jade County Sheriff's Department." He walked up the steps and looked down at the red and white bundle. "Is this what you called about?"

"Yes, he's dead."

Robinson pushed the body's fake beard over and checked the carotid artery. "I'd like for you to move off the porch so you don't continue to contaminate the scene." He gestured toward the steps.

"I need to go inside. I'm cold, and my friend is probably . . ."

No need to continue. At that moment, Jane opened the door and asked, "What's going on?"

"One of Harmon's detectives is here," I answered. "I'm coming inside with you."

"Unless there's a back door, she needs to come outside," the detective said. "I'll be putting crime scene tape around this porch."

"Crime scene tape?" Jane screeched, totally losing it like she always does when there's a corpse involved.

"She has a back door," I said and stepped toward Jane.

"I don't want either of you in there anyway. Both of you come outside. We'll need to check the inside of those apartments to be sure that's not the place of death." He paused. "And to find out if this person was here on a B & E."

"B & E?" Jane questioned.

"Breaking and entering," I explained. I read so many mysteries that I know what most of the terms mean. *Dalmation! A hundred and one dalmations and shih tzu!* I'd realized that Jane and I would be sleeping somewhere else that night—somewhere away from our apartments—because this man would have forensics techs go over the entire building and then probably ban us from our own homes with that yellow tape.

Courteous but firm, Detective Robinson walked us to his car, opened the rear door and said, "Sit here until I'm ready to take your statements."

"We'd rather sit in the Mustang," I said.

"No, get in the cruiser." His authoritative tone left no room for discussion.

We sat in the back while he sat up front and called for CSI and the coroner. He got out of the car and closed the door.

"What's he doing now?" Jane asked.

"He's putting crime scene tape all around the front of our porch."

"Is it a dead man or woman this time?"

"I didn't look close enough to tell. The body's wearing a white wig, false beard, and Santa Claus suit. No makeup, but the face is kind of feminine-looking."

"I hate this, Callie. I just hate it."

"I know you do. I'm not exactly fond of finding decedents away from work either."

"Won't they let us back in if they see that no one has been inside while we were gone?"

Then it hit me. I hadn't opened my door before I found the dead Santa Claus. Could the Santa have come to our place to rob us and died on the porch after trashing my apartment? The thought of cops searching my home wasn't pleasant even if there had been no invasion, and I hate cleaning up black fingerprint dust.

What's the likelihood Santa was at our place to steal from me or Jane? Not much, I answered myself. *Neither Jane nor I have any real valuables—not much real jewelry or silver or anything like that. Even our electronics aren't the current high-dollar kind. The most expensive thing I own is my Gibson banjo. Thank heaven it's at Daddy's.*

"What cha thinking about, Callie?" Jane asked.

"Just wishing Wayne was here. I'd be a lot more comfortable with him than this new guy."

Sometimes hopes do come true, because just then Sheriff Wayne Harmon arrived, hopped out of his car, and went up to Robinson. I watched Wayne nod a few times before he came over, opened the back door of the cruiser, and slid in on the seat beside me.

"Merry Christmas," the sheriff said.

"Yeah, a real good end to the day," Jane answered. "Callie here found another body."

"I know. I assume you met my new detective, Dean Robinson. He'll be heading up homicide investigations, including this one, but you girls know you can call me any time."

Girls! Wayne thinks of me as a child just like my daddy does.

"How long do we have to sit here?" I asked.

"We'll need to get statements, and I'll want you to look inside both apartments to see if there are signs you've been burgled."

"I guess then you'll expect us to go to Daddy's to spend the night, but John and his family are on the way here. It'll be awfully crowded if the four of them are there along with Daddy, Mike, and Frankie." I paused and then asked, "Did you know Jeff Morgan was killed in a car accident?"

"Yes, I was over at his mom's home when I heard about this. Miss Lettie is completely shattered. You know Jeff was her only child and his daddy died in Vietnam right before he was born. She went all to pieces when Jeff left St. Mary, moved to Rock Hill, and went to work right over the state line in Charlotte. You can imagine what she's like right now. Jeff's body will be brought from Rock Hill to Middleton's in the morning. When Otis or Odell picks up Santa Claus off the porch to take it to Charleston for the autopsy, I'm going to tell them I think it would be a good idea if you're there tomorrow when Miss Lettie makes the plans for Jeff's funeral."

"You know I don't usually sit in on planning sessions unless there's a question about clothes or hair."

The sheriff smiled at me. "I know that, but an elderly lady like Miss Lettie would probably appreciate having a female with her."

"So, knowing Daddy's house will be full, how long will you keep us locked out of our homes? I've been in Jane's apartment, and there didn't seem to be anything out of place."

"How long will depend on whether there's any evidence inside." He smiled. "Callie, since you found the victim, did you recognize him?"

"I moved the beard, and I didn't recognize the face, but I couldn't tell if it's a man or woman. Skin's discolored and the features are feminine if it's male, a little coarse if it's female."

"That's interesting. I just assumed it was a man. I guess because of the Santa Claus suit. Hadn't thought of Santa being a woman, but we'll know when the coroner gets here."

Jane shivered, and I asked, "Could Robinson turn the heater on in here? It's cold."

Wayne checked out my knitted red dress from shoulder to right above my knees where it ended. "That red looks pretty on you, especially now at Christmas, but you girls should wear coats when you go out in December." I didn't say anything about his calling us girls again, but I didn't like it. Instead, I tried to explain why neither Jane nor I had worn a coat.

"We went straight to Daddy's, and then right home. We've got heat at his house, our apartments, and in the car."

"Think about it, Callie. Your car is a 1966. Yes, it's a classic, and in great shape, but it could break down, and you two girls would be outside walking."

"Why do you call us girls?" He'd aggravated me. "We're both over thirty."

The sheriff laughed. "What do you want me to call you? Ladies? You don't always act like a lady."

"How about women?"

"How about I tell Robinson to turn on this car and give you women some heat? I'll send one of my deputies for coffee for everyone."

"There's a tin of homemade Christmas cookies inside my place," Jane offered.

"Did you or Callie make them?" Wayne asked and winked at Jane, though she couldn't see it.

"Jane did," I said. Everyone knows that even though Jane

can't see, she's a far better cook than I am.

Unfortunately, the activities of the next couple hours were old hat to me. I say "unfortunately" because this was not the first time I've discovered a corpse. Jane and I were more comfortable since Robinson had started the heater and another deputy brought us coffee and doughnuts. Jane entertained herself singing every Christmas song I've ever heard, some of them multiple times. That wasn't too bad because she does have a nice voice. I amused myself watching the law enforcement officials work the scene—photographs of the Santa as well as every inch of the porch from all angles. They also walked a grid in the yard, apparently looking for footprints. I doubted they found any because our yard is covered with grass that turned brown after the first frost.

I couldn't see as well when the coroner arrived because too many deputies blocked my view, so I was getting not just tired and sleepy, but also bored. I know that sounds bad, but I've been through this far too many times both as a part of my job and as an unwilling finder of dead people.

When the sheriff returned to the car, he said, "Jane, give Callie your back door key. You stay here while Callie and I check out your apartment." He coughed and I thought, *Maybe the sheriff needs a heavier coat himself.*

"Callie, come with me," he added. "I'm surprised you haven't been throwing a fit about getting in your place to take your dog out."

"Big Boy's not home. I finally took him to the vet to be neutered, and she found a small tumor in his abdomen. He had surgery day before yesterday, and I can bring him home tomorrow." I felt silly when a tear formed in my eye. "You have no idea how much I miss him."

I followed Wayne to the rear of Jane's side of the building. He checked her door before we went in, and there was no indication of illegal entry. Jane might have been a neat freak regardless, but because of her blindness, she's very particular about everything always being in the correct place. Her ceramic Christmas tree stood in the exact center of her round dining table. Jane's very proud of that tree. It was one of the smaller ones, a little less than a foot tall, but she'd painted and glazed it herself when we went through a crafts period several years back. Not too many visually handicapped people do ceramics, but Jane's always been amazing, and that tree is quite an accomplishment. I'd helped her with other Christmas decorations—red and green place mats on the table and live poinsettias in each room, but I'd never touched that tree. She always handled it herself. Wayne checked every room and closet. No sign of anything disturbed. On the way out, he picked up the Christmas tin of cookies.

A totally different picture next door. I'm not the best housekeeper under any circumstances. There are too many other things I love to do, like read a good book or change my hair color or try out a new makeup, whether for my face or for my job cosmetizing at the mortuary. I'd gotten up early that morning, but I hadn't finished wrapping the gifts for my family, so I'd needed to do that. Then I drank several cups of coffee and ate a MoonPie while reading the latest copy of *Mortuary Cosmetology News*. I hadn't finished with it by the time to go, so I'd taken it with me. I'd had to rush to be ready on time.

I watched Wayne stare at my dirty coffee cup along with dishes from the previous night still on my kitchen table though he didn't say anything. When the apartment was remodeled after a previous misfortune, I'd made a guest room out of the second bedroom, but it had rapidly filled up again with books and things that I didn't want to throw away. My bedroom wasn't as cluttered, but the bed was unmade and my nightgown lay crumpled on the floor.

"I can't tell," Wayne said. "It appears trashed, but then your place usually looks like this." Wayne Harmon was my older brother John's best friend when I was a kid, so we're comfortable with each other. I didn't take offense at what he said because it was true, although I would have said "cluttered" instead of "trashed."

After looking in the places where I hide the little bit of jewelry I own, which consists of some earrings I was able to trade my wedding rings for after my divorce, I found nothing disturbed. I assured the sheriff, "Nobody's been in here since I left this morning."

"Good. I'll tell Detective Robinson that you and Jane can go in and out your back doors and have use of your apartments. It appears the corpse was dumped on your porch."

"Or murdered on it," I commented.

"Jed Amick thinks the body has been moved since death. That would make your porch a secondary crime scene, but we won't know until the complete medical examination in Charleston." Wayne laughed. "My new homicide man's already told Jed that since it's so obvious that Santa's beyond rescue, the body should be transported with all clothing in place so the pathologist can remove it layer by layer while looking for evidence. Apparently he thought Jed had planned to disrobe Santa, but Jed's okayed us to call Otis and Odell to pick it up."

Amick is our tall, lanky Ichabod Crane of a coroner, which in Jade County is an elected official who isn't required to have a medical degree. Exams in unexplained or illegal deaths are performed at the medical university about an hour and a half drive away in Charleston, and Middleton's Mortuary where I work has the contract to transport individuals to and from Charleston. One of my bosses, Otis or Odell Middleton, would pick up Santa from my porch in a funeral coach (Funeraleze for hearse) when the forensics team and Amick okayed moving the body.

My mind locked in on that exam. Regardless of what Robinson may have assumed, when the person is indisputably deceased, Amick doesn't unclothe the body at the scene. He didn't need to be told that clothing would be removed layer by layer and photographed in case there are clues during the postmortem in Charleston. I'm not freaky, but I'd like to see Santa Claus unclothed. Did I really say that? What I mean is I wish that the corpse on my porch could have the Santa suit removed and see if anyone recognized who it was. At least, see if there was any identification on the body or even if it was a man or woman.

Robinson met Wayne and me on our way back to the cruiser where Jane still waited, and Wayne told him about letting Jane and me use our apartments.

The detective frowned but replied, "Yes, sir." He paused for a moment. "I understand that the body will be transported to

Charleston for the medical exam. I observed autopsies of my homicide cases in Florida, and I plan to attend this one."

"That's fine. Contact information for the medical center is at the office. They're usually pretty prompt for me on these things, so you'll want to check with them tonight or first thing tomorrow to see when it's scheduled. Ask Middleton to tell them we'll be sending someone when he delivers the body."

"Yes, sir." Detective Robinson walked back toward the front porch.

"When did you hire him?" I asked.

"Only a week ago. He's heading up the new homicide unit, and this will be his first case for us."

"Does St. Mary really need a department just for murder?"

"Gonna need two of them if you keep finding dead people." Wayne chuckled. Some folks might be offended that he was joking at a crime scene, but law enforcement is like mortuary science. Without a touch of dark humor at times, the job would be unbearable.

Jane and I were both happy when we'd finished giving our statements and were okayed to go into our apartments. I knew that the deputies would be busy interviewing neighbors, taking fingerprints, and investigating the scene as long as possible with their bright portable lights.

"Callie said you brought my tin of Christmas cookies out," Jane told Wayne. "You can have them."

Wayne's grin spread all across his face.

At our back doors, I asked Jane, "Do you want to come in and visit for a while?"

"No, and unless you're feeling needy, I'd rather you not come in with me. It's getting late, and Roxanne needs to work tonight."

Back inside my own place, I grabbed a box of MoonPies from the cabinet and a Diet Coke from the fridge. The apartment was lonely without Big Boy even though I could hear activity still on the front porch and I knew Jane was next door burning up her Roxanne phone line. I no longer have a landline in my home, so I pulled my cell phone from my bra, curled up on the couch, and took my first bite of MoonPie for the evening while dialing my friend in Orlando. Please note that I spell MoonPie without a space between Moon and Pie. I do that because that's the usual way the company in Chattanooga does it in their ads, on their website, and on most of their boxes.

I refer to Patel as my "friend," but I think he's turning into a "boyfriend." I met him a couple of months ago when the Jade County Fair was here. His real name is Jetendre Patel, but I call him Patel rather than his nickname of "J.T." When the fair left town, I was afraid I'd never hear from him again, but we talk almost every night by phone and plan to get together either here or in Florida after New Year's.

"Merry Christmas," his smooth voice answered. "I've wanted to call you since I awoke this morning, but I knew you were at your family's house, and I didn't want to bother you. Have you had a good day?"

"It was great but I had a bad evening. I found a body on my porch."

When I finished telling him about the dead Santa, he consoled, "What a horrible way to end Christmas day! I wish I was there to comfort you."

Now, in the South, "to comfort" has several meanings, including what some folks call "making love," "bonking," and "getting laid." My mind immediately went to my empty love life, and a little comfort that night would have been wonderful, but there were too many miles between us. No, I wasn't tempted at all to turn the conversation into phone sex. That's Roxanne, not me.

By the time Patel and I disconnected, I'd eaten almost a box of MoonPies. Better watch that or I'll be busting out of my jeans as well as the black dresses I'm required to wear at work.

Lying in bed, I could hear a murmur through the wall. Roxanne busy working while I tried to read myself to sleep to escape thoughts of why corpses follow me around.

ON THE SECOND DAY OF CHRISTMAS MY TRUE LOVE GAVE TO ME

TWO BROKEN HEARTS

Lots of magazine articles tell women to wear night bras to keep their ta tas from sagging in old age, but I sleep in only a T-shirt most of the time, so when James Brown woke me the next morning with, "I Feel Good," his voice didn't come from my bra, but from the bedside table where my phone was charging.

"Callie, did I wake you?" inquired Otis Middleton.

"Not really. I guess you heard there was a body on my porch yesterday."

"I was there to pick it up, but the hour was late and I assumed you were probably asleep. I took Santa to Charleston, and they'll be autopsying this morning." He paused. "How are you feeling?"

"I'm all right. I see dead people at work every day, but finding one on my porch *was* upsetting. Did you call just to check on me?" I pushed my shoulder up to hold the phone against my ear and stretched.

"I called because I know Odell gave you today off, but Jeff Morgan's being brought in this morning from Rock Hill where they did the autopsy, and I want you to get him ready before Miss Lettie comes to make arrangements at two. The sheriff also suggested I ask you to sit in on the planning session. Says Jeff's mama is out of her mind with grief. He thinks a female there will be helpful."

"What time do you want me?" I got out of the bed and headed to the bathroom, talking the whole time.

"I'll call you when I finish and we're ready for makeup and dressing. Keep your cell phone charged and on you." This was the only fault my bosses had complained about in the past. I used to have a hard time remembering to charge my phone and I lost it all the time, but my new routine of charging it overnight while it was by my bedside and carrying it in my bra was working out well.

"Okay, do you know any more about how Jeff died?" I gazed at myself in the bathroom mirror. I looked tired.

"He was in a car wreck four days ago. Of course, we won't know for sure until the autopsy report is completed, but when I talked to the medical examiner, he said not all the toxicology reports are back, but Jeff appeared to have a high blood alcohol content in his body. Said he could smell it. Thankfully, Jeff hit a tree instead of another car, so no one else was hurt."

"If it happened four days ago, why didn't we know earlier?" I wet a washcloth and began wiping my face, trying to make myself more alert.

"His identification showed only his address in Rock Hill just below Charlotte. The police up there had to interview lots of neighbors and coworkers to find anyone who knew where he was from originally and who his nearest relative might be. It took several days before they got that info and contacted Sheriff Harmon. He went to Rock Hill and identified the body before he went to tell Miss Lettie yesterday."

"Do you have any idea how bad the injuries are?" I asked. I don't do any prepping (Funeraleze for embalming), but my work dressing and making up the body includes using reconstructive techniques whenever necessary to make the decedent look as good as possible for loved ones. South Carolina allows me to work as a cosmetician (Funeraleze for cosmetologist) because I have a South Carolina Cosmetology License, but my bosses, Otis and Odell Middleton, taught me my reconstruction skills.

I'm also a certified primary school teacher, but I'll need two additional graduate level college courses to maintain my certification after next year, but I don't plan to go back to teaching anyway. My clients now lie still, don't talk back, and don't tee tee their pants like my kindergarten students did.

"I'm not sure," Otis continued. "Miss Lettie wants us to dress him in a suit from stock because none of his clothes are here. I'll leave that selection up to you, and she wants him ready so she can see him when she comes in this afternoon. I'll call and let you know when Morgan is here and about what time we'll be ready for you."

We both said goodbye.

What a way to start the day after Christmas! I wanted to call Jane and see if she'd like to go out for breakfast, but if she'd worked late last night, she'd still be sleeping.

At the exact moment that I stepped into the shower, James Brown belted "I Feel Good" from my phone again. I thought Otis must be calling back, but it was Daddy.

"Calamine, I've made a big pot of Brunswick stew. Can you pick it up and take it over to Miss Lettie's house?"

"Is John there yet?" After all, he was Jeff Morgan's good friend, while I hadn't really known Jeff since I was only eight when he moved away when he and John were about twenty years old. Besides, that would be a lot like working. My extra duties at Middleton's included taking register stands, folding chairs, and a silk floral wreath for the door to the homes of the deceased.

"John's here at the house, but he's too upset to go over there yet, and I want this stew over at the Morgan home as soon as possible. I was up before daylight making it. Couldn't sleep thinking about that boy. He was a good kid, hung around the house a lot with John when they were young, before Jeff got to drinking like he did. You know he grew up without a dad, and Miss Lettie was a basket case until Jeff was several years old." He cleared his throat. "Will you come get the stew? John's planning to go over there this evening, and I'll go with him then, but I want this food there early."

"Yes, sir."

By the time I finished showering and dressing, I was starving and I'd eaten all of my MoonPies the night before. I called Otis back and got the address and directions to Miss Lettie's farm house before heading to Gastric Gullah Grill on the way to Daddy's.

My friend Rizzie Profit owns the restaurant. She was cooking and Tyrone, the teenager who'd been raised like her little brother, waited tables. Rizzie is a voluptuous woman about my age with a great figure and skin like Godiva chocolate. Sometimes she dresses and speaks her native Gullah, but this morning, she wore jeans and a sweat shirt with "Gastric Gullah Grill – G3" and a fancy sweetgrass basket embroidered on it. It coordinated with the baskets and other Gullah artwork that decorate the walls of the grill.

The beautiful, intricately woven baskets made by the Gullah folk here are widely known far beyond where we live in the South Carolina Low Country. A lot of signs write Lowcountry as one word, but I like to do it my way. Both Rizzie and Tyrone can make the baskets, but Rizzie claims she enjoys cooking authentic Gullah food and creating her own Gullah-inspired recipes more than weaving.

"Hey, what's with the Gee Three?" I asked.

"It's my 'brand.' Gonna use it on a webpage and on menus—everything associated with the grill." Rizzie answered.

The restaurant was almost full. Even the favorite seat of regular morning customer Pork Chop Higgins, who probably weighs more than three hundred pounds, was taken. A young couple occupied Pork Chop's favorite booth, which is the only one with a movable table so he can create more space between the table and seats than the other booths have. Pork Chop sat on one of the stools at the counter with his huge round butt cheeks hanging off each side of the seat. He had on his usual overalls over a bright green shirt. Pork Chop owns a pig farm not too far down the road from my daddy's place. He's about an xxxxx-large man whose mere size is intimidating. I confess that I'd never want to be the one who tried to cheat Pork Chop or make him angry, but he's always been a gentleman around me.

I slid onto a counter stool beside Pork Chop and tried not to accidentally touch his overhang. Rizzie herself brought me a cup of coffee and glass of water.

"Where's your server this morning?" I asked.

"I let her have the day off because I didn't expect to be slammed. Guess everyone got enough of cooking yesterday and didn't want leftover turkey sandwiches for breakfast."

"Make me something fast and good," I told her.

"Do you want a Gullah breakfast?" Rizzie asked.

"No, just scrambled eggs and toast will be fine. I'm kind of in a hurry."

A copy of the *St. Mary Gazette* lay on the counter, probably left by a previous customer. I picked it up and began reading the obituaries. Middleton's Mortuary is the only funeral home in the actual town limits of St. Mary, but the *Gazette* carries obits from several surrounding towns as well, including Beaufort and neighboring islands. I write the death notices for Middleton's, and I'm always interested to see how other mortuaries are wording their news releases as well as who may have died in St. Mary but chose to use one of other undertakers in the area.

Tyrone slid a plate in front of me. "Scrambled eggs and toast" had become Rizzie's own version of Gullah Eggs Benedict with scrambled eggs piled on top of flash-fried oysters on a spicy corn bread flat cake. She'd topped the whole stack of culinary heaven with Bearnaise sauce instead of Hollandaise because she knows I absolutely *adore* tarragon. I dug in and was concentrating on my feast when a disturbance across the room drew my attention.

The *very* pregnant woman who'd sat in Pork Chop's booth was trying to slide out of the seat. She was a pretty girl who looked far too young to be pregnant. The boy with her hardly looked Tyrone's age, and he's only fifteen. The young man pulled on the girl's arms and got her to the edge of the bench, but each time she tried to stand up, she sank back onto the seat and screamed.

"Misty," he said, "we've got to get you out of here and to the hospital."

"I'm trying, Billy Wayne. I'm trying." She grimaced. "You don't have any idea how bad it's hurting."

Now, anyone who grows up on a farm in the South is very familiar with birth. We've seen it in farm animals and frequently assisted creatures when Mother Nature wasn't making delivery run smoothly. I confess, I thought about stepping in to help, but I hesitated, thinking the boy—excuse me, I mean young man—would get her to a hospital. I didn't know what stage by number, but I knew enough to realize that Misty was in advanced labor.

Eeeeeeyowwww! Misty arched her back and slid from the booth onto the floor—flat on her back. Now tears and sobs mixed in with her very regular screams. Billy Wayne stepped back, clearly awed and confused about what to do.

Pork Chop slid those monstrous hams off the stool and stepped over to Misty and Billy Wayne. "When's her baby due?" he growled in a raspy voice.

"Last week," Billy Wayne gasped.

Pork Chop turned around and pointed at me. "Get some towels or tablecloths," he barked.

Rizzie must have heard all the commotion because she came running out of the kitchen and grabbed an arm full of tablecloths from the linen shelf.

"Hold those sheets up around us and give this little lady some privacy," Pork Chop said. "And somebody call 911 and tell 'em we need an ambulance." He said it "am-boo-lance."

Rizzie helped some other diners and me hold the tablecloths like curtains around the young girl. Pork Chop's voice lost the gravel and became comforting.

"Now push just as hard as you can. I'll catch your baby."

A moan, a groan, a scream from behind the tablecloth drapes.

The next sound was a cry—a loud, lusty howl.

"It's a boy!" Pork Chop yelled joyfully. "I'm putting your son on his mama's chest," he said to Billy Wayne. "Cover him up with these clean cloths and make sure he don't slide off before the paramedics get here."

I confess that I peeked around the tablecloth I held. The baby was red and wet and wrinkled and had its eyes squenched shut just like newborn farm animals.

Silence reigned in the Gastric Gullah Grill for a moment, but a cheer went up when we heard sirens heralding the ambulance.

The paramedics proclaimed that mother and son seemed healthy but that they would take them to be examined by a doctor.

"Wow! Guess you learned to do that while helping birth those piglets on your farm," Rizzie told Pork Chop.

"No, by the time my ninth young'un was due, I'd gotten old and fat and lazy. When Mary Beth woke me up and said it was time to go, I figgered we had plenty of time, and I tole her I wasn't going anywhere until after I had my breakfast. I delivered my last kid on the kitchen floor." He grinned. "And my wife ain't never gone let me fergit it and she ain't cooked me no breakfast since then either. That's why I'm here every morning."

With that, Pork Chop went to the men's room. When he came out, he picked up his cup and plate from the counter and moved them to his booth recently vacated by the new parents. He sat down and rattled his spoon back and forth in his empty coffee cup while calling to Tyrone, "Can you warm this up for me?"

The prettiest thing about my childhood home is the long drive bordered on both sides by ancient live oak trees that bend across the road forming an overhead arch dripping with Spanish moss. The house itself is ugly, covered with dark gray shingles and black trim—both chosen by Daddy because they were on sale.

My dad had been waiting for me, probably very impatient, because I'd barely braked the car before he came out with Mike right behind him carrying a huge pot, which he placed on the floor of the front passenger seat. I noticed John's dark gray Mercedes in the drive and asked, "When did John's family come in?"

"We don't have time to talk," Daddy said. "I told you I want this stew over there right away." Behind Dad's back, Mike shrugged his shoulders and gave me a *What can I say?* look. Daddy has never allowed any of his six kids to even suggest what he should do, and that's become a problem since he had a heart attack and my brothers and I try to "help" him more. He's stubborn, and it's "my way or no way."

"I'm gone," I said and pulled away without ever stopping the engine.

When I arrived at Miss Lettie's, I was surprised to see only one vehicle in her driveway—a blue F-150 pickup truck. Around here, when someone dies, friends and relatives usually flock to the home. I went to the door and rang the bell without getting the stew pot from the car.

"Who is it?" someone called from inside. Not an old lady voice, it had the sound of a strong, young person, but the face of the woman who opened the door didn't match. Wrinkled and weathered would have described her appearance even if her skin hadn't been flushed dark red and tear-streaked. She stood tall and straight, again at odds with that angular, aged face. Her brown, long-sleeved, chenille bathrobe covered her head to toe, but I could tell she was lean and sinewy. Her hair—going gray, but with some lifeless brown still in it—was pulled tight into a scrawny ponytail in back.

"Is Miss Lettie Morgan home?" I asked.

"It's Miss Lettie or Mrs. Morgan," she answered. "I was married to Jeffrey Morgan Senior which makes me Mrs. Morgan." She stretched out the Mrs. to Missussss. "Somehow people just began calling me by my first name and stuck Miss in front of it, kind of like they do kindergarten teachers."

"Yes, ma'am. I'm Callie Parrish. I work at Middleton's Mortuary, and you'll be seeing me there when you come in this afternoon, but right now I don't represent Middleton's. John Parrish is my brother. He and your son were close friends growing up, and my daddy wanted me to bring you a pot of Brunswick stew this morning from our family." The words just poured out of me like they'd been rehearsed.

That wrinkled face beamed. "John Parrish? I remember. Him and Jeffrey Junior was good friends all through school and right up until my Jeffrey Junior got that urge to go and moved himself to Charlotte. Well, he didn't actually *move* to Charlotte. He went to work there and lived in Fort Mill just on the other side of the South Carolina line. Where's your brother now?"

"John lives in Atlanta, but he's coming here to see you tonight."

"I'll be happy to see him. I've hardly seen any of Jeffrey Junior's friends in all these years since he left. It's been, what? Over twenty years since Jeffrey Junior moved. Once in a while I see that red-haired girlfriend he had in high school shopping at the Walmart, but we never speak, and none of his friends ever came to see me."

I didn't answer that. I wondered if Jane's mother had lived and Jane had moved away, would I have gone over to visit Mrs. Baker?

After a moment of silence, Miss Lettie stepped back and waved her arm at the living room. "Come on in."

"Let me get that stew first."

The pot was heavy, making me glad Daddy hadn't tried to carry it out to my car since he now has a heart condition. I lugged it up the steps, and that old woman reached out and took it from me. "Hold the door for me," she said. "I'll just set this right on the stove and turn it on low. Some of the relatives and neighbor people will probably come over tonight. The longer stew simmers, the better it will be."

I couldn't believe that elderly lady could carry the pot, but she did it with a lot less apparent strain than I'd felt trying to bring it in. I followed her into the kitchen. When the stew was on the big burner and she'd set the temperature to its lowest setting, she motioned me to have a seat at the kitchen table.

"Let's have some coffee," Miss Lettie said. She poured two cups and set one in front of me before sitting across from me. Sugar, Sweet 'N Low, and powdered cream were already on the table along with several napkins and plastic spoons.

"Now, tell me about that brother of yours." She took a sip of the steaming-hot coffee.

"I have five brothers, but the one who was closest to Jeff is John. Like I said, he lives in Atlanta now, but he'll be over to see you this evening, and he'll be here for the funeral."

"I'm glad. I want to talk to people who knew Jeffrey Junior. I don't know any of his friends since he moved. How about your brother? Does he have children?"

"Yes, ma'am. He has a boy called Johnny and a girl named Megan. His wife is Miriam." I didn't bother to tell her that what had always been the best marriage in our family was getting rocky as John got older. I kept telling myself it was middle-age crisis. I wished he'd just trade in his Mercedes for a little red sports car and hurry up his male menopause.

"I hope he brings his chaps with him tonight." (Chaps is Southernese for children.) Miss Lettie's expression became wistful and wishful. "I always wanted Jeffrey Junior to settle down and give me some grandkids."

"Do you have any other children who might have families someday?" I stuck my foot into my mouth with that one. Her expression clouded.

"No, Jeffrey Junior is or I guess I should say *was* my only child. I never remarried or even wanted to date after his dad died."

Working at a funeral home, I'm familiar with people breaking down when talking about their loved ones who've passed away. I've been trained to be comforting, to pat shoulders or even offer an occasional hug, but I wasn't expecting Miss Lettie's sudden explosion.

She jumped up. Her face twisted into violent rage, and she threw her cup against the kitchen cabinet, splashing coffee all over the linoleum countertop. She flung her arm out and slammed everything on the table down to the floor. Thank heaven I held my cup in my hand or my hot coffee would have splattered all over me along with the contents of the sugar bowl.

"It's not fair!" she screeched. "God gave me everything and then took it all away. It's like I had two hearts, and both of them are broken. I loved Jeffrey Senior with all my heart, but he died. When Jeffrey Junior was born, I began growing another heart, a mother's heart to love that little baby boy. Now he's gone, and there's nothing left of him, not even a little bit of him in a grand-child for me to love. He won't live on anywhere except in my heart, and it's gone. Both my hearts are broken, destroyed, and will never mend."

I did what I've been taught to do. I put my arm around her shoulders, pulled her close, and let her sob all over my shirt, Buh-leeve me, I was relieved when the back door opened and an older lady stepped in without even knocking.

"Oh, Lettie," the woman, who looked like a white-haired Aunt Bea on Andy Griffith's old *Mayberry* show, said and reached for Miss Lettie, pulling her away from me and into her own ample bosom. "Cry. Let it all out."

"Are you kin to her?" I asked.

"No, just her neighbor Ellen, but we've been friends for years."

I pointed to the pot. "I brought some Brunswick stew. I need to go to work. Will you stay here with her until she feels better?"

"I don't know if she'll ever feel better, but I'll be here until she calms down. I plan to spend the day with her." She wiped a tear from her eye. "It's terrible about Junior, but I'll be with Lettie like I was when his daddy died." She continued patting Miss Lettie and dismissed me with, "Thank you for the stew. I don't think the funeral home has brought the food register yet, but when it comes, I'll write it down. Who did you say you are?"

"I'm Callie Parrish, but the stew is from my daddy. I work at Middleton's and we'll be bringing registers and chairs over this afternoon."

"I'll probably see you at the funeral home. I'll be going with Lettie to see Junior, and make arrangements for his service. You can leave now if you like. I'll stay here with Lettie."

She didn't have to tell me twice. I put my cup in the sink and left without offering to help clean up the mess.

I changed into a black dress, stockings, and low black pumps when I got home. That's my standard work uniform, and I figured I'd hear from Otis soon. I was right, though his brother Odell called instead of Otis.

"Callie," he said, "Otis has finished the prep and is ready for you to come in. This one is going to take a lot of work. His nose was smashed and part of it's missing."

"Be right there," I answered though I'd hoped to have time to visit with Jane before going to work.

Middleton's Mortuary is an old, but immaculate, white two-story house surrounded by a parking lot edged by as many live oaks with Spanish moss hanging from them as there are lining the drive to Daddy's house. The house has a verandah that extends from the front around both sides with white Cracker Barrel-style rocking chairs and clay pots filled with seasonal flowers on it. My bosses grew up in the second floor of the house with caskets stored in some rooms. No one lives up there now, and they recently moved all the caskets into a new storage building in back.

Odell met me when I stepped into the hall through the employee entrance. "Mr. Morgan is already in your workroom, and if you need any help, just buzz for Otis. I'm going out to pick up some barbecue sandwiches because it's probably going to push all three of us to have this one presentable by the time his mother arrives."

My bosses were born identical twins, but Odell is balding and probably fifty pounds heavier than his vegetarian brother who opted for hair plugs instead of baldness. Their personalities are as different as their current looks, but they both treat me and everyone except each other with courtesy and respect.

The minute I stepped into my workroom, I saw what Odell meant. Even covered by a sheet, it was obvious that Mr. Morgan's limbs jutted out at slightly unusual angles—evidence of broken bones. After pulling on my gloves and waterproof smock, I changed my mind and garbed in a full suit a lot like a hazmat. I pulled the sheet back and looked at the face. The Middletons don't like for me to refer to decedents as bodies or corpses. They prefer that the deceased always be called by their names, but it wasn't easy to think of what lay on my work table as "Mr. Morgan."

In addition to the black-stitched Y-incision on his chest and groin from the autopsy, the man was bald, which would make the postmortem head incision a problem. The entire body was discolored and covered with abrasions, and Odell might refer to Mr. Morgan's nose as damaged, but in my mind, his nose was missing. Making Jeff Morgan presentable for his mother would require a work of art and several procedures beyond sculpting wax.

"Be careful as you position him," Odell cautioned. "His left arm was amputated in the accident. They put some stitches in, but if you jar that arm, it's going to come loose." He hesitated and then added, "Otis is in the prep room if you need him. I'm going to pick up sandwiches, but after lunch, I'll help, too, if you need me." He handed me several photographs of a young man. They bore little resemblance to the corpse. In addition to decades of difference in age, the head in the pictures was covered with thick, dark hair.

"This is a rough case," Odell continued. "If you want to wait until we can work on him together for the face, you can pick out his clothes while I'm gone."

Normally I'm a self-starter at work, but though I've done my fair share of restorations, I've never actually rebuilt a nose. I decided to select clothing and hope Otis or Odell showed up to help before I began facial reconstruction. Most of our stock clothing for men is gray, navy, or black, but we had a dark brown tweed suit with a two-button jacket that seemed perfect for Jeff Morgan. In my mind, Mr. Morgan was linked with my brother John, so I chose clothes that I thought my brother would like—the tweed suit, a cream-colored shirt, and a brown, burgundy, and tan striped tie that was a lot like one I'd seen John wear.

The soft sound of an instrumental "What a Friend We Have in Jesus" signified that the front door was opened. I'd barely reached it when in walked Detective Dean Robinson. "Just a few questions," he said.

"I don't have time right now," I answered. "Jeff Morgan's mother will be here after lunch to make funeral plans for her son. She wants to see him when she arrives, and I'm nowhere near ready to dress him."

"We'll talk while you work," he said.

"Are you sure? I haven't done much toward restoration and makeup yet."

"I've been viewing autopsies for years as part of my work in homicide. I doubt seeing you put someone back together will be any worse than watching medical examiners take them apart."

"Okay, there are rules about who can be in my workroom, but I guess if it's legal for you to sit in on postmortems, it's all right for you to come on in."

When we stepped into the workroom, Robinson reached to the dispensers and took out a pair of disposable gloves and a mask. He pulled them on and stepped away from my work table.

I have to say this for Robinson—he made it a point to stay out of my way except when I needed to shift the body or the amputated arm. When assistance would help, he lent a hand without commenting or interfering with what I was doing. After several repairs with special wax, most of my work became air brushing except the nose, which I postponed until one of my bosses returned. The detective watched carefully.

"Had you put makeup on before I came in?" he asked. "The skin color is different, rosier, more natural than the bodies I've seen at autopsies."

"Most autopsies are performed before embalming. Mr. Morgan has been prepped. The embalming fluid changes the texture and the color of muscles and skin, makes them harder and pinker."

"You're good at this," he said.

"I try to create a good memory for loved ones."

"I wanted to ask you a few questions about yesterday."

"Go ahead." I continued working.

"Are you certain that body wasn't on your porch when you left to go to your father's?"

"It was big enough that I think I would have noticed it," I answered while correcting color coverage on Mr. Morgan's right hand. Special prep fluid adds some color to the skin, but doesn't eradicate damage from bruises.

"Did you touch her before you called 911?"

"Her? Then it's a woman?"

"Yes, white female, probably in her early forties. No identification and no identifying marks like tats."

"What does she look like?"

"Slim, attractive with long red hair. It's not always easy to determine eye color after death, but they appeared blue or green."

"Cause of death?" I stopped and looked him directly in his eyes.

"Of course we'll know more when the postmortem report is ready, but from watching, I'd say she was strangled. As the pathologist recorded his observations, he noted petechial hemorrhages in the eyelids. That's usually an indication of choking, and I noticed a deep ligature furrow on the neck, but this examiner wasn't as willing to discuss his findings with me as the ones who knew me before I came up here from Florida. He told me he'd get the official findings to us as soon as possible." Detective Robinson removed his gloves and took a small notebook like the one Sheriff Harmon carries from his inside pocket. "Of course, we won't know about blood ethanol or drugs until those screens come back."

"What did you want to know from me?"

"Do you have any female friends who have long red hair?"

I stopped dead still and set the airbrush on the counter beside my work table. "My best friend has red hair—very long hair. It hangs to her waist when she wears it loose."

"Would you be willing to look at the deceased when she's brought back to be sure it's not your friend?"

"Not necessary. My friend was with me when I found the body. She's the woman who lives next door to me. You saw her. She sat in your car with me."

"I don't remember her hair being long."

"She probably had it in a ponytail in back. Sometimes she braids it, and a lot of the time, she just loops it into a knot at the back of her head and pins it there. She may have pinned the ponytail up while she was inside her apartment before you arrived. I don't remember because I'm so used to seeing her that I don't pay much attention to how her hair is done."

"Do you know any other females in St. Mary with extremely long, red hair?"

"Not that I can think of."

I guess long hair is relative. Mine is barely shoulder-length now, which is long for me. Jane hasn't really cut her hair in years. Sometimes I trim the ends, but basically she wears that long, straight hair because her mother had long, straight hair. Her mom was a flower child who died around the time we finished high school. Jane wears a lot of her mother's vintage hippie outfits. I think it makes her feel close to her mom. My mother died giving me birth, and I have nothing particular that makes me think of her. Sometimes I wonder whether I would have enjoyed wearing her clothes if Daddy had saved them.

"Are you okay?" Detective Robinson asked. "You seemed out of it for a minute."

"Just thinking."

Thank heaven Odell stepped in at that moment.

"Looks good except for the nose," he said.

"I want you or Otis to help with that."

"No problem." He turned toward Detective Robinson. "I saw you over at Callie's house, didn't I? Aren't you the sheriff's new homicide man?"

"I'm new to the department, and I'll be heading up homicide cases. My name's Dean Robinson."

"Well, Deputy Robinson, I hope you haven't had lunch. I went to that new place, Bubba's Bodacious BBQ Barn, to pick up sandwiches for Callie, Otis, and me, but after I ordered, I saw they have pepper-vinegar, mustard base, and tomato base pork as well as chicken and catfish on their buffet. I couldn't resist it. I ate there, so I've got two extra sandwiches in a bag on my desk." He nodded at Robinson. "Help yourself to a sandwich while I work on Mr. Morgan's nose." He rubbed circles on his—well, in Odell's case, the only word for it is *belly*. "I'm stuffed."

Robinson must have been as hungry as I was eager to avoid having to rebuild Jeff Morgan's nose because neither of us wasted any time getting out of my workroom. Over coffee and barbecue sandwiches, he told me more about the Santa found on my porch.

"I watched the medical examiner carefully, and I didn't see any signs of violence other than the marks on the woman's neck. There was definitely a circumferential ligature furrow around her neck as well as small abrasions or contusions periodically on the furrow. The doctor didn't let me get my face right into what he was doing, but I could hear him dictating. He referred to petechial hemorrhages on the conjunctival surfaces of the eyes and facial skin. Are you familiar with petechial hemorrhages?" He took a big bite of his sandwich.

"I've read about them in mystery books. They indicate strangulation, don't they?" I took a bite, but not nearly so big as his had been.

"Yes. I'm positive that the autopsy report will be that she died as a result of being choked to death with some kind of rope or cord."

"You sound like a medical examiner yourself." Okay, I know that was stroking his ego, but the man was good-looking.

"I've watched and read a whole lot of postmortem exams in Florida." He sipped his coffee, and then beamed—a big, warm smile.

"You're not married, are you?" His eyes twinkled and questioned as much as his words.

"Not anymore."

"Are you in a committed relationship?"

I am about as far from a sweet, magnolia-mouthed, blushing Southern belle as possible, but I think my cheeks may have flushed bright pink.

"I don't think so," I answered.

"I didn't see a man at your place Christmas night. Are you living with someone?"

"No, I was getting serious about a doctor, but that faded. Then I met this man in October. He had to go back to Florida, and we talk on the telephone almost every night, but it's not really any kind of relationship." I paused but felt compelled to add, "He talks like he's really interested and keeps saying he's coming back to South Carolina to see me."

The detective smiled again. "Sounds to me like you might be free enough to have dinner with me Saturday night. How about it? I'm fairly new in town, and you could tell me the best place to get my dry cleaning done and all those little things. I know where you live. I can pick you up around eight o'clock. You choose where you want to eat, and we'll share our baggage."

"Share what?"

"Baggage. You know—the things in the past that have made us cautious in the present."

Now, if Patel and I had shared more than just a kiss and he was calling me *every* night, I probably would have had even more hesitation about going out with Sheriff Harmon's new deputy, but to be honest, the way Patel went on about being attracted to me, I'd been disappointed he hadn't come to South Carolina around the holidays. Face it. Christmas hadn't turned out so great when it ended with me finding Santa dead on my porch.

"That sounds nice," I answered. "Of course, I never know when I'll be called in to work."

"And I plan to be off that night, though developments in this case could change that, but barring unforeseen work changes, I'll pick you up at your place at eight."

He finished his sandwich and walked briskly out of the room. I heard "Just a Closer Walk with Thee" when he left the building.

I should have cleared off the sandwich wrappings and gone back to my workroom immediately to see if Odell needed me and check why Otis hadn't shown up for his sandwich. Instead, I acted like a fourteen-year-old and called my BFF.

"Callie here," I said when Jane answered.

"I think after all these years I recognize your voice. You left early this morning. Are you at work?"

"Yes, but I called to tell you I have a date for dinner Saturday night."

In my mind, I saw the big grin on Jane's face. "J.T. Patel's coming back to town?" she asked with a lilt in her voice, but the expression was a statement rather than a question.

"No. Do you remember the homicide detective who was at the house last night?"

"The one who made us sit in his car?"

"His name is Dean Robinson, and he asked me out."

"Where'd you see him?"

"He came by Middleton's to ask some questions."

"What about J. T. Patel?"

"What about him?"

"I know you're not really in a relationship with him, but aren't you two trying to hook up?"

Thank heaven a call-waiting beep interrupted the conversation because I didn't know how to answer that question.

"Got a beep coming in. I'll call you or see you tonight." I hit the "flash" button on the telephone.

"Callie," the smooth, velvety voice of J. T. Patel greeted me. "You've been on my mind since I woke this morning, and I wanted to see how your day is going. Sometimes thinking about you makes me feel like a sixteen-year-old kid in love for the first time."

We chatted for several minutes, and no, I didn't tell him that I was going out to dinner with another man on Saturday night.

"Just As I Am" called me from the front door.

"I've got to go," I said. "Someone's in the hall."

"I'll call you tonight," Patel promised, and then added, "We've got to make plans to get together."

The call from Patel made me wonder if I should cancel the date with Detective Robinson. Patel and I'd never told each other that we weren't dating other people, but since we talked most nights, it was obvious that neither of us was getting busy in the evenings.

No time to pursue that line of thought. I stepped into the hall where tall, thin Miss Lettie awaited with her short, slightly plump neighbor Ellen. *What time is it?* I thought. *I haven't dressed Mr.*

Morgan yet. Surely it's not two o'clock already!

The first thing Miss Lettie said was, "I want to see my baby!"

Odell joined us before I had time to open my mouth, much less consider what to say.

"You've come early, but of course, you'll see your son," he said in that calm, professional undertaker tone he uses. He took her arm at the elbow and guided her into the first conference room. We've recently added paintings of Southern flowers on the walls of the planning rooms and named the rooms for the décor. We sat around the mahogany table in the Wisteria Room, named for the cluster of silk wisteria centered on the round table and an oil painting of lavender wisteria on the wall behind the side table.

"I want to see him *now*!" Miss Lettie protested.

"Let me assist you in planning how to best respect Mr. Morgan with a beautiful funeral or memorial service." Odell continued as though she hadn't said anything.

"I know what I want, and I want to see my son!" Miss Lettie objected.

Watching the sometimes gruff, growly Odell Middleton tame that lady was a lesson in professionalism. He convinced her that she'd want to see Mr. Morgan in the casket she selected. In no time, with only occasional encouragement from her friend Ellen, Miss Lettie selected a solid cherry casket that we stocked. Odell sent me to tell Otis what had been chosen and that Mr. Morgan should be casketed as soon as possible.

I found Otis in my work room finishing dressing Mr. Morgan. His nose looked great! We brought the coffin in from the storage building, put Mr. Morgan in it, and placed him in Slumber Room A, which hasn't yet been renamed.

By the time I stepped back into the conference room, Miss Lettie had set the visitation for Saturday, at one p.m. in Middleton's chapel with service to follow at two p.m. and interment beside Jeff Morgan's father in the St. Mary Cemetery. She considered and then flatly refused offers to have the visitation catered with finger foods, saying, "People can eat before they come."

As she nor Ellen had any church affiliation, Miss Lettie told

Odell to hire a preacher and someone to sing "Onward, Christian Soldiers" and "Battle Hymn of the Republic" because those were the songs performed at her husband's funeral. She requested a red, white, and blue casket spray, and then asked emphatically, "Are we done now?"

"As soon as you sign these papers," Odell said and placed a clipboard of paperwork in front of Miss Lettie. She scrawled her name everywhere Odell indicated and swatted Ellen's hand away when Ellen reached for the clipboard, probably intending to read what her friend was signing.

"Now I want to see my son," Miss Lettie demanded.

Odell raised an eyebrow and glanced toward the door. I nodded "yes," and Odell said, "Callie here may need to ask a few more questions for the obituary, but if you'd like to see Mr. Morgan before that, we can see him before finalizing the announcements."

Fully expecting Miss Lettie to be a body-grabber, I stood close to her when she reached her son. The top half of the casket was open, but we'd draped a thin, almost transparent cloth over it—not that it would physically prevent anyone from seizing or embracing the decedent, but we've found it's a good psychological barrier when there's facial damage.

Straight and tall, Miss Lettie looked like that woman in Grant Wood's picture "American Gothic." Everybody's seen it—a solemn, plain woman standing beside a farmer holding a pitchfork with a barn in the background. I always thought they were man and wife, but I've read that the woman was his daughter. Miss Lettie looked just like her with hair beginning to gray, and for the first time, I saw that even in December, Miss Lettie had a farmer's tan browning her hands and the back of her neck.

She narrowed her eyes and stared at Jeff Morgan without making any effort to touch him.

"My baby," she finally said. "He was my beautiful baby, and he looks just like his daddy." She turned toward me. "Why did you shave his head?"

"No, ma'am. His head isn't shaved. He's bald." I knew this because I'd rubbed the top of Mr. Morgan's head myself out of curiosity. Shaved heads on men are stylish now, and I like the look, but Mr. Morgan's head had shed the dark hair I'd seen in his youthful photograph. Her question did make me wonder how long it had been since she'd seen her son though.

"His daddy's hair was thinning. If he'd lived long enough, he probably would have been bald, too," Ellen said.

"I guess so." Miss Lettie's voice lowered, barely audible. She turned toward me. "I don't want a long write-up. You can say that Jeffrey Junior was killed in a car accident and announce the time and date of the service, but that's all."

Taking Miss Ellen's hand, she said, "Take me home now," in a child-like voice.

Confusion filled my mind when Miss Lettie and Ellen left. I was definitely tired, both physically and emotionally after beginning my day witnessing a birth, but the thought of that newborn baby boy made me feel good. I was a little excited at the idea of going to dinner Saturday night with that good-looking, hot deputy, but guilt feelings crept around inside my head. Would it be cheating on Patel? Was it even possible to cheat on someone after only a few dates and kisses? He'd been so sweet when he called earlier. I put that thought on my mental shelf and got to work.

Jeff Morgan's obituary was soon completed, posted on our Internet page, and emailed to the local newspaper. Sometimes families want funeral notices sent to *The State Newspaper* as well, but Miss Lettie had said *St. Mary Gazette* was the only one she wanted.

Next I made several phone calls. First was to the florist to order the casket spray and Middleton's usual sympathy wreath. Then I needed to arrange the service.

The first pastor I called was Dan Christianson who frequently performed services for us when a family asked Middleton's to arrange for a preacher. Pastor Christianson wasn't available, so I called Pastor Mark Holt. He's a Hospice chaplain, and at the last service he preached at Middleton's he'd said, "Call me if you ever need me. I'd be glad to help whenever I can," so I took him at his word and called.

"Pastor Mark," he answered.

"This is Callie Parrish at Middleton's Mortuary. We have a decedent with no church, and his mother wants a pastor to perform the service. Would you be interested?"

"I always want to help, but I already have a funeral tomorrow for one of my Hospice patients. What time is this scheduled?"

"It's not tomorrow, but Saturday with visitation at one p.m., service at two p.m.—both here at Middleton's. Interment will follow at St. Mary Cemetery."

"I'm available for that. I'm driving right now. Let me call you back and get the information when I'm stopped and can write. I'll want to visit with the family tonight."

"Fine. I'll be right here."

My next call was to Ruth Gates. She's got a great voice, can sing anything, and her charges are reasonable. Ruth was available Saturday also and would have no problem with the songs Miss Lettie had requested. Our usual organist, Linda Jonathan, had played often when Ruth performed and was pleased to put us on her calendar for Saturday. This was going well. Pastor Mark called back for information about Jeff and his mother.

Otis or Odell usually set up arrangements for opening graves and transporting the awning and chairs to the cemetery, but I still had to deliver folding chairs, an artificial white silk wreath for the door, as well as both guest and food registers to Miss Lettie's house. I decided to do that immediately.

When I told Otis I'd booked Pastor Mark, Ruth Owen, and Linda Jonathan as well as talked to the florist, he suggested that after I went to Miss Lettie's, I could take off the rest of the day. "I'll be here all afternoon to greet visitors, and with Mr. Morgan the only decedent here, it probably won't be busy until tomorrow when the obit's in the paper. Didn't you say you're picking up Big Boy from the vet? No reason for you to drive back here for your car. Just take the van. Your gigantic dog will be more comfortable in that than in the car anyway. You can switch vehicles tomorrow."

I had everything loaded and was on the road in no time.

Ellen answered my knock on Miss Lettie's door.

She made the *shhh* sound for silence and held her pointing finger up to her lips. "Come on in, but please try to be quiet. I've given Lettie one of her pills and put her to bed. She's asleep." I didn't ask what kind of pill, just tiptoed in, carrying the guest register stand. I stood it just inside the front door and placed a burgundy guest register and one of our pens on it. Before I began working at Middleton's, they chained their pens to the stands, but I'd talked them out of that because it was too much like going to the bank.

Ellen helped me bring the folding chairs in and set them up in the living room. When I gave her the food register, she said, "You don't have to show me how to do it. I've been down this road too many times before. I put the numbered sticker on the food container and write who brought what beside that number in the book, right?"

"Yes, ma'am."

"Come on in the kitchen, and we'll put sticker number one on your daddy's pot. I tasted the stew. It's delicious. Does your father do a lot of cooking?"

"Yes, he does."

"I remember he raised you and five sons all by himself, so I guess he had to learn to cook."

"Yes, ma'am."

"I used to tell Lettie she ought to take a nice chicken casserole or something over to your daddy's house and get to know him. She'd have been a lot better off joining up with him to raise six boys and you than she was running this farm all by herself and raising Junior as an only child. You'd of thought that child would have been spoiled, but she went the other way. Wanted to make a 'man like his daddy' out of him. Smothered him, absolutely smothered him with her rules and regulations. It just about killed Lettie when he moved off." She sniffled. "And now he's gone for good."

Even though part of my profession is consoling loved ones, I was glad Miss Lettie didn't wake up before I left. As I drove away in the van, I glanced in my rearview mirror at the wreath I'd hung on her door. Odell frequently said, "Morticianing is a sad job, but somebody's got to do it." I agreed, but at times I wonder if I want to spend the rest of my life being somebody who does it.

• • •

"He's still going to be a little sore," the vet said when she helped me lift all one hundred and fifty pounds of Big Boy into the back of the van. "I'll have the biopsy report next week, and I'll call you, but it didn't look malignant. Sometimes these tumors just happen, but it was better to get it out."

Big Boy looked up at me with an *I want to go home* expression. I've had him since he was a puppy, and I'd been missing him something fierce while he'd been in the hospital. I scratched him behind the ears and closed the van doors.

I was a little concerned about Big Boy lying on the floor of the van. I had a special harness seat belt installed in my Mustang for him, but when I glanced back at him, the dog was asleep. He was comfortable. I just hoped it was safe.

At home, when I opened the van doors, Big Boy jumped out, then dropped to the ground and whimpered. I patted his head. "I know, I know that hurt," I soothed and then led him slowly through the back door which appeared to confuse him, but he seemed happy to lie down on his special rug and eat a banana MoonPie. I was out of chocolate MoonPies, so I had a banana one with him.

I'd finally taken Big Boy in to be neutered after my whole family about nagged me to death to do it. The vet had found an abdominal tumor that meant instead of a day visit, he stayed and had surgery plus several days of recuperation before I could bring him home. I'd recently dug out an old Kinsey Millhone book from a basket of books in my spare room, so I curled up on the couch to read while Big Boy slept some more.

The story was interesting, but I couldn't keep my mind on it. I kept looking over at Big Boy and being grateful he was home. I was also a little scared. What if the biopsy came back positive? The more I thought about it, the more inclined I was to spend the rest of the day at home with my dog. I called Daddy.

"When are you coming over here, Calamine? I've got supper cooked, and we're all going over to Lettie's house in a little while. Do you know when the funeral is?"

"Yes, sir. The service is Saturday afternoon." I waited a full minute. My dad doesn't like it when I change plans on him. "Listen, Daddy, can I get a rain check on supper? I'm really tired, plus I brought Big Boy home, and I don't want to leave him here alone right now."

"We'll go ahead and eat then, Calamine," he said, "but you don't get a rain check. I made a rib roast dinner, and you know it'll all be gone by tomorrow."

I laughed, told him goodbye, and went back to my book, waiting for my call from Patel. About nine o'clock, I broke down and called his cell phone. No answer. When I went to bed at eleven, I tried again. Still no answer. I'd be hard-pressed to say if I was more disappointed or angry.

★ ON THE THIRD DAY OF CHRISTMAS MY TRUE LOVE GAVE TO ME

THREE RED WREATHS

"How's your latest murder?" I knew the words were Mike's because I recognized his voice on the phone and because he's the only one who actually teases me about finding dead people.

"It's not *my* murder. How's *your* job search?"

"Oh, that was cold," he answered. "John said ask if you want to meet for lunch since you didn't come to dinner last night."

"Sure. Is everybody going?"

"Just you, me, John, and Frankie. Miriam is taking the kids shopping, and Pa's busy in the kitchen making bourbon balls to take to Miss Lettie. She bragged so much about his stew that now he wants to show her he can bake, too. I reminded him there's no baking to the way he makes bourbon balls, but he just said, 'She won't know the difference.'"

"I have to work, so I'll need to meet you somewhere at twelve-thirty."

"Let's eat at Rizzie's. She always has good specials."

"See you then and there."

I helped Big Boy out onto the back stoop and watched him step gingerly down the steps. He eyed the van, and I wondered if he wanted to go for another ride in it or if he was dreading my putting him in it. Then I actually hoped that Big Boy had realized he was a boy dog and might hike his leg by the van's tire, but he squatted like he always had. Back inside the apartment, he took a few laps of water and then lay down on his rug again. When I left for work, he was sleeping.

My first task at Middleton's was to carry plants and floral arrangements from our flower room to Slumber Room A and arrange them around the bier under Jeff Morgan's casket. Two florists had already made early morning deliveries.

Otis and Odell were both in their offices, and since I didn't have anything to do at the moment, I pulled a mystery from my desk drawer and read. We don't have to keep anyone near the entrance because the front door lets us know someone is there by activating recorded hymns any time it's opened.

I'd just gotten interested in the book when the phone rang. "Middleton's Mortuary. Callie Parrish speaking. How may I help you?"

"This is Lettie Morgan. I've been thinking, and while I appreciate you picking such a nice suit for Jeffrey Junior, I want him buried in an Army uniform. Do you have one there?" Miss Lettie sounded very businesslike.

"No, ma'am. We don't stock any uniforms."

"I've been to funerals there when the dead person wore a uniform." Her voice changed to a whine.

"We can dress Mr. Morgan in a uniform if you supply it, but we can't get it for you."

"I'll see what I can do then, but don't take my son's clothes off until after I bring you something else for him to wear."

"Yes, ma'am."

I went back to my book, but I don't believe curiosity will kill me, so I phoned my brother John at Daddy's house.

"Little Sister, glad it's you. I was about to ring you," he said when Daddy called him to the telephone. John didn't know about my telephone no longer ringing—it sings "I Feel Good" in James Brown's voice.

"I called to ask about your friend Jeff Morgan."

"What about him?"

"Was he ever in the military?"

"Are you kidding? Jeff's father died in the Army and left him at the mercy of his mom. Jeff had all kinds of emotional turmoil about that—grief, sorrow, and anger at his dad. He wasn't interested in the military at all. Wouldn't even do ROTC in high school. Why?"

"Miss Lettie wants him buried in a soldier's uniform."

"She seemed a little ditzy when we went over there last night. I wondered if maybe her doctor had put her on a tranquilizer, but then, she was strange even back when we were kids. That's why we always hung out at my house instead of his."

"What were you going to call me about?" I had my answer, so I changed the subject.

"Miriam insists I go with her and the kids, and Pa's making something to take over to Miss Lettie's tonight. Instead of lunch, let's meet at Rizzie's for an early dinner. That way everyone can go. What time will you be off?"

"About five today. I can be there by five-thirty."

"Fine. We'll see you there."

I was back into my book when the phone rang again.

"Middleton's Mortuary. Callie Parrish speaking. How may I help you?"

"Is the casket spray there yet?" I recognized Miss Lettie's voice.

"Yes, ma'am, and it's beautiful."

"Oh," her tone was disappointed. "Ellen is going to bring me over there to see my baby again, and I'm going to bring you the flag they gave me when we buried Jeffrey Senior. I thought about having it draped over the casket, but I'll just leave it with you to present to me tomorrow. I called the Veterans Administration and they said they can't send out any soldiers or a new flag unless I can prove Jeffrey Junior served in the armed forces."

When she ended the call, I went to Otis's office. "Miss Lettie called," I said. "She wants a flag presented tomorrow at Mr. Morgan's service, but he was never in the military. She's bringing us the one she got at her husband's funeral."

"Never done that before, but Odell and I will present it to her. I don't see anything wrong with that since the flag belongs to her anyway. So long as what they want isn't against the law or decency, you know we always aim to please the bereaved."

"Yes, sir."

Otis looked thoughtful. "Callie, I've been thinking about renaming our slumber rooms."

Dalmation! What now? I don't think any widow is going to want her big, strapping truck driver husband lying in the Rose Room. Or maybe paint the rooms colors and call them names like at the White House. Mr. Jones is in the Blue Room and Mr. Smith is in the Green Room. Actually, that might not be too bad.

"A lot of funeral homes call their slumber rooms 'state rooms.' That sounds good—like royalty or the Pope lying in state. I think families might like that," Otis explained.

"Sounds good." That's my answer to any suggestion made by either of my bosses unless I think it's really terrible. After all, they sign my paychecks.

"Peace in the Valley" announced an arrival. I met Miss Lettie and Ellen in the hall. Ellen handed me a flag folded in the traditional triangular shape. Miss Lettie stopped by the display case exhibiting Print Memories and Remembrance jewelry. Print Memories are gold and silver items with the deceased loved one's fingerprints. We've sold a few of those, but not a lot. Remembrances are gold and silver chains and bracelets with translucent colored plastic pendants containing a tiny speck of ashes. Of course, lockets to hold cremains have been available for years. I haven't sold any Remembrances yet, but cremations have increased lately, so someone will probably order one soon.

"That's what I want," Miss Lettie said and pointed at the display.

"Printies?" I asked, accidentally calling the Print Memories by the nickname Odell called them. "I can take Mr. Morgan's prints and have one made for you."

"No, I want the other thing. One of those pretty necklaces with the plastic drop with some of Jeffrey Junior in it."

"Mrs. Morgan," I said, pronouncing Mrs. as Missssusss like she had earlier, "those are for cremains."

"Cremains? What's that?" Miss Ellen asked.

"Ashes. Mr. Morgan isn't being cremated, so there won't be any ashes."

"Put some other part of him in it then," Miss Lettie insisted.

My mind immediately went into senseless mode. Did she want me to cut off something like part of her dead son's little finger to put into a piece of jewelry? Might begin a new business. We could call them "Pinkies." After that thought, I should have prayed, "Lord, please keep my mind respectful as it should be so nothing like that ever pops out of my mouth and causes me to lose my job."

"Put a lock of hair in it," Miss Lettie suggested. Once more, my mind went off in outlandish directions. The man was bald!

"I'll check with Mr. Middleton and see what we can do."

Apparently Miss Ellen's mind had been where mine was because she suggested, "How about fingernails?"

I didn't reply. We could have done that if we'd known before we'd cosmetized him, but I certainly hadn't saved any nail clippings. That would have felt like voodoo or root doctoring.

For sure, I'd turn the situation over to Otis or Odell.

Still expecting Miss Lettie to collapse or grab the body, I escorted them to Mr. Morgan's casket. Exclaiming over the beauty of each plant and flower, they read the cards aloud.

"Don't you take these off and give them to Lettie so she can send thank you notes?" Ellen asked.

"The florist puts two on each floral tribute," I answered. "We keep the duplicates in an envelope and will give them to Mrs. Morgan after the service along with enough thank-you notes for her to send for flowers, food, and anything else she wishes to send appreciation."

"I knew Middleton's would do a good job."

I wasn't sure that even an inferior funeral home would neglect to give floral cards to the family, but for a wonder, I kept my mouth shut.

When they left, I reported the conversation to Otis.

"I doubt seriously that she'll order any Remembrance jewelry," he replied. "But just in case, let's go in and retrieve something to put in it if she does."

He brought a pair of scissors with him into Slumber Room A. We were standing there surveying the situation when Odell came in. When we explained what we were doing, Odell took the scissors from Otis.

"Close that door." Odell motioned toward the entrance to the slumber room.

He lifted one of Mr. Morgan's hands. "Can't get anything here. The nails are clipped too close to take anything. We'll go with hair."

Now my mind went from senseless to the gutter. *Where* was the hair he planned to clip?

Odell loosened Mr. Morgan's shirt, stuck one hand with the scissors under the body's arm, cupped the other hand in Mr. Morgan's armpit, and brought out a very small lock of hair.

"Straighten his shirt and tie," he told me. "I'll save this in a zipper bag in Mr. Morgan's file folder in case his mother does order something." He turned away, but immediately looked back at me. "I've got some papers to send to the sheriff. Come get the package and you can take them by his office on your way to lunch."

That's how I wound up at Wayne's office just before lunchtime. He sat behind his big, shiny mahogany desk, and I sat facing him.

"No word yet on who Santa is," he commented and tapped the pencil in his hand on the surface of the desk.

"Your new homicide man said that it's a female—a red-haired woman." I smoothed out the wrinkles in the skirt of my black dress.

"Yes, apparently strangled to death." Wayne set the pencil into a cup holding pens and pencils.

"That's what he said."

"When did you see Detective Robinson?" He must have been nervous because he took a Sharpie from the cup and began tapping it on his desk.

"He came by Middleton's. He told me about her and wanted to know if I knew anyone who fit that description. She sounded like Jane, but thank heaven Jane was inside Christmas night, not lying dead on our front porch." I trembled at that thought.

"Want to ride over to Gee Three for lunch?" he asked.

"Gee Three?"

"Yes, haven't you heard the ad on the radio? Rizzie's advertising the Gastric Gullah Grill as Gee Three." He returned the Sharpie to its place with the other pens. "She and Tyrone had on shirts with that on them when I was in there for breakfast yesterday."

"She's developing a logo for her 'brand'. That's the buzzword these days—brand. Last time I talked to her, she said she's going to ask you to help her put up a webpage for the grill," he added.

"Sounds good." I know that's my standard answer for my bosses, but I use it with the sheriff also.

"You can ride along if you like," Wayne said. "This will probably turn out to be nothing. By far, most missing people reports about adults wind up being cases where the disappeared person went somewhere else by choice. That's why an adult usually has to be missing over seventy-two hours before it's an official missing person case."

We'd been sitting in the grill discussing what to order when a call from Wayne's office had interrupted us.

"Who's missing?" I asked as we got into the sheriff's cruiser.

"Amber Buchanan. The call came from Safe Sister, the haven for abused women and children."

"If someone's missing from there, she could have just decided to go home or move on," I commented. "How will you investigate this? I understand that no men are allowed on the premises of Safe Sister."

"We're not going to the shelter. Amber works for Safe Sister in their office, not on the shelter premises, but we're going to her home. She'd volunteered to help Christmas morning at a party for the kids at one of the safe houses, but she didn't show up. She was off yesterday but scheduled to work today. When she didn't come in again and they still couldn't reach her by telephone, someone at their office called and asked us to check on her."

"Why don't you send a deputy?"

"Because her home is near here. Besides, I remember her, went to school with her. She was a pretty girl, quiet, and kind of big—not fat, just pleasantly round."

The house wasn't far away—just a few blocks. A single-family dwelling. Amber Buchanan was as enthusiastic about decorating for the season as I'd been. Not that she had a monster tree on the porch like Jane and I did, but colored chaser lights had been strung all around the eaves of the house. Lit even now in daylight, they twinkled—sparkling bright reds, yellows, and blues everywhere except right around the door. Three red plastic wreaths with outdoor lights hung at the entrance—one on the door and two more on each side. The wreaths were lit with red bulbs. A string of brilliant green and red lights dangled down from over the door.

The burgundy Saturn in the drive was probably a 2009 or so, one of the last ones made. The doors were locked, but we peeked through the windows. The car was completely empty—of people as well as clutter.

Wayne would probably be right. This wouldn't be a kidnapping. Maybe the lady just wasn't ready for the holiday to end, had left her Christmas lights on, and gone off with a friend.

But as we walked closer to the house, I saw red-and-white-striped candy canes scattered over the porch, and the string of lights dangling from over the front door, still lit, were definitely out of place.

Then I noticed something significant—a lady's purse. Not an expensive brand, it probably came from Wally World. Zipped closed, black imitation leather, it lay on the edge of the step. I pointed it out to Wayne at the same time he must have seen it because he stepped over to it.

He picked up a stick from the ground, stuck it through the straps on the purse, and lifted the handbag just like cops do on television.

"Something's happened here, but I don't know what at this point. I think we need to go into the house to be sure Amber's not in there sick or injured."

Dalmation! I wished I was anywhere but here with the sheriff. The way my luck goes, we'd find this woman neither sick nor injured, but *dead* in her house, and I'd feel like it was my fault. *Shih tzu!* That was ridiculous. I didn't cause people to die around me.

Wayne stepped to the door and pushed the dangling string of illuminated lights over with the stick. The green wire snapped back at him and slapped his finger. He snatched his hand back and let out a mild cuss word. Then he put his finger to his mouth. "Burned just a little," he said.

He knocked and rang the doorbell, but no one answered. I've known the man my whole life, and I could almost *see* his brain working, considering what to do next. Action was swift when he made up his mind. I expected him to kick the door in, but, instead, since there was no dead bolt, he jimmied the lock with a credit card from his wallet and the door swung open.

Inside, everything appeared decorated and immaculate. An empty cereal bowl and coffee cup in the sink were the only things not spotless in the kitchen. The single bed in her bedroom was made with corners folded in military precision and ornamental Christmas cushions spread across the top. She had Christmas trees and nativity scenes in every room along with ceramic figurines of angels and Santas.

"Not to hurt your feelings," Wayne said, "but I want you to stand still while I check this out. The purse on the steps bothers me, and I'd feel better if her car wasn't in the driveway."

The sheriff oozed tension into the air. Something was wrong. He knew it, and I knew it, but we didn't know what had happened or what he might find as he opened every closet door and inspected the contents. When he finished, he came back to me and said, "The only evidence of foul play is her handbag on the porch. Everything in here looks fine, and her car in the driveway isn't necessarily an indication of anything wrong, but the purse is."

"Those candy canes all over the front porch aren't a good sign either," I commented. "She appears to be a good housekeeper, not the kind of woman who'd drop things and leave them lying all around."

Wayne took the broom from the kitchen and swept the candy canes on the porch into an evidence bag from his car.

"Are you doing that in case there are fingerprints on the cellophane wrappers?" I asked.

"Just in case."

He put the broom back, then locked the door behind us as we left.

By the time we'd finished at Amber Buchanan's, neither of us had time for a sit-down lunch at Rizzie's. We went through the McDonald's drive-through and picked up sandwiches before he took me back to his office to get my car.

• • •

My niece Megan and nephew Johnny ran over and gave me great big bear hugs when I went into Gee Three that evening. I'm really trying to use Rizzie's "brand," and Daddy or John were supporting it because one of them had bought the kids Gee Three sweatshirts which they wore. Daddy, John, Miriam, Mike, and Frankie nodded at me and said "hello," but none of them are into hugging me hello or goodbye like the kids are.

"Where are Bill and Molly?" I asked when I sat down at the biggest table Rizzie has in the grill.

"He called and said they wouldn't make it," was Frankie's answer.

Tyrone arrived at the table with eight glasses of sweet iced tea and asked, "Are you ready to order?"

"Not yet," Daddy said. "Does Rizzie have a special today?"

"Yes, she calls it the 'Split Po Boy.' " Tyrone paused.

"What's that?" Daddy asked.

"It's a twelve-inch sub on crusty French bread. What makes it a split is that she puts oysters on one end and catfish on the other. You can get it dressed with lettuce, tomato, pickles, and onion or undressed with just meat and either tartar sauce or remoulade sauce." Tyrone delivered this in a monotone, making it obvious that Rizzie had made him memorize it.

"What's remoulade?" my nephew asked, mutilating the pronunciation of the name of the sauce.

"It's a special mayonnaise kind of thing that Rizzie makes. It has a little mustard and pickles and something that makes it pinkish-colored. Oh, and horseradish, definitely has some of that in it." Rizzie clearly hadn't rehearsed him on that.

Most of us decided to try the Split Po Boy but Johnny and Megan both asked for hamburgers.

After turning in our orders, Tyrone came back to our table. "You should have been here yesterday morning," he said to everyone. "Callie helped deliver a baby."

"What?"

"Callie and Pork Chop Higgins helped Misty Bledsoe have her baby right here in the diner. It's a boy. Billy Wayne came by while ago and said he was on the way to the hospital to pick them up."

Megan screwed up her nose and made that "eeuhh" sound teenaged girls sometimes use to express distaste. "We're not eating at the table where she had the baby, are we?"

"Nah," Tyrone answered, "Misty was actually lying on the floor over there by the first booth."

Thank heavens Rizzie called him then to pick up an order. I really didn't want a blow-by-blow description of birth from a fifteen-year-old. Johnny's the same age though, and I could see that he was interested.

Our food was scrumptious, and the only thing wrong with a Split Po Boy is that it's impossible to tell which side tastes better—the catfish or the oysters. Rizzie came to the table just as we all finished eating. "How about dessert? I have some home-made fruit cake and several kinds of cookies."

The adults all ordered cake, and the kids wanted cookies. "Granpa wouldn't let us eat any of the bourbon balls," Megan said as she licked the frosting off a bell-shaped sugar cookie. Then, with a proud as punch expression, she said, "But he's making Aunt Cutie's Peanut Butter Blossoms for us tomorrow." I grinned at that and made a mental note to go by Daddy's tomorrow. Those were my favorite cookies growing up.

"Don't be offended," I answered her with my mind back on the Bourbon Balls. "He won't let me drink beer at his house and probably wouldn't let me eat bourbon balls either."

Daddy grinned. "Start sharing my bourbon balls with everyone, and I might run short after I take some over to Miss Lettie. Did you know that woman ran that farm by herself since the Vietnam War?"

"Better be careful," Frankie said. "From the way she behaved last night, Miss Lettie may already be noshing on some bourbon balls."

"I think maybe the doctor had given her something to keep her calm," John defended his friend's mother. "Until Jeff moved, she was really a paradox. She was very demanding and strict, yet she smothered him, too. I hadn't seen her in years until last night, but this has to be as awful for her as her husband's death was, and that was a major subject at their house the whole time Jeff and I were growing up."

"Losing a spouse that you love isn't something a person ever gets over," Daddy said. "Then to have a child die has to be dreadful."

"And Jeff was her only child," John commented.

"That don't matter a whole lot," Daddy said. "Do you think I'd grieve less for one of my children than someone who only has one? You can't replace a child, no matter how many you have."

"You could replace a wife *and* a child, Granpa," Johnny suggested. "You could marry somebody new who had a child or your new wife could have a baby."

Daddy's eyebrows lifted in that way he does sometimes when he's surprised. The rest of us laughed at the thought of Daddy with a new baby. "And I might just do that someday, but a new wife would be just that—a new wife, but not a replacement, and I'm perfectly happy with the kids I've got, though a few more grandchildren would be nice." With that, he cut his eyes toward me.

At that moment, James Brown embarrassed me by shouting from my bosom.

"Hello," I answered.

"This is Otis. What's the chance of your coming back by here when you finish dinner with your family? Didn't you transfer all the prepaid funeral files to the computer?"

"I did."

"Where are the original folders?"

"In boxes upstairs on the second floor."

"Frank Patterson is coming over, and we're going to need to access some files. It'll be easier if you're here and can pull this stuff up on the computer instead of having to dig out the box and paperwork."

"I'll be back soon. We've finished eating, and Daddy's going over to Miss Lettie's again."

Otis may have needed me to find what he wanted on the computer, but when I arrived, he was bringing a big box of files down the stairs from the upstairs room that had been casket storage until recently and the Middletons' living room before then.

"What's going on?" I asked.

"Have you heard of that new natural burying ground?"

"The one in the green cemetery where we buried that lady's husband and planted the crape myrtle tree?"

"No, this is even newer. They advertise that 'you can be your own undertaker' and not involve anyone except the owner of the ground."

"What's the name of this cemetery?"

"It's not a cemetery! It's a field where they're burying people without caskets, not even those cardboard or basket ones; no vaults of any kind, not even concrete blocks around the body to keep the earth from sinking; no memorial markers, don't even plant a tree; no service at all. The burying ground man just digs a hole, dumps the body in, and covers it up. The family doesn't pick the spot. He's got them lined up and 'planting' bodies side by side, back to front, so he doesn't drive his tractor over an existing grave because he's packing them in as close as possible. It's a field, just a common field. Go look it up on the Internet. I think it's called Fields of Flowers Green Funeral Services."

I did as I was told. Fields of Flowers had a webpage fit for a rock star. Across the top in sparkle letters was, "Save $ and our environment with natural burial." Below that, a picture of beautiful wildflowers served as background for bold goldenrod-colored letters: FIELD of FLOWERS NATURAL CEMETERY. For under a thousand dollars, Field of Flowers would sell a plot and provide opening and closing of the grave. For an additional one hundred dollars plus seventy-five cents a mile, they would transport the body from place of death or the morgue to the cemetery with no stops. Since embalming, caskets, vaults, and memorials weren't allowed, those were the only choices. They also provided (for one dollar) a brochure explaining how to obtain death certificates. As each section of the cemetery was filled, the owners would plant it with wildflowers. Sweet, simple, and cheap without having to pay a preacher or musician either.

I have to admit that if I wasn't involved in the mortuary industry myself, it would sound pretty good to me, but I'd been with Middleton's long enough that I believed in the value of a funeral service where the family and loved ones could be comforted by their pastor and remember the deceased together.

Would places like this take over the business? I wondered. I'd assumed that Otis was exaggerating and Fields of Flowers would turn out to be a funeral home and cemetery that was simplifying the funeral business by cutting out the "extras," things like catering and jewelry, but I'd had no idea that it would be cut as drastically as it was described. They should have named the place "Bare Bones" because that's what their amenities were stripped to and that's what their "cemetery" would hold quite quickly as they buried unprepped bodies either clothed or wrapped in natural fibers like cotton as the webpage specified.

"Precious Memories" announced Mr. Patterson's arrival, so I closed out the Internet and went to meet him at the front door.

"I don't have time to waste on this. Just refund my money. My mind's made up. When Emma Lou dies, I'm going to bury her at Fields of Flowers."

"I'm sorry, sir, but I don't make any decisions or handle business here. You'll need to talk to one of the Middletons." I smiled and turned. "Follow me, please."

I led Mr. Patterson to Otis's office. Otis was seated at his desk with the big file box in front of him. When we entered, he appeared to be frantically going through the files, but he stopped and stood when he saw us. "Let's go down to a consulting room," he said in his Funeral Director 101 voice.

"I demand my money back right now!"

Otis ignored him until we were seated at the conference table. "Now, sir, before we can discuss refunding your money for the prepaid funeral, I need some information." He took a clipboard from a small table beside the chair and placed it in front of him. "Your name?"

"I'm Frank Patterson, and my wife was Emma Lou Riley."

"Was? Then your wife is deceased?"

"No, but she's dying, and I've decided to put her in that flower place they advertise on television where it costs less than a thousand dollars. Emma Lou tells me her first husband prepaid Middleton's for both their funerals before he died. She says all I have to do is call you people when she kicks the bucket and you'll take care of everything."

"If her services have been prepaid, that, sir, is all you'll need to do. If she's in the hospital or a nursing home, please tell them to call us as soon as she's pronounced. We'll remove her and then you can finalize the arrangements." I cringed when Otis said, "We'll remove her," because that's one Funeraleze word I don't use. The term "remove" is what most morticians use to refer to bringing the body from the place of death or medical examiner's facility to the funeral home. I use the term "pick up." I don't know exactly why, but it sounds more respectful to me. When I die, I'd rather be picked up than removed.

"Can't you understand what I'm saying?" Patterson sputtered. "I want the money back. I'm not going to use your services." His face turned dark red.

"I believe, sir, that if you read the contract, you'll find that the prepaid services are not refundable except under certain conditions."

"Emma Lou doesn't know where the papers are. She told me to check with you about them, but I'm telling you I want the money back."

"You're going to need to talk to my brother Odell, but I assure you that there can be no refund to you if you're not who bought the service."

"He's dead. I told you that her first husband made these arrangements. You buried him almost ten years ago. I'm her husband now. The money comes to me."

"Not unless she's dead, and even then, for you to get a refund for a prepaid funeral, the person must not only be dead but also have no remains to be interred."

"Now, how is Emma Lou supposed to be dead but have no remains?"

"Sir, that's to cover situations like when the deceased is lost at sea or dies in an explosion—something like that."

"She's not even able to get out of bed. She's certainly not going to be out in a boat or anywhere there's a bomb. I just want my money back."

"It's not your money until you inherit from your wife. Then it will become yours, but right now, you have no say at all." This sounded rude coming from Otis. He stood and said, "Call tomorrow and make an appointment to see my brother Odell. He can explain this better than I can. You need to read the contract."

"I've already told you, I can't *find* the contract! You have to give me another copy."

"I can't do that. The prepayment belongs to your wife."

"She's a dying invalid."

"Call and make an appointment with Odell."

"Can't you make the appointment?"

"No, sir. It's time for you to leave now. It's past closing time."

"I didn't know funeral homes ever closed. Isn't someone here all the time?"

"Not anyone who can handle money matters." That was an unspoken lie. It would lead the listener to believe that *someone* was always on the premises, and it used to be law in South Carolina that someone was always at funeral homes, but that law changed years ago. Now if we have no decedents, we put the phones on call-forwarding and go home at night. Of course, we're always available and if a pickup call comes in, Otis, Odell, or one of the part-timers goes immediately to bring the body to Middleton's. I've even been on a few pickup calls myself.

Without touching Mr. Patterson nor telling him to come on, Otis led him to the door and locked it after Mr. Patterson left.

"Why didn't you want me to make a copy of the contract?" I asked.

"Because I can't find it. I first wanted you here to see if you copied it into the computer when you converted these files. Then I decided that from the way he'd sounded on the telephone, insisting to come this evening and all, I'd rather Odell handle the whole thing."

"Where is Odell?"

"Your guess is as good as mine. I'm on duty and he's not answering his cell phone."

Before I left Middleton's, I pulled up the prepayment file for Emma Lou Riley on the computer. The prearrangements had been finalized and paid for almost twelve years previously. Plans were for a very expensive casket, quality vault, and top-of-the-line accessories. Of course, the price that had been paid wouldn't touch that service at today's prices. I printed out copies of the front and back of all the planning forms and the contract for Otis before I went home.

Big Boy didn't meet me at the door like he usually did. He looked up when I talked to him and rubbed his head against my hand when I petted him, but he stayed on his special rug and seemed too tired to play.

I lay awake trying to read, torn between worry that Big Boy wasn't acting normal and that Patel hadn't called back since saying he would. I was also angry with myself that I hadn't remembered to buy myself more chocolate MoonPies. *Sometimes life sucks,* I told myself, *but it's a little more bearable when I have a MoonPie to nibble.*

★ ON THE FOURTH DAY OF CHRISTMAS MY TRUE LOVE GAVE TO ME

FOUR FALLING FLAKES

I couldn't believe it! I stepped off the back stoop and stuck my tongue out as far as it would go while Big Boy dang near knocked me over trying to get back into the apartment. My dog's lethargy from the night before was gone. He'd tried to climb up on my bed before I even thought about getting up. He obviously felt much better as he licked my face, and I'd ignored him as long as I could before pulling on a pair of jeans, sweatshirt, and Nikes.

When he was a puppy, I sometimes let Big Boy sleep beside me in bed, but now that he was pushing one hundred fifty pounds, he was too big. Besides, he'd had that surgery. I didn't want to risk my dog hurting himself even more. Since I'd brought him home from the vet's, there'd been times when he'd moan and whimper when he moved certain ways. I've never had surgery, and if I ever do, it won't be by choice. I'm scared of the knife, or should I say scalpel? That's why I wear my inflatable bras instead of opting for augmentation surgery. Being cut on has to hurt.

I'd clipped Big Boy's leash to his collar and dragged him to the back door. He'd pulled back, trying to get to the front door where he usually went in and out.

When I pushed the door open, Big Boy jumped out, obviously in a hurry for his morning bathroom break, but as soon as he saw and felt something falling from the sky, he turned around and almost knocked me over getting back into the apartment.

My yard was beautiful—looked like a Christmas card!

South Carolina doesn't get much snow. Oh, it snows occasionally up toward Greenville, and once in a long while, the middle of the state around the capital city Columbia has an inch or so, but on the coast, it's very rare. This morning my yard was covered with snow. To be honest, it probably wasn't more than half an inch, but there was enough of the wonderful stuff to hide my dead grass.

The few times I'd seen real snow before, it had fallen during the night, and I'd awakened to see it the next morning. This time was different. It fell all over me as I stood there with my tongue stuck out, hoping to taste the white flakes.

Then it hit me. *Dalmation!* Miss Lettie wasn't going to be happy about this. The only people on the coast of South Carolina who can drive with even a minimum of ice or snow on the roads are transplanted folks from up north. Even the smallest accumulation creates holidays for everyone. Officials cancel schools for the day and close government offices. The only activity on a snow day would be at the grocery stores where customers immediately bought a month's supply of batteries, peanut butter, bread, and milk in case the weather created power outages or the roads became impassable. Actually, for us, any snow or ice at all makes driving hazardous. Not only because we can't drive in it, but because other folks on the road can't either.

Miss Lettie wanted a big crowd for Mr. Morgan's funeral. She wouldn't like anything interfering with her plans.

I thought about that for a few minutes before deciding there was nothing I could do about Miss Lettie, so I might as well enjoy this unexpected blessing. I knocked on Jane's door, and when she didn't answer. I hammered it as hard as I could.

"Who is it?" A soft voice from inside.

"It's me." Okay, I know that the grammatically correct statement would be, "It is I," but to say that around the Low Country would sound pompous and preposterous.

"Put your clothes on and come out back," I added. "I want to show you something."

"Oh, no, don't tell me you found another body."

"No, it's a good thing."

Jane stepped outside wearing a purple terry-cloth bathrobe over pink flannel pajamas and fuzzy slippers. "It's cold," she said as the delicate flakes touched her face.

"It's snow!" I shouted.

Back when I went to the University of South Carolina in Columbia, we'd had rare accumulations of an inch or so of snow, but this was the first time Jane and I had experienced it together.

"Tell me what you see," Jane commanded and danced around, doing her version of a victory dance, though in her case, it must have been a hippie dance because I remembered her mother jumping like that when she was very happy, and Jane's mom was as hippie as hippie can be.

"Be careful. You'll slip and fall. The ground is slick," I warned my friend.

"I want to build a snow man." Jane continued her joyful dance.

"Not enough yet, but if it keeps falling, we might be able to make snow angels."

When Otis Middleton walked into our back yard, Jane and I probably looked like full-blown idiots. There wasn't enough snow for a snowball fight, so Jane and I were gathering up handfuls of the powdery stuff and smashing it into each other's faces like some brides and grooms do when they cut their wedding cakes.

"So, here you are," Otis said. "I've been trying to call you. When I couldn't get an answer, I drove over, checking out the ditches on the way to be sure you hadn't run off the road on the way to work. I'll drive you. I'm in one of the family cars, much heavier than your Mustang."

Work? A hundred and one dalmations! I'd forgotten all about it.

"I'm sorry. Just give me a few minutes, and I'll be ready," I apologized.

Otis nodded in agreement and then turned his attention toward Jane.

"You need to go inside and put on a coat," he told her. "It's too cold to be out here in what you're wearing."

Jane shivered, obviously exaggerating the motion. "You're right, Otis. There's fresh coffee inside if you want to come in for a cup while Callie gets dressed over at her place."

They went into Jane's while I headed to my door. Big Boy's bladder had finally won out over his fear of all things that fall from the sky. When I opened my door, he darted outside, looked around for a tree to hide behind, and then gave up and squatted right by the back steps. Of course, the stitches in his abdomen may have made lifting his leg painful, but the truth is that regardless of how big he is, my dog still acts like a puppy. He *never* lifts his leg, and if there's a tree or anything to hide behind, he'll be sure to get on the other side of it, oblivious to the fact his head sticks out on one side, while his wagging tail shows on the other.

I confess that while I felt quite confident that I could drive as well in our scant covering of snow as Otis could, I didn't mind having a ride to work that morning. No telling when some other Southerner who'd never driven in snow or ice before might careen into me, and I do *not* want my 1966 Mustang hit. I've got a new ragtop on it, but it still has scratches and gouges from vandalism not too long ago, and that's already too much damage.

"Are you certain that Miss Lettie will want to have the funeral today with this weather?" I asked Otis as he carefully backed out of the driveway.

"I'm not sure, but we need to be ready regardless of what she decides."

I laughed. "At least we don't have to worry about this being one of those redneck funerals Jeff Foxworthy talks about."

"What do you mean?"

"Foxworthy says you might be a redneck if you wear shorts to a funeral. There'll be jeans there, but I don't expect shorts." In the summertime, we've had people wear shorts to funerals. Odell has joked about handing out long pants like some restaurants lend ties to men who don't fit into their dress requirements.

On the way to the mortuary, we passed a couple of vehicles that had skidded off the road and landed in ditches, so I was surprised when Otis pulled over to the side of the road for no apparent reason.

"I'll just be a few minutes," he said as he stepped out of the car. "I want to check the tires. One of them doesn't feel right."

He walked slowly around the vehicle, pausing and looking at each tire. We'd hardly gone a mile farther when he did the exact same thing again. Before we reached the mortuary, Otis had stopped to check the tires four times. I didn't mind because once we were actually in St. Mary, the big silver tinsel stars the town had put on each streetlamp were perfect with the snow on the ground. Sad that we make our world so beautiful for Christmas and then take it all down.

Odell met us at the employee entrance. "Mrs. Morgan has already called."

"Is she postponing?" I asked.

"No, she wants everything as planned, but she made a strange comment about anyone who fought in a war wouldn't cancel because of the weather. Did Mr. Morgan serve in the military?"

"No, but she wants us to present a flag during his service. She's bringing the one she received at her husband's funeral. I told Callie we'd do a little ceremony with it," Otis reminded Odell.

"No problem. Like we always say: If it's not illegal or going to hurt someone, we do whatever the loved ones ask. How are the roads?"

Otis suddenly turned and walked quickly away from us down the hall to his office, so I answered, "Not very bad."

"I didn't think the streets were a real mess or the florists wouldn't have delivered already. Everything in the flower room is for the Morgan services. Take them into Slumber Room A."

"Sure. Let me take off my coat first."

"Otis will stay here, and I'll take the new family car to Mrs. Morgan's to pick up her and her friend."

"You might want to take the older car. Otis felt something wrong with the tires and kept having to stop to check them."

"Did he have to stop and walk around the car?"

"Yes. That's exactly what he did."

Odell burst into a roaring guffaw. "Ain't nothing wrong with the tires. He went out and ate enchiladas and refried beans last night. Otis has been pulling that stunt when he has gas since he was a teenager. Now me, I just let it rip."

Typical of South Carolina snowfall, most of it had melted off the streets by noon though trees, bushes, and lawns were still blanketed in a thin layer of white. I took Mr. Morgan's casket to the chapel and double-checked his appearance before moving all the floral tributes from the slumber room to the chapel.

I held the door open when I heard the family car pull under the covered portico. Miss Lettie was talking fast and loud. "Just look at that beautiful snow! My Jeffrey Junior was always special, and this snow on his day proves it. I want to see my boy again."

With Odell on one side and Miss Ellen on the other, she hurried to the casket and this time she lifted the drape. I saw Odell's hand rise as she reached toward the body, but she gently stroked Mr. Morgan's cheek and crooned, "My baby, my baby boy." Miss Ellen must have been aware that we'd had to do reconstruction because she touched her friend's hand and moved it away from Mr. Morgan's face.

"Come, Lettie. More flowers have been delivered. Let's see who sent them."

Nowadays, lots of families suggest donations to churches or charities in lieu of plants or arrangements at a funeral, but Miss Lettie hadn't wanted that, and there were over thirty sprays, baskets and wreaths as well as a few poinsettias.

The chapel was packed when the visitation began. Here in St. Mary, many businesses close if there are even a dozen flakes of snow. Stores that sell the snow essentials of bread, peanut butter, and batteries in case the power goes off, close as soon as supplies are gone. The roads were clear, and I guess all those people who were off work that Saturday showed up to pay their respects. Miss Lettie had requested that the coffin be closed at the end of the chapel service instead of between the visitation and the funeral. At two o'clock, Otis and Odell circulated around quietly requesting everyone to be seated for the service.

I'd seen Daddy and John speak to Miss Lettie, then mingle and socialize with the crowd. For the service, they sat right behind the reserved seats. I didn't expect them to sit with me in the back. They understand that my responsibility during funerals is to sit where I can keep an eye on everyone in the event someone faints or behaves in a manner not appropriate to the funeral service. Pastor Holt gave an inspiring sermon, and Ruth Gates sang beautifully. They'd added a few more songs, and she did one of my favorites, "God's Other World." Eulogies have become more frequent recently, so I wasn't surprised when Sheriff Wayne Harmon stepped forward. His words were touching. He spoke of Jeff Morgan's childhood and their friendship through the years. When he mentioned that Jeff's mother had raised him by herself because of his father's death in Vietnam, Miss Lettie jumped up and ran to the casket.

"You never knew him! You never knew him!" she screamed. I thought she was saying that Wayne hadn't known Jeff, then that Jeff Morgan hadn't had a chance to know his father, but I was wrong.

"He was such a beautiful baby," she shouted, "and you went off to Vietnam and didn't come home to help me with him! If you'd been here, maybe he wouldn't have moved away and he wouldn't be dead now." I realized her words were directed toward her husband, dead all these many years since Vietnam.

Both Miss Ellen and Wayne hugged her shoulders and tried to ease Miss Lettie away from the coffin, but she collapsed against the casket and they almost had to carry her back to her seat.

Wayne wrapped up the eulogy with just a few more sentences. I don't know if that was all he'd planned to say or if he'd cut it short to keep from upsetting Miss Lettie even more.

During Pastor Holt's benediction, Odell leaned over my shoulder. "Callie, I've decided to go with Otis and the part-timers to the cemetery and leave you here in case a call comes in. Otis and I will present the flag graveside. I don't expect Patterson back today, but if he shows up, don't discuss anything. Tell him he has to talk to me."

I helped load the flowers into the van and stood by the door watching everyone but me drive away.

"Callie, I want to talk to you." I jumped. I hadn't realized anyone was still there.

"Well, talk to me." I turned around to face the sheriff.

"How about talking over a cup of coffee."

"No problem. Go on into my office and I'll brew two cups." We have a thirty-cup pot, a ten-cup pot, and a one-cup coffee maker.

Wayne and I sat across from each other at my desk with fresh cups of Pecan Torte Gevalia in mugs, not the fancy Wedgwood cups I use when Otis or Odell wants coffee served to clientele.

"There's been a development in Amber Buchanan's case."

"The missing woman?"

"The body in the Santa suit that was on your porch is Amber."

"How do you know? I thought Amber was a plump girl. Detective Robinson described the body as a slim woman with long red hair."

"Callie, you of all people, know that size and hair color are very changeable attributes, especially in women." He motioned toward my honey blonde hair. The only reason I'm never a redhead is because dyed red hair fades more rapidly than other colors. I've been every shade from platinum to jet black, and all it takes for me to change my hair color is a change of mood.

"Why was she on my porch wearing a Santa Claus costume?"

"We're not sure, but Amber planned to give out the presents at one of the Safe Sister houses. No men are allowed in there, and we think she may have decided that the kids would enjoy having Santa deliver the gifts. I have a deputy checking with the costume store to see if Amber Clark rented the outfit there. Of course the store's closed because of the blizzard here." He laughed. Just like Wayne to say that because sometimes he exaggerates as big as I do.

"Amber Clark?" I questioned.

"I mean Amber Buchanan. She was a Clark when we were in school together."

"How'd you get a fingerprint for Amber and how'd you get it so fast? I thought that would take several days."

"IAFIS—the Integrated Automated Fingerprint Identification System. You've probably seen it used on those CSI television programs you watch. It provides automated fingerprint searches through their data which includes criminal prints as well as employment background checks and legitimate firearm purchase prints. Amber's prints were on file because she worked in a place that houses minors and requires fingerprints and background checks. The body's prints were taken and submitted in Charleston."

"Still that was awfully fast. I thought it took more than a week."

"Takes a lot longer for DNA testing, but matching fingerprints is almost instantaneous these days."

"I appreciate your letting me know all this, but why are you sharing? Usually, I have to drag info from you."

"A week before Christmas, a man named Norman Spires got into a raging argument with Amber at the Safe Sister office. He insisted she let him see his wife, Naomi Spires, and that he was going to get his daughter Betsy out of Safe Sister to spend the holidays with him. Amber refused to even discuss whether Naomi and Betsy were at Safe Sister. They're at Safe Sister because Spires abused both of them. He cussed out Amber and then pushed her. She didn't hesitate to call 911 and press charges for assault. Norman Spires got out of jail on bond Christmas morning."

"What does that have to do with me?"

"Amber's body will be brought back here from Charleston and kept in Middleton's cooler until released by us to the next of kin when we identify who has rights to the body. Another consideration is Amber's husband, Randy Buchanan. He's incarcerated for robbing a jewelry store. When he was convicted, he insisted that he'd given some jewels to Amber to hold for him. She swore in court that he was lying. He's in jail for robbery, but he's mean. The reason she was drawn to work at Safe Sister was that she'd been there herself when Randy beat her. I just want you to know these are not nice people we're dealing with. Don't be daydreaming when you should be alert to your surroundings."

"Well, thank you for your concern." Sarcasm is one of my faults, and my tone of voice showed it.

"Don't be such an intelligent derriere. I'm serious. I have a female deputy over at Safe Sister right now, talking to Naomi Spires, trying to learn as much as possible about Norman and where he might have gone when he bonded out of jail."

"If it's that serious to you, I'll take it more seriously, too. I'll be careful of who comes in here and be aware of my surroundings wherever I am." Okay, I said it just like a little girl says, "Yes, sir," to her daddy when she knows she won't be home on time, but I consider myself very aware at all times.

"That's exactly what I want. I don't like the fact that the door here is unlocked all day so that people can just walk in."

"You'll never talk Otis and Odell into locking our front door. We welcome the families of deceased loved ones any time they want to be here."

Wayne laughed. "You sounded just like Otis when you said that." He finished his second cup of coffee, stood, and stepped toward the door. He turned back toward me.

"Callie, I heard you're going out with Detective Robinson. I'm not too happy about that."

"Why?"

"The only reason he accepted my offer was because he wants to live in a small town on the coast. He's got more education and experience in homicide than anyone else who applied for the job, and I'm already seeing that he's a superb deputy even when we're not working a murder. I want him to stay here."

"What does that have to do with me?"

"Face it, Callie. Your track record with men hasn't been fantastic since you moved back. Your relationships haven't lasted very long. I don't want you two getting serious real fast, then Robinson leaving when you break up."

"Your deputy's just taking me to get something to eat. Don't go thinking we'll get involved at all, much less soon. And furthermore, Dr. Donald's been calling and trying to get me to date him again. He claims he's commitment-shy and got scared he was getting in too deep, but now he wants to pursue our relationship."

"So why are you going out with Robinson?"

"I don't know if I want to date Donald again, and going out with Robinson is more like welcoming him to town. He said we'd talk about things he needs to know about St. Mary like where to get his dry cleaning done."

"Wherever he's been taking his laundry is fine. His uniforms are always immaculately pressed and when he's in civilian clothes, they're impeccable." He shrugged. "I'm just saying don't scare him off by chasing him or breaking his heart. I want to keep him with the department."

Truth was—I'd been considering canceling the date with Robinson, even though Patel still hadn't called and didn't answer when I rang him. Wayne Harmon's warning me not to associate on a personal level with one of his employees infuriated me. Forget about canceling. I'd be home and looking as good as possible at eight o'clock.

"How'd it go?" I asked Otis when he came in.

"Glad this one's over. Odell has driven Mrs. Morgan and her friend home in the family car."

I almost asked if he'd taken the new one and were the tires okay now, but Otis is a sensitive man, and he'd be upset to know Odell had explained the tire business to me.

"Did you present the flag to her?"

"Yes, and I don't think she even noticed we weren't military. I don't know what kind of tranq her doctor might have given her, but by the time we got to the cemetery, she was even more out of it. She claimed the snow was a beautiful white blanket for her baby, and in the next breath, she was talking to her dead husband telling him she wished he could see Jeffrey Junior. Her friend tried to tell her the boy's with his daddy now, but she still rambled on." He turned out of the hall into his office door.

"Have we had any calls?" he called over his shoulder.

"No pickups, but the sheriff says they've identified the Santa Claus body and it's Amber Buchanan, the missing employee from Safe Sister. She'll come back here until she's released to next of kin."

"We'll pick her up tomorrow morning. You can go now. I'll be here until we lock up."

Big Boy hobbled to the back door when I went into my apartment. Usually he greets me joyfully and has to be reminded not to jump up on me. He's big enough now that when he does that, his paws reach my shoulders. That afternoon, he moved slowly and I swear he had a pained expression on his face instead of the smile he normally wears when he greets me. Yes, there's no denying my dog uses human expressions. He smiles when he's happy. I also noticed that his food bowl was still full and very little was missing from his water bowl. I emptied and refilled it. Big Boy took a few laps and lay down on his rug. I couldn't understand what was going on with him. He acted normal at times, and then he behaved like a very old dog unable to move much or respond to me.

I rubbed my dog behind his ears. "What's wrong, Big Boy? Still feeling puny?" The vet had said to leave the bandage over his incision until he went back to her Tuesday, but I was tempted to take it off and look at his stomach. I understand the theory that keeping an operation bandaged avoids infection, but it also hides contamination if it's already there.

By the time I'd bathed and done my hair and makeup, Big Boy was snoring again. I put on cream-colored wool slacks and a dark crimson sweater with a new single strand of white pearls—real ones—that John's family had sent me for Christmas. Looking at myself in the mirror, I decided to enlarge my girls just a bit more. That involved taking off the sweater, removing the blow-up bra, and carefully inflating both sides so that one ta ta didn't look bigger than the other one. Back into the bra. Back into the sweater. Flip the pearls from under the sweater so they showed. Comb the hair again. Modesty is a virtue, and I try to be virtuous—at least most of the time—but my mirror told me I rocked!

For a moment, I thought about the ugly yellow crime scene tape stretched around my front porch, but it didn't matter since Detective Dean Robinson was my date. He was the one who'd put it there. He knocked on the back door five minutes early.

"Hi, come on in." He looked even better than he had in uniform. I saw what the sheriff meant. The deputy wore dark gray, perfectly pressed and creased slacks, a light gray pinpoint cotton dress shirt, and a silk tie with stripes that varied from white to black. Under my indoor lights, instead of looking sandy blond, his short hair appeared more like a light prematurely gray. He was monochromatic except his lively blue eyes. His smile seemed genuine.

"You look fantastic," he said. "Have you decided where you'd like to have dinner?"

I knew where I'd like to have dinner—at Andre's, the fancy French restaurant I'd been to with Dr. Donald Walters and J. T. Patel. I have no idea what the sheriff's department of a small county like ours pays its officers, but I had no intention of eating half this man's paycheck on Saturday night, so I suggested Rizzie's place. I even remembered to call it Gee Three.

"Gee Three? What does that stand for?"

"Gastric Gullah Grill. My friend owns it and does the cooking. She serves Gullah foods, but you can get plain country cooking there, too."

"Let's go there next time. A new place just opened near Beaufort that you might enjoy." Hesitation showed on his face as though he'd just thought of something. "You're not a vegetarian, are you?"

"Not me." Were we going out for a meatless meal? I had friends in Columbia who were vegetarians and vegans, and there are vegan restaurants there, but we always went to restaurants that offered both—frequently Indian restaurants because they have vegetarian dishes as well as those with meat. The thought of Indian food brought Patel to mind. Why hadn't I heard from him? Why didn't he answer my calls? Was he commitment-shy like Dr. Donald Walters or had he just lost interest already?

"Callie?" Dean waved his hand in front of my face. "Are you okay? You blanked out on me for a minute."

"I'm fine, and I'm happy to try the new restaurant, Detective Robinson."

"Detective Robinson? I thought this was a date."

I smiled. "I believe it is."

"Then you should call me Dean so that I don't have to start calling you Miss Parrish."

He not only helped me on with my coat, he held the door open for me to get into his Ford Ranger. I believe in equal rights for women, including equal pay and the right to think for ourselves, but I like that old-fashioned Southern gentlemanly behavior as well. During the ride, we chatted about St. Mary. I told him about growing up here, then moving to Columbia where I attended the University of South Carolina, taught kindergarten, and married.

"But you're divorced now?"

"Yes. After my divorce, I moved back to St. Mary and used my South Carolina cosmetology license to work at Middleton's."

"Then you're not a licensed funeral director?" he asked.

"No, I don't do any of the actual mortician's work. I do hair, makeup, dressing, and some office chores. What about you? How'd you get into law enforcement?"

"All I ever wanted to do is be a cop, but my family's full of lawyers and judges. I went to college, then law school, but that didn't suit me at all. I worked in New York City for a few years and then moved to Florida. The city I was in was fine so far as the police work, but I didn't like the fast pace of life in general there any better than I had in New York. I read Sheriff Harmon's ad and since my background was exactly what he said he wanted, I applied. So far I like it, but I haven't really been here long enough to know for sure."

We rode in silence for a while. Finally, I said, "Tell me about the restaurant."

"Have you ever been to a Brazilian steakhouse?"

"Nope, never even heard of it."

"First off, it's all you can eat, so I hope you're hungry."

"I am. Is it all you can eat steak?"

"Yes, as well as pork, lamb, chicken, and fish. Gauchos, which is just a fancy word for cowboys, go through the room offering diners some of everything. All the meats are grilled or cooked on a rotisserie over wood. They also have a tremendous salad bar and several hot side dishes like seasoned rice and potatoes."

As soon as he finished with what sounded like a commercial to me, I said, "Sounds great to me." I almost asked if he could afford this place, but that would be rude. Maybe he had a grand opening coupon or something. He knew enough about it that I assumed he knew the cost also.

The building was new and fancy, displaying lots of flashing neon including cowboys dressed in red and black who whirled lassos that appeared to move. I was glad I'd worn winter white pants instead of black or I'd have matched both the neon cowboys on the outside and the living ones we saw when we stepped inside. A hostess in a silky black dress greeted us and led us to our table. The salad bar ran through the entire center of the room, end to end. The live cowboys inside were young men in black pants and red shirts moving around the room carrying carving knives and huge skewers of meat over trays.

The hostess took our drink order and waved toward the center of the room. "Help yourself to the salad bar and hot side dishes." She placed a red coaster beside each of us. She lifted mine and held it up so that we could see that the back was green. "This is your signal to the gauchos whether or not you wish to be served meats. We have fifteen cuts of beef, lamb, pork, and chicken as well as fish.

"While you're having your salad or when you're busy with a previous entrée, place the card beside your plate with the red side up. That shows the gaucho that you don't want to be interrupted or served more at that time. If you turn your card green side up, the gaucho will offer you what he is serving. You may accept or decline, but don't worry that you'll miss anything because it's a continuous rotation."

Dean and I went to the bar, which featured, among other things, smoked salmon, extra large shrimp, fresh mozzarella cheese, chilled asparagus, and one of my favorites—hearts of palm. I noticed that Dean dipped more pre-made items like pasta salad, potato salad, and tabouli. I put a nest of fresh spinach leaves on my plate and then piled lots of good stuff on top, including a generous amount of cold cuts and cheeses.

Back at our table, Dean seemed to enjoy everything. I'd made a rather substantial salad, but the sight of those good-looking men in their red shirts going from table to table carving what smelled and looked like juicy, succulent meats made me hungry for more than salad. I flipped my red card over so that the green side was upright and set my salad plate to the side.

"Ma'am, would you care for garlic steak?" the first gaucho to our table asked. He looked Hispanic, but his accent was pure Low Country, South Carolina.

"Yes, thank you."

I noticed then that Dean and I each had a stack of small plates by our drinks. The man placed one in front of me and carved several slices of steak on it. I tasted it. *Wow!*

"Is it good?" Dean asked.

"Delicious. How did you know about this place?"

"I've been to Brazilian steakhouses in Florida. This is a different franchise, but the concept is the same."

Beef tenderloin; filet mignon, both plain and wrapped in bacon; beef ribs; *picanha*, their house special Brazilian steak; *linuica*, a Brazilian sausage; pork loin; lamb chops; leg of lamb—I tried everything but the chicken. I can eat chicken any time. All meat servings were sample-sized, but more than a bite or two. My favorites were the filet mignon in bacon and pork tenderloin crusted in parmesan cheese, and I had several servings of each of those.

I loved that restaurant! The only problem was that so long as the card was green side up, there was a man offering something every few minutes. That constant flow of service didn't contribute to soft get-to-know-each-other conversation. Dean flipped his card to red before I did, and he ordered coffee. He'd had several cups by the time I finally turned my card to red.

"Would you like dessert?" he asked.

"No, thank you." I didn't say it, but all I wanted at that moment was to be home in bed. I'd had a full day from its beginning when I played in the snow through working Jeff Morgan's funeral. Now my stomach was completely full, almost *too* full, and sleep would be welcome.

Dean deftly paid the bill without my seeing what the cost had been, helped me into my coat, and left me sitting in the entry area while he brought the car to the door. I tried to make polite conversation on the way back to St. Mary, but suddenly I realized that Dean was saying, "We're at your place, Callie."

I'd been *asleep!*

"Good grief, I am *so* sorry. I was *so* tired and the food was *so* good. I can't believe I took a nap on the way back."

He laughed, but it was a sweet laugh. "Just wait until your friend and my boss, Sheriff Harmon, finds out that you ended our first date snoring."

"I don't snore," I protested, then added, "do I?"

"No, you did make a little sound, but we won't call it snoring. Let's just say you 'purr' in your sleep. I won't tell the sheriff anyway. He'd get the wrong idea."

At my back door, I wasn't sure what to do if he wanted to

come in. I was so embarrassed about going to sleep in the car that I felt I should be polite and offer him a cup of coffee, but there really was no room in my stomach for even a breath mint, certainly not anything else, and besides, he'd already had plenty of coffee.

Dean stood patiently while I unlocked the door and then reached for me. I'd decided there would be no harm in a simple goodnight kiss, but instead he gave me a gentle hug and said, "Thank you for an enjoyable evening. I'll call you and we'll do it again." He waited while I stepped in and locked the door. I listened to the sound of his footsteps off the back porch and his car leaving my yard.

Now, I was tired, I was full, and I was sleepy, so tell me why I was a little disappointed and puzzled that he hadn't wanted to stay and talk or at least kiss me. I'd eaten a whole lot of garlic steak. Could that be why?

I went to Big Boy first thing. He was asleep again, but he looked comfortable and he wasn't moaning or grimacing. I pulled my sweater over my head and dropped it on the couch, thought about it, and took it into the bedroom where I folded it and my slacks and put them on a chair. The inflatable bra and fanny panties came off, and I pulled on my comfort gown. It's old and warm and used to be fuzzy. Now it's just soft and cozy.

My telephone rang as I got in bed and pulled the covers up to my chin. My heartbeat jumped to a more rapid speed, and I grabbed the receiver.

"Hello."

"Dang it, Callie, what are you doing? You sound like Roxanne." Jane didn't give me a chance to answer. "You must have thought I was going to be Mr. Patel."

"Maybe 'hoped' is a better word than 'thought.' He still hasn't called."

"So tell me about your date with the cop."

"He's not a 'cop.' He's a homicide detective."

"I don't see a thing wrong with the word 'cop.' What they don't want you to call them is that old expression, 'pig,' but I personally like pigs. I like them when they're little and cuddly, and I like them when they're all grown up and turn into bacon and ham."

"Why aren't you working?"

"I am. I just decided to take a break when I heard your date bring you home. He didn't stay long."

"No, I was wondering what to do if he wanted to stay, but he didn't ask."

"You should have known he wasn't planning to come in."

"Why?"

"He left his car engine running when he walked you to your door."

"I didn't notice that."

"You need to be more aware of your surroundings, and speaking of surroundings, is there any snow left?"

"Maybe in the woods, but the streets have been clear all day and by late afternoon, it began to melt in the yards."

"That was fun this morning."

"I thought so, too."

"Tell me about your date. Where'd you go?"

I described the entire evening—how Dean looked and acted, all about the restaurant, and the food and how it had been served.

As I talked about food, a low growl rumbled through my abdomen. In a few minutes, a sharp pain joined the sound.

"Gotta go, Jane. I think I'm going to throw up."

"You only do that when you're scared or overeat. Did you make a pig of yourself on your very first date with the cop?"

I didn't answer, dropped the phone, dashed to the bathroom, and felt mighty glad that Dean hadn't wanted to come inside.

★

ON THE FIFTH DAY OF CHRISTMAS MY TRUE LOVE GAVE TO ME

FIVE STOLEN RINGS

I believe in the Bible, and I was brought up attending Sunday School and church every weekend. I don't believe I could do my job at Middleton's and be around so many people who've passed away if I didn't believe in an afterlife and that the people I cosmetize are just shells that I work on to present good memories to their loved ones until they see them again. That said, I confess that I don't go to church as often as I should. Daddy scolds me about that, but I just can't get back in the habit. He also thinks I should be teaching Sunday School, but I was tired of teaching before I changed occupations from kindergarten teacher to mortuary cosmetician.

Big Boy had eaten better that morning. I'm aware I'm not supposed to feed him people food, and most times I don't except for his banana MoonPies, but I'd cooked grits and scrambled eggs right after I got out of bed. On the farm, Daddy never let us feed the animals eggs because he claimed a dog that ate eggs would get into the chicken coop. Personally, I don't think my dog is smart enough to make the connection between scrambled eggs with cheese grits and a raw egg in the hen house. He'd eaten better, but now he lay on his rug like he was exhausted.

After the television channel discontinued *Six Feet Under,* I bought every season on DVDs from the Target store. I figured Jane had been Roxanne all night and would sleep late, so I snuggled up in a blanket on the couch and started watching my favorite episode. I've seen those shows so many times that I know every spoken word, but a knock on my back door irritated me. I looked down at my old flannel nightgown and called through the door, "Who is it?"

"Wayne Harmon."

"Hold on. I'm not dressed yet. Let me get a robe."

I was back in just a few minutes and opened the door.

"Don't you *ever* tell a man at your door that you're not clothed," he scolded.

"But the door was locked, and it was *you*," I argued.

"Doesn't matter if the door's closed. Some men would knock your door down to get to a nude woman."

"I wasn't naked. I had on my gown, just not a robe. Besides, it was *you*!"

"And I would never hurt you, but it's not a good idea to say that even to men you know." He looked down at Big Boy. "What's wrong with your dog?"

"He doesn't feel good. He goes back to the vet Tuesday, but I'm going to call her. I was drinking a Diet Coke. Want me to make a pot of coffee?"

"No, I've had plenty of caffeine already this morning. How was your date?"

"He's nice, and no, I didn't even kiss him goodnight." I didn't bother to tell him I'd been tempted, but Dean Robinson hadn't even tried for first base.

"Want to ride back over to Amber Buchanan's house with me?"

"Why?"

"I've got a warrant now for a thorough search, and I thought you might take a look around with me—see if you spot anything unusual from your feminine point of view."

I laughed. "I didn't see anything unusual before except that she's a danged sight better housekeeper than I am and she must have more Christmas decorations than Wally's World."

"Need to talk to you about something else, too. I'll tell you about it on the way. I've got Jane's cookie tin in my car. I'll run it over there while you get dressed."

"Just leave it here. She worked late last night and is probably still asleep."

• • •

"You're going to *deputize* me?" I couldn't have been more shocked.

"I want you to go inside with me on this warrant, and to keep it legal, you need to be deputized. I don't do this every day, but I've done it before for special services for the department. I'll do it when we get to Amber Buchanan's apartment.

Being deputized was an exciting idea, but it really didn't amount to much. It's not like I'd have a uniform or anything. We stood on Amber's porch. Wayne asked me a few questions, and then told me I was now a temporary deputy with the Jade County Sheriff's Department.

"Do I get a badge?" I asked.

"I assumed you'd want one, but you have to give it back when you're no longer a legal deputy." He handed me a shiny Jade County badge. I pushed my jacket aside and pinned it to my shirt.

I grinned. "I just wanted to have one, even if it's only for a day. Will you take my picture with my cell phone?"

"Give me your telephone."

I took it out of my bra and handed it to him. Wayne rubbed the phone and smiled. "It's very warm."

I ignored him, held my jacket aside, and smiled for my picture wearing a badge. He handed back the phone and I checked the photo. I liked it. Might even use it on next year's Christmas card. This year's card was of Big Boy standing with me, front paws on my shoulders.

"If you agree, you'll be a deputy for more than just one day." Wayne unlocked the door and held it open for me.

"What do you want me to do?"

He handed me a pair of latex gloves from his pocket. "We're looking for anything that seems odd because something unusual in here could be associated with her homicide. You're a fine amateur sleuth, and I want a female vision on this."

We began in the bedroom, and I felt guilty looking through Amber Buchanan's personal belongings. One thing for sure—she didn't shop at Victoria's Secret. Her undergarments were what I'd expect to find in an old lady's drawers. I don't mean drawers like underpants. I'm talking about the storage areas of her dresser. No bikinis or thongs, and even the word "panties" was too feminine and racy for her belongings.

I was carefully refolding clothing as I put it back, but Wayne said, "You don't have to do that. People expect things to get messed up when their places are searched."

"It seems disrespectful, especially with her being dead."

"I'll finish in here. You begin the kitchen."

Amber Buchanan's kitchen was decorated for Christmas with garlands suspended from the ceiling and several live poinsettias on countertops. Tiny wreaths on each cabinet door. A bouquet of mistletoe and ribbons hung from the overhead light fixture. Figurines of a kissing Mr. and Mrs. Santa Claus and a holly-shaped spoon rest on the stove top. A miniature Christmas tree centered the table. Not a ceramic one like Jane's, Amber's was made of artificial greenery and decorated with miniature red bows. At some time, Amber or someone close to her must have been into ceramics though because little ceramic Christmas doo-dads were everywhere.

Opening the cabinets, I found that her cooking utensils were as orderly as the rest of her home. Every knife, fork, and spoon was in the correct compartment of her flatware drawer. I gave up on that at my place long ago and threw my divided holder away. I just dump everything into the drawer and pick through them when I want something.

I didn't see anything unusual among the tidy stacks of dishes or pots either. Wayne came in and watched me peeking in the cabinets and refrigerator.

"Nothing here," I told him as I opened more cabinet doors with boxes lined up neatly. Some had been opened, but the tops were sealed back with masking tape.

"You won't know that until you sift through whatever's in those boxes. Does she have ice trays in the freezer?"

"She has an ice maker." I opened the top refrigerator door and pointed.

"I didn't ask that. I questioned whether she has ice trays. Lots of people hide things in them, then fill them with water, thinking the police won't have enough sense to defrost the ice cubes."

"No ice trays."

"Now I want you to find her colander or strainer and sift that pancake mix and anything else that's been opened."

"Can I throw away the mix after I sift it?"

"No, sift it into a container and when you finish, put it back in the box or bag it came in. Check anything that's not in a sealed can even if it doesn't appear to have been opened. It's doubtful, but as sure as we throw anything away, the pathology report will come back showing some kind of poison and I'll want to have everything here analyzed."

I looked inside another cabinet filled with stacked canned goods as well as more boxes and bags carefully lined up side by side and asked, "Are you going to help me?"

"Not right now. I had her car towed in, but it puzzles me why she had it parked in the driveway when she has a garage. I'm going to check out that garage. I'll be back in here soon."

Sometimes I'm more than curious. I'm downright nosy, but sifting dry goods through colanders and then pouring the contents back into their original containers fast became boring. It also became untidy with tiny spills of cornmeal, cake mix, and coffee spattered on the table where I'd begun working. They clung to the Christmas tree centerpiece like a dusting of snow. Using a funnel I'd found among Amber Buchanan's pots and pans helped get the goods back into their containers, but I still made a mess

Duh! I moved the entire operation to the kitchen sink which made cleanliness much easier. *Why didn't I think of that when I started?* After I completed each bag or box, I used the spray attachment to wash away my spills.

"Having fun?" Wayne asked when he returned.

"Not really. This is too much like cooking."

He laughed. "I saw why the car was parked in the drive. She used the garage for storage with lots of boxes neatly stacked and labeled. About a dozen empty storage bins are marked "Christmas."

I waved my arm around to encompass the entire kitchen. "She has more Christmas decorations in this one room than Jane and I have in both of our apartments combined."

"It's that way all over. She even has a Christmas tree in the bathroom. I don't mean something ceramic or artificial on the countertop, she's got a live tree decorated in there. I barely had room to stand."

My turn to laugh. "Don't tell me you contaminated the scene."

"No comment to that silly suggestion. Are you finished?"

"Everything except those canisters." I pointed to four ceramic reindeer of varying sizes lined up from big to small across the back of the counter beside three tall clear-glass cylinders."

"What are you going to do with them?"

"Empty and sift just like you told me. The reindeer are Christmas canisters. We'll have to see if she filled them or just put them out for decoration."

The smallest reindeer was full of tea bags. No problem. Emptied them on the countertop, looked through to be sure there was nothing hidden, then gathered them up and stuffed them back in. A delicious aroma of cinnamon and nutmeg floated up to my face when I opened the second. Some blend of Christmas coffee. I wished I could brew a pot right then, but Wayne would never have agreed to that. I sifted the coffee out, then funneled it back. Third and fourth reindeer were full of sugar and flour. Nothing else.

The only thing left was the set of three tall glass cylinder canisters with clamp lids. Since the glass was clear, I could see what each contained—grits, rice, and little dry elbow macaroni. Same old routine with the rice. The macaroni wouldn't go through the strainer, so I poured it into a large bowl and went through it with my fingers.

When I poured the grits into the colander, I heard a clinking sound. "Wayne," I called. I poked my fingers around in the grits that hadn't gone through the tiny openings, and then I screamed, "Come here!"

I held up a miniature plastic bag. No more than an inch and a half square and sealed with tape as well as the zipping mechanism, the transparent sack gave me a good view of what was in it—rings! Either diamonds and emeralds or cubic zirconium and fakes.

Wayne took the little container from me with a pair of tweezers.

"Are we going to open it?" I asked, eager for a better look.

"No," the sheriff said and dropped the tiny bag into an evidence envelope. "Forensics will dust and examine the outside before it's opened." He grinned. "You took me at my word that we wouldn't be leaving this place as immaculate as we found it."

"I tried to be as neat as possible. Are we doing anything else?"

"No, I'm ready to go. Amber's husband, Randy Buchanan, is incarcerated for armed robbery of a jewelry store. He swore in court that he'd given her some rings from the robbery, but she testified he was lying. I've considered that one of Randy's friends or enemies murdered Amber because she wouldn't tell where the rings were. You can figure from what we did to this place searching it that no one's been in here rummaging through Amber's belongings and left it as neat as we found it. Of course, someone could have questioned her about the jewelry and killed her accidentally. That might have scared the perp too much to search the house. "

As we got into Wayne's cruiser, I asked, "Am I finished being a deputy?"

"Nope. Naomi Spires is in Safe Sister. Last week, her husband Norman Spires, got into a confrontation with Amber Buchanan. He became combative, shoved Amber, and she pressed charges for assault. He's out on bail, but we can't find him. I sent a female deputy in to talk to Mrs. Spires, but the woman won't say a word. She's scared to talk to law enforcement."

"What does that have to do with me?"

"You know all about makeup and you're always poking your nose into places it doesn't belong. I want you to make yourself up to look like somebody trounced you. Black eyes, bruises—you'll know how to do it. We're admitting you to Safe Sister and you'll be Naomi Spires's roommate. Your assignment is to get her to talk. We want to know where her husband might be and if she thinks he might have killed Amber Buchanan."

I have to confess the thought of being an undercover deputy excited me.

• • •

"If your father or brothers saw you right now, they'd be looking for someone to kill," the sheriff said.

At home I'd taken him at his word and spent several hours becoming a battered woman. My left eye appeared totally blackened, and there was a large makeup bruise on my right cheek. My left arm was in a sling with multiple fake contusions on the hand. I'd concentrated the made-up injuries on the left side so that I didn't risk rubbing off makeup when using my right hand.

"Do you have a new name and a story for me?" I asked Wayne.

"No, it's not like we're putting you into witness protection. You can make up your own story for this. You'll probably need to spend the night there to gain Naomi Spires's trust. One thing I didn't tell you though is that her child is only ten months old and the crib is in Mrs. Spires's room, so you may not have a very peaceful night."

"Oh, great!"

"Usually mothers with kids at Safe Sister don't have roommates if the children are sharing a room with their moms, but holidays seem to cause more abuse, and they've had to add single beds in with the mothers who just have an infant or toddler in a crib. Mrs. Spires knows that, so she won't be surprised when they take you in and introduce you."

"Okay. What else do I need to know?"

"We're going to wire you."

"Wire me?"

"Well, with today's technology, the device doesn't actually involve a wire, but we still call it that. I'm thinking the best place for the microphone is on the back of your arm inside the sling."

"Do I have to turn it on and off?"

"Nope. Just don't take the sling off in front of Mrs. Spires."

"Are you taking me over there?"

"No, too many people know me, and I don't want anyone seeing me through the window and letting everyone know the sheriff brought you. Detective Robinson is taking you over there in civvies and his personal truck. The story is that he's your brother who picked you up from your house after your boyfriend attacked you."

Just then, my front doorbell rang. "Who could that be passing by the yellow crime scene tape?" I opened the door and saw Dean Robinson standing there with a wad of yellow tape in his hand.

"This can come down now. Are you ready to go, Sis?"

"She will be after we attach this," Wayne said and held up a tiny electronic device. I slipped my arm out of the sling and he attached the wire, which, like he'd said, wasn't a wire at all.

Dean asked, "Are you ready?"

"Yes, I've got a gown and change of clothes in here." I handed him my overnight case. He shoved it right back. "Women who run from their homes to escape violent men don't usually have time to gather up things into a nice little case like that."

"Sure they do," I answered. "I've seen too many shows on television that advise women to have a bag packed and hide an extra set of car keys so they can get away fast when necessary. If I'm going to pretend to be a victim of domestic violence, I'm going to pretend to be a smart one."

Wayne laughed. "I warned you, Dean. She's feisty at times." He turned toward me. "Being prepared is one way to be wise, but the smartest thing for a battered woman to do is to get away for good as soon as abuse begins."

"You're right," Dean said and grinned. "I would say, 'but she's pretty,' except right now she's not. That's very convincing makeup."

"I do this in reverse for a living."

"In reverse?" Dean questioned.

"Yep, I cover bruises and discoloration to make decedents look better and alive. This time, I've created bruises and discoloration to make me look worse and lucky to be alive."

The three of us stepped out on the front porch. I couldn't help glancing down at the chalk outline where Amber Buchanan's body had lain in her Santa suit. Now that the tape was removed, I wanted to take the tree down ASAP. In fact, I was ready to remove all Christmas décor from my apartment.

Wayne drove away before Dean and I did. "What's your story going to be?" Dean asked as we got into his car.

"I thought about making up a fake name to go with my tale, but I realized that almost everyone in St. Mary attends a funeral at

Middleton's at some time or other, and one of the women at Safe Sister could recognize me, so I'm using my own name."

"Then you can't accuse a husband for those bruises. Someone might know you're not married. Gonna say your boyfriend did it?"

"I don't know. That would be like when a person cuts school and says their grandmother died. I was always afraid to say anyone who wasn't dead had passed away for fear that it would come true."

"Then please don't say your new boyfriend beat you up because I'd never hurt you and I'm hoping to become your new boyfriend."

No answer for that. I still hadn't heard from Patel, and though I was confused, I had to confess that there did seem to be chemistry between Dean and me.

I was surprised when Dean parked beside a small yellow building and escorted me toward the door.

"I don't think you can go in," I told him.

"This is the office building. Men can go inside. It's the residence houses that are restricted to women and children. Of course, there *are* males in there—young boys who are sheltered with their mothers."

My paperwork had already been completed by my "brother," and a nice, middle-aged lady named Evelyn said she'd drive me to the transition house where I would be staying. I hadn't realized that Safe Sister had more than one residence, but Evelyn said none of them were located in the same part of town nor within walking distance of the office. When I asked why they were called "transition" houses, she said, "Because we don't plan for women to live there indefinitely. Our purpose is to help them change their lives so they can be self-supporting and stay away from whoever has abused them."

We went out a back door into a parking area with a tall wooden fence around it. Evelyn's nondescript car was an ugly shade of green not quite repulsive enough to be memorable.

"I'm filling in for Amber Buchanan. It's just awful that she's left us." The way Evelyn said it might have implied that Amber had quit her job, but I knew Amber was dead and that in the

South, "left us" is another euphemism for "died," like "passed away," or "kicked the bucket."

"Where is this place you're taking me?" I asked.

"We have several locations. You're going to one that already houses six women. Two of the women have one room, but the other four share with their children. Since Mrs. Spires only has one child, an infant in a crib, we've added a single bed in Ms. Spires's room for you. There are no numbers on the house, and we don't give out the street address. We also discourage our ladies from using their cell phones while staying with us, but it isn't forbidden. It's not that we think an angry husband or boyfriend might trace someone, but we've learned through experience that some men can talk a woman into giving them too much information."

I self-consciously touched my cleavage where my cell phone rested comfortably between the girls, who were bountiful due to my inflated bra. Without that underwear, I have no cleavage. Evelyn put on her turn signal and slowed down in front of a small brick house. When she turned into the drive, I saw that it was brick across the front and wood painted white on the sides. She parked in the backyard and used a key from her purse to let us in.

Elegant? No. Fancy? No. Warm and inviting? Definitely yes! We went through a long, narrow kitchen with a refrigerator decorated with children's Christmas drawings—lots of triangular trees and round Santas—to a large living room where several women sat on comfortable-looking couches and recliners. Bruises in various stages of healing showed on some of them, and one woman had a cast on her right leg. Children sat on the braided rug playing with dolls and Tonka trucks, and some gift-wrapped packages remained under the Christmas tree.

"Ladies and children," Evelyn said. "This is Callie. She's going to stay with us and will be rooming with Naomi." When she said that, the ladies turned and looked at a thin, blond-haired woman whose nod and smile silently told me she was Naomi. She motioned toward a curly-haired infant in a playpen.

"Will ya'll watch Betsy? I'll help Callie get settled in." Naomi stood and led Evelyn and me to a room that opened directly off the living room. "This is your bed," she said and motioned toward the single bed farthest away from the portable crib. "The routine here is that they left clean folded linens for you on the bed. I went ahead and made it for you. We share the chest of drawers, so I moved all of my things to the bottom drawers. You can have the top two. I'm sorry about all the baby things in here, but I need them for Betsy."

"Oh, no, the baby things don't bother me at all, and I'd rather you take the top drawers." I held up my overnight case. "This is all I brought."

"Well, Safe Sister supplies soap, shampoo, a new toothbrush, and toothpaste. I put your box of supplies on the shelf in our bathroom. If you need something else, I'll be glad to share, and anything I can do to make things easier with that arm in the sling, please just tell me."

Naomi was so nice and welcoming to me that I felt guilty for deceiving her. Evelyn told us goodbye and left.

I followed Naomi back into the living room. "Have you had dinner?" she asked.

"No, have you?"

"Not yet, but it's about time for me to feed Betsy. Let me introduce you." She named off each of the other three women. I didn't bother to try to learn their names. The house was pleasant, but knowing why these people were here touched my heart, yet made me uncomfortable. I wanted to get Naomi to talk so I could get out of there. "Judith and Sylvia are in the kitchen," she added. "We have a schedule for who cooks each meal."

I stayed in the living room while Naomi went to the kitchen to feed Betsy. The other ladies tried to include me in their conversation, but I wasn't really interested in most of their chatting, which was about their kids. Don't get me wrong. I like children or I wouldn't have wanted to be a teacher, but I haven't been blessed with any of my own, so nonstop talk about when each one potty-trained didn't interest me a whole lot.

Dinner was sliced ham, oven-fried potatoes, carrots, and a crusty apple dessert. The food tasted good, but the conversation stayed primarily about children with an added discussion about haircuts. A couple of them wanted to make arrangements with

Evelyn to either go to a beauty shop of have a beautician come to the house. I'm trained in cutting hair, but I didn't volunteer. Mainly sat and listened.

At eight o'clock, the mothers went to their rooms to put children to bed. I sat with Sylvia whose kids were grown and lived in their own homes, not at Safe Sister.

"Weren't you one of the cooks tonight?" I asked.

"Yes, I made the Apple Brown Betty. Not a lot of people make that dish anymore, but I learned the recipe from my mother, and I like it."

"It was delicious." Now if Jane had been there instead of me, she and Sylvia could have talked about cooking and recipes all night long, but my family and friends can assure you that I, Calamine Lotion Parrish, am not much of a cook. I swear I can make a dish exactly by the same recipe as Jane or someone else, and mine never tastes quite as good.

"Is there a set time for adults to go to bed?" I changed the subject.

"Not really, but almost everyone winds up in bed by ten or eleven. The others will be back here in the common room after they get the kids to bed. We sometimes play games. Would you like to play Scrabble?"

I hadn't played that game in years, but anything would be better than just sitting around, so I said, "Sure."

Sylvia hadn't warned me that she was the Scrabble Queen of Safe Sister. I used to beat my brothers regularly at Scrabble, but that woman knew more words than I could imagine, and they were *real* and spelled correctly. I know because I checked most of them in the dictionary she'd brought out from the cabinet with the Scrabble board. I'm not about to share the score, but Sylvia whipped my padded fanny totally and completely.

By the time we completed the game, the other women had joined us and were standing around watching. I was relieved when they cheered the grand finale as Sylvia finished her last word with a "q" on "triple word score."

Before long, the ladies had separated into two small groups—three of them playing Yahtzee, at the game table while the others flipped open a portable card table and pulled out a deck of cards.

Now that's a different story for me. I've played cards with my brothers and Daddy since I learned my numbers.

"Want to join us?" Naomi asked.

"I'd love to." I helped open folding chairs and place them around the table. Then it hit me. *What if they play bridge or something like that? I'm good with cards, but we always played gin rummy, canasta, or poker.* No problem! These ladies played poker for pennies—just my game!

Not only did I hold my own, but when Naomi and I went to our room, I'd won most of the pennies. There are some advantages to growing up in a house full of brothers.

"Do you shower at night or in the morning?" Naomi asked after she peeked in the portable crib at Betsy who looked beautiful sleeping with a smile on her face.

The truth is that I like to shower both before bed and when I wake each morning, but I answered, "In the morning is fine. I had a shower at my brother's before he brought me to Safe Sister. You go ahead. I'll brush my teeth after you finish."

"Okay. Will you call me if Betsy cries? I don't always hear her when I'm in the shower."

"Sure."

That gave me the perfect opportunity to get into my gown while Naomi was out of the room so I wouldn't risk her seeing me move my arm the wrong way for the sling or catch a glimpse of the device the sheriff had attached to the back of my arm. He hadn't said anything about how long the "wire" would work without recharging, and I hadn't gotten any real information about anything.

Standing in front of the dresser mirror checking to see if I'd smudged any of my artificial bruises and injuries, I heard a whimper that turned into a soft cry. I turned and looked at the portable crib. Betsy was sitting up, looking around her, and her face crumpled into tears.

I'm not totally ignorant about babies. After all, I baby-sat John's children when his family came up from Atlanta while Megan and Johnny were little. I picked Betsy up and snuggled her against my shoulder. I'd forgotten how wonderful it feels to hold a soft, sweet-smelling tiny one hugged close. I began to sway back and forth a little, trying to create a rocking feeling for the baby.

She cooed! It was the sweetest sound I'd ever heard.

Betsy lifted her head away from my shoulder, looked me in the face, and smiled a big, gorgeous smile. I was hooked! Betsy had to be the most lovable baby in the world. That's when I saw it—the slightly yellow remains of a healing bruise on her neck. I only caught a glimpse of it because she snuggled her head back against my shoulder.

I rocked Betsy back and forth until her breathing became the regular sound of a sleeping child, and I was gently placing her in the crib when her mom came back into the room.

"She woke up for a few minutes," I said. "I think she's asleep again now."

"Thanks," Naomi answered, but she eyed me with a questioning expression, stepped over to the crib, and tenderly touched the curls on Betsy's forehead. I guess when your baby has bruises on her neck, a mother is cautious about strangers touching the child. "The bathroom's all yours. I'm going to try to snooze now. Betsy doesn't always sleep through the night since we moved here. I hope she doesn't wake you."

"Don't worry. I'm used to Big Boy waking me sometimes."

"Is Big Boy your husband?" Naomi's expression changed to curiosity. She tucked Betsy's blanket around the baby and then slipped into her own bed and pulled the covers up to her chin.

"No, he's my puppy." I laughed. "Not really a puppy anymore. He's a Great Dane, and he weighs more than I do, but I'm worried about him. I took him to the vet to be neutered. She found a tumor in his abdomen and had to operate."

"Where is he now? Does your husband have him?"

"I'm not married, but my brother has my dog while I'm here." That wasn't a real lie, only a slight distortion. So far as Safe Sister knew, Detective Dean Robinson was my brother, but actually, Wayne had promised to take Big Boy to Daddy's that evening, where both brothers who lived there—Mike and Frankie—would care for him and spoil him even more than I already had.

"I don't want to pry," Naomi apologized with one of those things we say when we know we're about to cross a line. "But," she continued, "who hurt you?"

She'd just given me a perfect opportunity to lie. I was a deputized representative of the law of Jade County, and I'd come here to gather information for them, so I could make up a story and lie, lie, lie without feeling guilty. I'd be doing something bad to accomplish something good.

"I have a new boyfriend, or at least, I thought I did until this happened." I used my right hand to point at the sling and then my face. "He seemed perfect, and our relationship was going fine until I made him mad and he beat me up. My brother thinks I should stay here for a while until things cool down."

"Cool down?" Naomi laughed, but there was no humor in it. "I used to think that if you let him cool down and think everything's going to be all right, it would be okay, but the other women here say that you'll wind up back in here more than once, and sooner or later, he'll kill you."

"Oh, I don't think he's that bad."

"They tell me it will get worse," Naomi assured me. "But I don't know what to believe."

"What about you?" I asked.

"I don't want to talk about it. For right now, I like it here at Safe Sister. It's kind of like Girl Scout camp with all the women around helping each other and sharing the chores." She turned to face the wall. "Let's go to sleep."

"Sure," I answered. "Good night."

Betsy cooed, but Naomi snored, and either she was faking it or she dozed off instantly.

I lay there thinking how lucky I am.

My ex-husband, Donnie, is a cardiologist in Columbia. Our marriage ended badly, but he never threatened to hit me or hurt me physically. Don't confuse Donnie with Dr. Donald here in St. Mary. I've dated the local physician Dr. Donald off and on for a while, but the truth is the man is a womanizer as well as being what he calls "commitment-shy," which means that no matter how handsome and charming he is, Dr. Donald isn't a good candidate for a long-term relationship.

The men in my life haven't been great romantic success stories yet, but the only males who have ever hit me were when my brothers and I occasionally got into arguments and fights when I was little. That came to a screeching halt long before I matured into a woman. My daddy had "the talk" with my brothers, which meant that no matter how obnoxious I was as a sister, none of them laid a hand on me once there was the first sign that my boobs were developing. To Daddy, those ta tas meant I was becoming a woman, and "you *don't* hit women!"

Give me a license, and I'll use it. I lied when I said no man has ever hit me. Well, it wasn't really a lie. I'd forgotten about Eddie. I dated him when I was sixteen, and he slapped me one time. Note I said *one* time. When my brothers heard about it, the four of them living in St. Mary at the time confronted him and taught him a lesson about "messing" with their sister. It was a hard lesson, delivered in the woods behind St. Mary High School, but Eddie recovered with no permanent injuries and a definite knowledge that our dating was over and that he'd better be polite to me at all times.

I don't know if I developed better taste in males after that or word got around town that Callie's brothers didn't take kindly to anyone hurting her. Come to think of it, during high school and college, I did date a few guys who may have turned out to warrant those "wife-beater" shirts they wore, but there were red flags about those types, and I generally didn't date them more than once or twice.

For anyone who's not familiar with what a "wife-beater" shirt is, it's a shirt with the sleeves torn or cut off, generally a white T-shirt with the sleeves removed. I don't know why they call them "wife-beaters" unless it's because they look so redneck and in the past, some men who earned the name redneck thought their genitalia entitled them to knock their women around. Thank heavens times are changing about things like that. I'm proud that though my five brothers have all acted redneck at times and their marital track records aren't the greatest, none of them has ever physically mistreated a female. I say "physically" because a couple of them aren't known for their faithfulness, and I consider infidelity a form of mental abuse.

I lay in bed thinking about men and women and why relationships can sometimes be so painful. The sounds Betsy and Naomi made in their slumber kept me conscious of where I was and how grateful I was not to have ever needed to escape to a place like Safe Sister in real life.

My mind was too busy with memories and speculation to let me go to sleep. The closest I probably ever came to getting involved with someone who could have been a disaster was right after my divorce in Columbia. Lying there in a refuge for battered and abused women, I relived that date.

When the divorce was final, I was miserable in a lot of ways. Sometimes I felt that I should have been able to save my marriage. Other times, I felt stupid for having married someone who could do what Donnie did that made me divorce him. Anyway, this was before Internet sites to match people became so popular. I joined several singles groups which were supposed to be places to meet nice people to date. Some of my friends married guys they met at those groups.

One night, a pleasant man asked me to dance several times and by the end of the party, I'd given him my telephone number.

"Hello, is this Callie Parrish, that fantastic lady I met last night at the group dance?"

I was thrilled to hear his voice the next evening.

"Sure is," I answered.

We talked for a while and he ended the conversation with, "Let me take you to dinner tomorrow night. Where do you live?"

"I'd love to have dinner with you, but I have a policy about new dates. I'd rather meet you somewhere the first time we go out together."

"That's both fine and smart. How about The Stone Pit?"

The Stone Pit was a fancy restaurant not too far from my house. I agreed to meet him there at eight the next night.

This man was so smooth and charming. He was waiting for me at the door to The Stone Pit and escorted me to the table he'd reserved. When the waitress came to the table, he ordered for us —shrimp cocktails, Caesar salad, and filet mignon with garlic potatoes. Champagne to drink. Strange how I can remember everything we had to eat that night when there are days I don't remember what I ate for breakfast that morning.

The meal was great and the conversation was good, but he

seemed to mention his ex-wife a little too often for me. *Probably recently divorced,* I thought. I knew that the first few dates I'd had after Donnie, I'd seemed compelled to talk about him.

He ordered dessert—cheesecake with blueberries on top—even though I would have asked for cherry topping if he'd given me a choice. "Would you like to go somewhere to dance?" he asked before the server arrived with the desserts.

"That would be nice, but I'm kind of tired, and I have work tomorrow. Maybe we could go dancing one weekend."

"I'd planned for us to go out to dance after dinner." He sounded offended.

"Another time," I answered, not liking the sound of his voice.

He leaned across the table. "I don't like it when women disagree with me." The words were whispered, but they were sharp and threatening.

"You remind me of my wife." He almost spat the words. "Do you know what I used to do when she wouldn't do what I wanted?" He laughed. "I tied her to a tree and shot my rifle over her head. It never took much of that to convince her to see things my way."

My eyes must have almost popped out of my head.

"What's the matter? You don't like my methods? You'll learn to because I like you and plan to spend a lot of time with you. Now let's enjoy our dessert when it comes and then go dance the night away."

I almost choked. "Excuse me. I'll be right back."

He reached across the table and wrapped his hand around my wrist—tight. "Where are you going?" he demanded.

"To the ladies' room." I said and, as difficult as it was, I smiled.

On the way to the restroom, I stopped our waitress and asked her, "Will you page Callie Parrish and tell me that I need to call my father because my mother is sick?"

"I sure will. I've seen that man you're with lots of times in here, hardly ever with the same woman more than once though. He gives me the creeps. I'll have our doorman walk you out if you like."

"Please do"

I was hardly reseated before the server went around the room asking if anyone was Callie Parrish. When I replied, she told me that my father had called and my mother was being rushed to the hospital with a major heart attack.

"Your father said to meet him at Palmetto Hospital," she said and pulled my chair out for me.

"I'm sorry," I told the man who tied a woman to a tree and shot at her, "I have to leave."

"I'll drive you there," he insisted.

"No, stay here and enjoy the cheesecake." I grabbed my purse and went out with a big man behind me. When I reached my car, the man said, "I don't know what the problem was, but lock your doors."

I hadn't thought of that incident in years, but it had been why I quit going to singles dances and rarely considered Internet matching. It was proof to me that a woman can't be too cautious, and not only was I glad that my address wasn't in the phone book, I'd also changed my telephone number and became much more guarded about giving it out.

When I finally went to sleep, I dreamed about that awful man tying his wife to a tree.

★ ON THE SIXTH DAY OF CHRISTMAS MY TRUE LOVE GAVE TO ME

SIX TONGUES A'WAGGIN'

Howling woke me from a sound sleep. I'd finally stopped dreaming about bad men and had been dreaming about two good ones—Patel and Dean Robinson. No, I wasn't dreaming they were fighting over me or that I was having a hard time choosing between them. In my dream, the two men had become one man with no name, a combination of the two. He was kissing me, and I was feeling warm all over. Don't know what might have happened if it had been possible to sleep through the noise.

My first, half-asleep, thought was that Big Boy was howling, but this wasn't a dog howl. Then my half-awake mind wondered if this was some Girl Scout yell. I never went to Girl Scout camp, never even belonged to the Girl Scouts. When the school sent home flyers about joining scouts and I asked Daddy to let me join, he said, "If you want to go camping, I'll take you." I protested that they did lots of other things, too, and that I could learn a lot about cooking and nature while earning badges. He told me, "There's nothing they can teach you there that you can't learn at school or from me and your brothers."

All of that leads to the fact that when Naomi had said living at Safe Sister reminded her of going to Girl Scout camp, being around the other females and sharing the chores, I'd had no comparison in my mind, but I doubt crying babies are a part of Girl Scout camps. Betsy had pulled herself to a standing position holding on to the side of the portable crib and was screaming as though her heart were broken.

Now, I've been around a lot of children while I was a kindergarten teacher, but being the youngest in my family and not yet having any children of my own, my personal experience with babies was limited to when Megan and Johnny were little and holding that precious bundle last night. The problem was that the night before, Betsy wasn't screaming. What did she need? Would picking her up quiet her? Did she need a bottle or her diaper changed? The only way to know was to check. I stood up and headed toward Betsy. Not sure exactly what I planned to do. Should I lift her out of the crib or pat her on the back like we do to soothe the bereaved at Middleton's? Saved—not by the bell—but by Naomi rushing into the room with a plastic baby bottle. Betsy stopped crying the minute Naomi lifted her from the crib and popped the nipple in her mouth.

"I'm sorry. I know you probably needed to sleep late today. I'll try to get up early tomorrow and have her bottle ready when she wakes up. She was sleeping when I went to the kitchen for it."

"No problem. Do you mind if I shower now?"

"No, go right ahead. Do you need any help with that sling?"

I hadn't thought of that. Guess I'd thought I would just slip it off behind the locked bathroom door. Problem was *the makeup*. What I'd used wasn't water soluble, but it would probably need to be touched up. Another problem was *the wire*. I probably shouldn't get it wet, and I didn't know how to take it off and then put it back on.

"I'll be fine," I assured Naomi as she and Betsy went to the door.

"We'll be in the common room, but pull that little help cord in the bathroom if you need us." She looked down at her watch. "Breakfast will be ready in thirty minutes."

I settled for what Daddy used to call, "a good wash-up," without getting into the shower. I'd only brought one change of clothes, so there was no problem deciding what to wear. Clean jeans and a sweater with a snowman printed on it. I also checked all the makeup.

By the time I stepped out of the bedroom door, the women were headed toward the dining room. I followed.

Naomi put Betsy in a high chair beside her and put several

Fruit Loops on the tray. Her chubby hands grasped the cereal and crammed it into her mouth.

When the others were all seated, Sylvia led the group in a prayer of thanks before they began serving plates and passing platters and bowls. A woman whose name I didn't remember looked toward me and said, "Callie, I've made the chore schedule for the week and worked you into it. Since today's your first real day, I didn't put you down for anything today, but you're on breakfast duty tomorrow morning."

"Fine," I answered though I had no idea how long I'd be there. The problem was that I didn't know how to bring up Naomi's husband to her and she'd told me point-blank that she didn't want to talk about what had happened to her.

I wondered if the children at Safe Sister went out to school or if they were home-schooled, but it didn't matter because as one of the little girls told me, "Guess what, Miss Callie? We have another whole week off from lessons because it's Winter Holiday."

"Then what will you do today?" I asked.

"Play with our new toys and watch television and my mommy is on supper duty, and she promised I can help her make a cake this afternoon."

"Sounds like fun. What about the grown-ups? What will we do today?"

The child grinned. "Oh, grown-up stuff like reading and cleaning house and maybe some laundry."

Naomi laughed at my surprised expression. "Don't worry, Callie. There's plenty to do here—all the chores that are necessary to run a home plus several of us are studying for our GEDs and Lacey is working on her thesis in psychology and will probably corner you sooner or later for an interview."

The morning was busy, but after lunch, the children went back to the common room to play, and the adults stayed around the table drinking iced tea and talking. I hoped I'd finally hear something useful.

"Does everyone here know about Amber?" Sylvia asked, looking straight at me.

I didn't say anything.

"Amber Buchanan worked for Safe Sister. She'd planned to

come here Christmas morning dressed as Santa Claus," Sylvia explained, looking around at everyone, though it was obvious she was talking to me. Did she suspect anything about me? "She didn't show up and we learned yesterday that Amber was killed Wednesday morning at some girl's apartment. She was wearing the Santa Claus suit. Those unopened gifts under the Christmas tree were for her."

"I'm sorry for your loss," my standard response to hearing of a death, didn't seem appropriate under these circumstances. "That's awful," I said instead.

"The reason I brought this up is because I want to know if anyone here has any idea *why* somebody would murder Amber." Tears filled her eyes and she looked straight at Naomi.

What was happening? Was Sylvia undercover also? Had two of us been put in here for the sheriff to try to learn about Naomi's husband?

"You don't have to tiptoe around to ask me," Naomi said. "That policewoman who came to see me has already asked me point-blank if I think my husband Norman might have gone after Amber when he got out of jail. How should I know? I've neither seen nor talked to him since I came here. Evelyn told me about Norman demanding to see me and take Betsy home for the holidays. She said Norman and Amber got into a loud fuss and Norman shoved Amber. She pressed charges, and that would definitely have made Norman furious, but I don't think he would *kill* anyone."

"Bet you didn't think Norman would ever cause a bruise like the one that was on your baby when you came here either," another woman said.

Naomi burst into tears. "It was awful, just horrible. He grabbed her by the neck. He squeezed it!" She put her head on the table and sobbed.

"Was Betsy crying and wouldn't stop?" Sylvia asked.

"No, she didn't do anything. It was my fault, my fault. He did it because he was mad at me. Upset because I burned the baked chicken." Naomi's words were barely audible as she sobbed.

"And you came here?" Sylvia asked. "Did you go to the police?"

"No, I just brought Betsy here." Tears filled Naomi's eyes. "Well, actually we went to the office and they brought us here."

"Why didn't you go to the police?" Sylvia persisted.

"He didn't mean to. It's just how he is."

"If he was my husband, he'd be dead," Sylvia snapped.

"Then why are you here instead of in jail?" another woman asked.

"Because my husband never touched my kids, just me," Sylvia said. "Naomi, all I want to know is do you know where your husband is now? Where he might have gone when he got bailed out of jail? I heard that policewoman asking you, and you refused to tell her anything. That's not fair to the rest of us if you stay here."

"Are you telling me to leave Safe Sister?" Naomi murmured.

"No, but if you won't help the cops, maybe it would be better if they moved you to another safe house."

Naomi jumped from her chair and ran to our bedroom. Betsy began to cry when her mother ran past her, so I picked up the baby, followed Naomi, and then closed the door behind us.

Reaching her arms out for Betsy, Naomi sat on her bed and sobbed. When I handed the infant to her, she cuddled Betsy to her shoulder.

"Thank you." Naomi's voice was soft, and she sniffled again to stop the tears.

I sat on my bed and asked her, "Do you want to talk about it? Last night you didn't feel like it, but sometimes telling a person about things helps."

"Maybe so. I love Norman. That's why this is so hard. Sure, he's hurt me before when he got mad, but I never thought he'd harm the baby. Norman brags that he's 'rude, crude, and socially unacceptable,' but he's good in some ways. My parents were both alcoholics, and my sister and I never knew if there would be food on the table or not. Norman's a good provider. He's not like the husbands of some of the other women here who won't work and expect their wives to pay the bills." She sniffled. "But the counselor here tells me that he'll hurt me and Betsy again if I go back to him without Norman getting some treatment."

Tears streamed down her face. She wiped them away with a

tissue and continued, "Norman holds down a regular job and buys groceries every week. He doesn't even want me to work, just stay home and be a housewife. He's so good when life goes well. He whistles all the time. Then I'll do something wrong, and he explodes."

"Did he ever hurt you before you married him?"

"Only a couple of times and not too bad, but it was my fault every time. He's never hurt me except when I do something wrong."

I doubted that, and it sounded to me like Naomi was living in that surreal world I'd read that some abused women created for themselves. My mind flashed back to the man who tied his wife to the tree. Had his wife thought she'd caused the way he treated her?

"What made you come here this time?"

"Look at her." Naomi held Betsy out toward me. "How can a tiny being like this deserve to be choked because her mama burned the chicken? Norman always expects his dinner to be ready as soon as he's home from work. That day, Betsy was still napping, and he came home all frisky and wanting some loving. The chicken stayed in the oven too long, and it was too brown when I took it out. It was still okay to eat, but he said it wasn't juicy enough. He screamed at me and threw me across the bed. Betsy was still asleep, but he yanked her up and squeezed her neck. He didn't stop until she started turning blue. Then he let her go and stormed out of the house. I called a taxi and went to the church I attended before I married Norman. The pastor paid my cab fare and brought me to Safe Sister. I don't know how Norman figured out where I was when he went to Safe Sister's office and demanded to see me and get the baby."

I almost said, "And you love this man?" but, for a wonder, I held my tongue.

"Do you know how Amber Buchanan died?" I asked instead.

"Nobody's said."

"She was strangled to death."

Silence. Stone-dead silence.

"How do you know that?" Naomi asked.

"Somebody told my brother. Doesn't what happened to

Betsy and knowing that Norman was enraged at Amber make you stop and think about what Norman is capable of doing? If the police want to know where he is, and you have any idea, maybe you should tell them. It might keep him from hurting you or Betsy again, especially if he had anything to do with Amber Buchanan's murder."

"Maybe you're right, but I don't want Norman in jail. How would I pay the rent and buy Betsy's diapers? He's missing us or he wouldn't have confronted Amber. I think this will teach him a lesson and he'll change—not be so mean when he gets mad." Betsy had gone to sleep, and Naomi placed her in the crib and covered her with a light blanket embroidered with A, B, C blocks on it.

"Have you thought about moving away from here and getting a job to support you and Betsy?" I pointed toward the sleeping infant. "That little girl needs her mother, and you can't take the risk that he'll wind up killing either of you."

Naomi began weeping again. "Maybe you're right, but I don't want to talk to the police. If I tell you where I think Norman might be, will you ask your brother to tell them?"

"As soon as I see him."

"Norman goes hunting a lot and there's an old abandoned hunt club near Summerville. That's where I think he would go if he ran away. There's no electricity there, but he used to camp a lot before we got married. He might stay there like he was camping."

"Do you know the directions to get there?"

"No, but it used to be the Porter Hunt Club. I'll bet the police could find it from that."

I felt like shouting "Hooray!" I'd found out exactly what Wayne wanted, and I wasn't about to correct Naomi that who needed the information was the sheriff's department, not the police. Wayne sometimes gets irritated at folks who call his branch the police, but I didn't want to embarrass nor irritate Naomi.

Now I wished my wire was two-way communication though I don't know how that would be handled technically. *What else would the sheriff and Dean want to know?*

"What about guns?" I asked.

"He loves guns," Naomi answered. "We have several at the

house, but he keeps them locked up in the gun safe. See? He loves Betsy. He's says it's never too early to be careful about guns around children."

Wonder if that makes anyone safe when Norman's the one with the key? I thought.

A knock at the door interrupted our conversation. "Naomi? Naomi?" The voice was Sylvia's.

"Come in," Naomi answered.

"I'm sorry I exploded on you like that. I'm just nervous."

Naomi stepped toward Sylvia, arms outstretched. I left the room while they exchanged a sisterly hug.

"With a little more time, I might have learned more," I said to Dean as he drove me away from the Safe Sister office.

Evelyn had come for me not long after Naomi told me about the hunting lodge. She'd explained that my brother had made arrangements for me to stay with another relative out of town. Dean Robinson had been waiting for me at Safe Sister's office.

"You got what we needed, and I disagree with Norman Spires's wife. I think he's fully capable of murder."

"Then why didn't you want me to find out more from Naomi?"

"You'd already got what we wanted."

"How did you know?" I was puzzled.

"Everything you said, did, or heard was recorded at headquarters because the device on your arm transmitted all sound. We had a deputy listening when she told you about the hunting lodge."

"Glad I didn't do anything embarrassing."

"We had what we needed, and the Middletons have been calling Sheriff Harmon complaining that they need you at work." Dean's driving was fast, but safe.

"Somebody must have died," I commented.

"Two people."

"Who?"

"Sheriff Harmon said that you'd know these people, but I didn't until last night. We got a call from a Mrs. Corley that her daughter Patsy had phoned her and said she'd shot her boyfriend and was going to kill herself. Said they'd been fussing for two days over what to buy with their tax refund."

"Tax refund? People don't even have their W-2s yet. They couldn't have already filed taxes."

"They hadn't, but they'd worked it out enough to know they were getting a refund, and he wanted to buy some kind of sports equipment, but she wanted to get a new living room couch."

"That's nothing to kill someone over."

"There's nothing worth killing for," Dean said.

"So, did you arrest Patsy?" I remembered when Patsy's daddy, June Bug Corley was killed, and Jane and I'd ridden to Charleston to find a suit and shoes large enough to fit him. Patsy was built like her father, and in my mind, I'd called her Fatsy Patsy. Her sister Penny was tiny like their mother, and I'd thought of her as Skinny Penny.

"No, Mrs. Corley called from Patsy and her boyfriend's mobile home. She'd got there and the doors were locked, but she had a key. The bathroom door was locked and she could hear Patsy sobbing and screaming. When she tried to talk Patsy into coming out of the bathroom, she heard a gunshot, then silence. That's when she dialed 911."

"You said two deaths. Patsy is dead, too?"

"Yes, she put the gun barrel in her mouth and pulled the trigger. It was a gruesome scene and awful for Mrs. Corley. The sheriff said her husband died of a gunshot, too."

"Yes, he did." I thought for a few minutes. "Back when I worked with the Corley family when June Bug died . . ."

"June Bug?" Dean's questioning expression lifted his eyebrows.

"That's what everyone called Patsy's daddy."

"What about back then?"

"I think Patsy was living in Charleston. She and her sister Penny were visiting their parents when June Bug was killed."

"Her mother said she's been living in a trailer with her boyfriend."

"Please don't call it a trailer," I said, "a trailer is something you pull behind your truck to haul more stuff. What people live in are 'mobile homes.'"

"A trailer is also a brief film that advertises a movie and is usually seen before a movie instead of after it. That reminds me—would you like to see a movie with me sometime?"

"Sure, but I want to know more about Fatsy Pats . . ." I shook my head in embarrassment. "I mean Patsy Corley. Who was her boyfriend?"

"A man named Eugene Rodgers. He was quite a bit older than she was."

"Gene Rodgers? Snake Rodgers?"

"Snake?" Dean chuckled. "I'm not sure I want to know how he got that name."

"It's not what you think. He grew up with his single mother. When he was about thirteen, she told him to go up into the attic to get something for her. He came scrambling back down hollering, 'Mama! Mama! There's a snake up there.' She sent him back up with a gun full of snake-shot. Gene got so excited that he fired that gun off all over the attic and made a lot of bullet holes through their ceiling. His mama made him spend his own money for spackling and try to patch the holes, but he slipped and fell through the ceiling—right into their kitchen. They used to call him Snake Killer, but it got shortened to Snake before he grew up."

Dean smiled. "Not what I expected." He paused. "Of course, it's an open-and-shut case, not much to investigate, but both bodies have to be autopsied. I'm sure you know the laws on that. The point is that the Middletons *insist* you're missing too much time from work 'hanging out' with the sheriff, and that Mrs. Corley is demanding that she have you there to dress Patsy and to consult with them on planning."

"She seemed to take a fancy to me back when she planned her husband's services, which was strange because she insisted on a special oversize casket and had him dressed in clothes like a picture she had of him when he was young. He always went barefooted, and I had to locate shoes that would fit him. We cut off his long hair and shaved the beard so he'd look more like he did when they were young. She approved of everything, then had him cremated."

"I'm glad to know I'm not the only one who thought she was weird. I tried to get her to sit in the car, but she had her nose in everything. She'd stand in front of the boyfriend's body and cuss, then she'd go back to that bloody bathroom and cuss at her dead daughter. She wants you there when she goes in to make arrangements tonight at six, and since you'd already gotten the information we wanted from Naomi Spires, Sheriff Harmon told me get you out of Safe Sister. Where do you want to go? Your place or the mortuary?"

"My apartment. I never go to the mortuary unless I'm dressed appropriately, which means a black dress, black stockings, and low-heeled black shoes." I laughed. "And I'd better remove all these bruises, too. I'll call Otis and Odell when I get home."

"Tomorrow's New Year's Eve." Those blue eyes sparkled at me.

"I know."

"I just wanted to tell you that I'd love to take you out tomorrow night, but the sheriff has everybody on duty, including me, with or without a homicide. Guess I'll be pulling DUIs unless someone gets killed. Could I take you out for a late New Year's Eve celebration on my next night off?"

"When's that?"

"I don't know yet, but I'll call you."

Just my luck. Another man who planned to call me. I hoped his calls wouldn't be like Patel's had been lately.

At five o'clock that evening, I arrived at Middleton's in black clothes. After scrubbing the makeup away, I'd spent most of my time at home making telephone calls: to Daddy to check on Big Boy (he was fine); to Jane to check on her (she was resting up so Roxanne could talk all night); and to Otis to check on Mrs. Corley (he said she was as eccentric as ever). I'd also called Wayne, and he'd bragged on what a good job I'd done as an undercover agent. That made my chest puff out almost as much as my inflatable bras do; however, he'd insisted on stopping by to pick up the badge and pronounce me no longer a deputy.

Otis met me in the hall before I'd even reached my office.

"I don't know why Mrs. Corley has to make arrangements today. With New Year's Eve and New Year's Day, we may not get Patsy's body back for several days, but she's adamant she come today and that you be here." He cut me an inquiring look. "What have you been doing with the sheriff?"

"Just giving him some female ideas about investigations. What do you want me to do?"

"Mrs. Corley is scheduled to come in at six. We don't have any decedents here right now, so you can catch up on your paperwork."

"I don't have any until we talk to Mrs. Corley, and even then, we can't put funeral plans in the obituary until we get the body back."

"Until we get Miss Patsy back," Otis corrected me. Sometimes I slip up and don't call the decedent by name. He laughed. "I was talking about the paperwork you hide in the bottom drawer of your desk."

I just smiled. I keep my books and other reading materials in that drawer. That sounded tempting, but instead I offered to make coffee and to heat water in case Mrs. Corley wanted hot tea.

In the kitchenette, I took out the best silver serving pieces and Wedgwood china cups and saucers. The Middletons like to use their mother's china when serving coffee during a consultation though we each have personal mugs for when we don't have any of the bereaved with us. I made coffee and set up everything on a silver tray before I headed back to my office. An instrumental version of "He Arose" played softly over our sound system announcing someone at the front door. Sure enough, Mrs. Corley had arrived almost thirty minutes early.

"Why, Callie child, I haven't seen you since Jimmy Lee died." Mrs. Corley had looked anorexic the first time I'd seen her, and she was even thinner now. She'd been the only one who called June Bug by his given name, Jimmy Lee, and the only one who called me "Callie child."

Back when we went to pick up her husband's body, the first time I saw her she'd been wearing a yellow chenille bathrobe with those pink sponge rollers in her hair and had reminded me of a canary with her little beaked nose and bird-chirpy voice. Today she had on a long-sleeved navy blue dress with white eyelet collar and cuffs. She'd looked old before; now she looked ancient.

"Is anyone meeting you here?" I asked. There were several more children besides Patsy.

"No, I told Penny and the others I wanted to do this my way. Walter, my youngest, drove me here, but I made him stay out in the car."

"Yes, ma'am. Come into this planning room." I motioned toward the door and she was seated before Otis joined us. "Would either of you like some coffee or hot tea?" I asked.

"Coffee will be fine," Otis replied.

"I'd rather have some Coca-Cola on ice if you have it," Mrs. Corley said in that bird-chirp voice. "I don't guess you have anything stronger to put in it," she added. "Since Jimmy Lee's been gone, I've started having a little nip sometimes."

"No, ma'am," I answered, "but I'll be glad to fix you a Coke on ice."

"Can you stick your head out the door and call Walter in here for me?" she asked.

"Certainly." I was thankful she'd changed her mind about letting him come inside to assist her with plans, but once again Mrs. Corley surprised me.

Walter grinned when I walked up and told him his mother wanted to see him. A tall, gangly man, Walter had the most pockmarked face I'd ever seen, must have been scars from acne when he was young—an almost terminal case. He followed me into the consultation room and sat in the chair beside his mother. Otis had stepped out, but he returned in less than a minute with a tall glass of iced Coca-Cola which he set in front of Mrs. Corley.

"Boy," the tiny woman said to her tall son like he was a three-year-old, "I didn't call you in here to sit down. Bring me that blue and white crocheted carry-all bag off the backseat."

"Yes, ma'am."

Otis removed two forms from a drawer: a planning sheet and a general price list. "Before we begin your selections, Mrs. Corley, let me get some information from you. He quickly asked some preliminary questions and wrote her answers on the paper. Mrs. Corley wanted write-ups in the St. Mary paper and the Charleston paper. "Patsy lived in Charleston for several years before she met that Snake and moved back here. I want her friends there to know she's left us."

She looked up as Walter came back in and handed her the tote bag. She reached in and pulled out a pint bottle of rum. She uncapped it and tipped it over her glass of Coca-Cola, shook the glass a bit though I offered her a spoon, and took a long drink. "You know, I never consumed alcohol when Jimmy Lee was alive. He drank enough for both of us, but I've found since then that a little drinky-poo makes me feel better. You don't mind, do you?"

"No, Mama," Walter said.

"I wasn't talking to you, boy. I was speaking to Mr. Middleton and Callie girl here."

"I'm sorry."

"You can go back out and get in the car or you can sit here and keep your pie hole shut."

"Yes, Mama." That's the first time I ever heard a woman use the expression "pie hole," though I'd heard men say it before.

"Was Patsy married?" Otis asked. We like to be sure we're dealing with the next-of-kin when making plans. If Patsy died a married woman, her husband would be responsible for funeral plans instead of her mother.

"She was, but she divorced before she moved back here."

"A legal divorce? Not just a separation?"

"It was legal," Walter said. "I seen the papers."

"I told you to be quiet. If you keep that up, I'll call Penny to come get you, and I'll drive myself home."

"Yes, ma'am."

"Did she have children?"

"You asked me that already, and I said no. The closest relatives Patsy had was her mother, that's me, and her sisters and brothers. That makes me next-of-kin, doesn't it?"

"Yes, it does. Another question, before you select a casket, we need to know if you plan to have Patsy cremated like you did Mr. Corley. If so, we have special choices for that."

"No, Patsy didn't like me having Jimmy Lee cremated. Said it gave her the heebie-jeebies just thinking about us doing that to her daddy. I'll want to bury her in the St. Mary Cemetery, the old part with the stand-up stones. Jimmy Lee and I bought plots there a long time ago. I brought the deed for them with me." She took a folded blue paper from her purse.

"You'll need to go by the cemetery and show them which grave you want opened, but that can wait until Miss Patsy is back here in St. Mary."

"Where is she?" Walter asked. Mrs. Corley cut him a look that made the worst schoolteacher look I ever shot anybody look like a smile.

"They took her to Charleston for a postmortem exam," Otis said. "Since we can't set a time and date yet, would you like to select the casket next?" He pulled out a notebook of plastic-covered sheets with casket pictures and specifications. "These are the ones that we stock here at Middleton's, but I also have catalogs with others that we can order for you. If you'll step with me into the room next door, I can show you some examples."

"I don't have to look at sample coffins. I'll pick one out from the book here." She began flipping through the pages. Walter leaned over to look, too, but she pushed him away. I wondered if she'd been like this with her children when they were little.

"Are you the one who took Patsy to Charleston?" Mrs. Corley asked Otis.

"No, ma'am. My brother Odell did that."

"You know, she's a heavy girl. We had to have a special-sized casket for Jimmy Lee. Do I need to get something special for her?"

"I don't believe so. Odell would have mentioned that if the size would be a problem."

Mrs. Corley went through the book several times and finally settled on a pale gray steel with silver handles and shirred pink interior. The page showed several sample, mostly pink, casket sprays, and she selected one of those also.

"What about clothes?" Otis asked. "Will you supply them or should I have Callie shop for something?"

I confess the thought of being sent to Charleston on a shopping trip excited me. Jane and I love to go to Victoria's Secret in Charleston, and that would be even more fun now that Jane had quit shoplifting and I didn't have to worry about what she might try to pull in the store.

"No, Callie girl won't need to shop. Patsy bought lots of clothes after her divorce. I'll go to the trailer and get something from her closet."

I didn't bother to tell her to call it a mobile home, and I didn't mention that the place might be roped off with yellow crime scene tape making it impossible to get in there for an outfit. I figured that poor woman had enough to deal with, and it was better to let her face any complications as they came instead of suggesting some that might not exist. Dean had said that the investigation was closed. Maybe he'd already removed the tape.

Otis went through each step thoroughly, letting Mrs. Corley take as long as she wanted to make choices. She decided on a service in our chapel, with her nephew, whom she called "Preacher" as though that were his name and an organist, but no soloist.

"And food," she said. "I want a catered reception. Can we do that here?"

"Yes, ma'am." Otis took out a brochure showing lunches and finger foods. Around here, family and friends take food to the home of the bereaved, but there are caterers who will provide food at the funeral home.

Mrs. Corley's eyes lit up. "Did you see that article about the man who died and his funeral procession went through one of the short-order places and everyone received one of the dead man's favorite burgers? I saw it in one of those little newspapers they sell at the grocery store."

"No, ma'am. I don't think I did."

"Well, that's what I want to do. Instead of having food here, we'll take the procession to a drive-through window and have them give each person something."

"Do you have a particular restaurant in mind?" Otis didn't miss a beat.

"I don't know yet."

"What was her favorite food?" I asked.

"Shrimp." Walter barely had the word out when Mrs. Corley glared at him.

"Most places with drive-through windows don't serve shrimp," Otis said, "but we'll let Callie figure out that problem and get back to you."

Just my luck. Now they expected me to find a McDonald's or Burger King that sells shrimp-burgers.

Mrs. Corley turned to me. "Now, I want that same oak stand you brought to my house before because it matches my furniture. I want a white wreath for the front door and one for the back door, also, because lots of our neighbors come around there." She wiped her brow and wrinkled her face even more than it already was. "Oh, and the registers, don't forget those."

"Callie won't forget anything," Otis assured her.

"I want this stuff brought out *tonight*," Mrs. Corley emphasized. "There was an article in the paper this morning about Patsy's death, calling it a murder-suicide, but people are being kind and have already started bringing food to the house. It's a shame they have to print that stuff in the paper like that. I'd think they'd give us a little privacy, what with me having to bury my child. It's not right for kids to go before their parents. It's not the natural way of life."

"No, ma'am, it's not, but we just have to do what needs to be done to respect and remember our loved ones," Otis said as he slid the papers over in front of Mrs. Corley and showed her where to sign them.

After Mrs. Corley and Walter left, I loaded folding chairs, silk wreaths, an oak stand, and both a guest register and food register into the van. When I was ready to leave, I asked Otis, "Can I take the van home and bring it back and trade it for my Mustang tomorrow morning."

"Are you working tomorrow?"

"That depends on whether we get any clients in, but I can bring the van back whether I'm working or not." All I knew was that I wanted to get Big Boy from my daddy's house, and I thought he'd ride more comfortably in the van than in my car.

"Okay, I'll call if we have a pickup."

Mrs. Corley had changed since June Bug died, but the house remained about the same. Everything was precise. In the kitchen, pots with shiny copper bottoms hung from black wrought-iron racks over the range top, but I'd bet the pots they cooked in were under the cabinets. Almost every surface in the living room sported those starched, crocheted doilies with stand-up ruffles. I thought about Mrs. Corley's crocheted tote bag where she kept her bottle of rum and wondered if she did all that needlework herself.

Penny and one of her brothers helped me unload the chairs and set them exactly where Mrs. Corley told us to. Like before, she complained that the oak register stand was lighter than her furniture. Once again, I restrained from explaining that her furniture was older than the stand and had darkened as it aged. When Penny told me, "Just leave the flowers and registers. We'll put them where they belong," I was glad to get away.

I stopped by Daddy's on the way home. He asked a bunch of questions about where I'd been and why the sheriff had brought Big Boy to them to dog-sit. I skirted the issues and didn't actually tell him anything. Mike and Frankie helped me put Big Boy in the van, and I was glad to see that he seemed more lively and in less pain.

Jane's door opened when I pulled into the driveway in front of our side-by-side apartments. "Where have you been?" she called out. "Did you spend the night with that homicide cop?"

"No, been working. Do you need anything?"

"No, I'm working right now. You wouldn't believe how many calls I've had tonight. Call me tomorrow and we'll have coffee, but not before noon."

Jane's use of the word "call" made me eager to check messages to see if I had a message from Patel. Nothing. After feeding Big Boy and scoffing up a few of his banana MoonPies myself instead of even heating a can of soup, I called Patel. The phone rang and rang. No answer.

ON THE SEVENTH DAY OF CHRISTMAS MY TRUE LOVE GAVE TO ME

SEVEN DOGGIES HOWLING

Rain pelting my rooftop made me want to stay in bed, and even all scrunched up in my blankets, I felt it was going to be a watery, cold day. The last thing we needed on New Year's Eve was slick roads drenched with rain. I glanced at the clock beside the bed and was surprised to see it was almost ten. Normally Big Boy would have been by my bed licking my face before then. I'd promised Daddy I'd go by his house before I reported to work at noon and I should have gotten up already.

I wanted to talk to Jane and see if she had any plans for the evening—New Year's Eve—the night every single woman wants to have a date, and I had none. Here I'd been worrying about whether I should feel guilty about the flirtation and attraction between Dean and me because of my previous budding relationship with Patel, but I was as dateless for New Year's Eve as any old spinster I'd ever read about. Probably wouldn't even have a phone call that night. At least, Jane would have calls, maybe more than she could handle. From what she'd said lately, Roxanne was burning up the phone and earning bigger checks than ever.

Big Boy was nowhere to be seen when I went to the bathroom and had a shower. I wrapped a towel around me and went through the apartment looking for him. That's not hard to do because my place isn't large—two bedrooms, kitchen with eating area, living room, and one bathroom—and none of the rooms are big. My single bed fits fine in the larger bedroom, but a double would crowd it, and a king-size would be impossible. I used to describe my apartment as being "probably the only one left in St. Mary with olive green shag carpet." That changed after several unfortunate events which resulted in bloodstains and my getting new paint and carpet throughout. I chose cream walls and dark beige berber carpet.

The floor plan of Jane's apartment is a mirror image of mine, but she keeps hers much cleaner and knows exactly where everything is. I admit that my method is to put things wherever it's convenient and then look around when I need them again.

Big Boy wasn't lying on his special throw rug in the living room nor by the stove in the kitchen. Both of those were favored spots though he'd prefer lying on my bed or my new couch if he didn't know that would bring down my wrath. I saw the door to my second bedroom was slightly open. That's supposed to be a guest bedroom, but after I clean it up, I never have any overnight guests, so I wind up stacking books and things in there, and soon it looks like those houses on the hoarder television shows again.

My dog lay in the middle of a pile of unfolded laundry I'd thrown on the bed, planning to deal with it later. He's not a puppy anymore, but a chewed book lay beside his mouth. When I lifted it, slobber dripped off.

"Big Boy?" I said and scratched him behind his ears. "Big Boy?"

He looked up, but there was no recognition in his eyes. I swear that dog is the most expressive animal I've ever known. He laughs and cries, and sometimes, he rolls his eyes like a thirteen-year-old. Now, even with open eyes, he had an unconscious look. I screamed with shock and frustration. Big Boy didn't react at all.

When I tried to rouse him enough to get off the bed and stand, he flopped like a soft-filled teddy bear. I did what most girls do when there's trouble. I called my daddy.

"We'll be right there," he assured me. "Don't you try to lift that giant dog. You'll tear up some of your inside parts, and I'm still hoping for more grandchildren. Mike and Frankie can put Big Boy in the truck and take him to the vet. No telling what's wrong. You didn't let him get into any poison after you took him home, did'ja?"

"No, Daddy, and he was fine when I went to bed."

"We're on the way there now. Just stay by him and pet him."

I'm the first to acknowledge that I don't always do what my daddy tells me. This was no exception. I went to my room and dressed. I almost pulled on jeans, but I decided I'd better dress for work because time might run short between taking Big Boy to his vet's office in Beaufort and getting to Middleton's by noon.

Daddy and my brothers insisted on riding with me in the van to the vet's office even though I protested that the assistants there could help me. When we arrived, we heard a cacophony of howling, mostly dogs with a few cat screeches included. I just love the word "cacophony." I've used it whenever possible since I learned it in a high school vocabulary class. Two of my other favorite words are "elusive" and "lackadaisical." Those words are delicious in my mouth.

A sign on the door informed us, "Closed New Year's Eve and New Year's Day. Call 555-3417 if this is an emergency." I rang the number and an answering service advised me to go to the emergency vet service across town. I told them that something must be wrong because it sounded like every dog in the boarding section was howling. She informed me, "The boy who comes in to feed the animals has car trouble. He called and said he'll be there as soon as possible." Those dogs were hungry. I wished I could get inside and feed them, but if I tried, I'd be sure to wind up in jail for breaking and entering. One thing for sure—I wouldn't board Big Boy there. I'd continue to leave him with Daddy when I needed dog-sitting. Besides, it's cheaper.

I was totally frustrated, but Daddy entered the address for the animal ER on his GPS and drove us there while I sat in back and petted my dog.

Frankie and Mike carried Big Boy in with Mike complaining that they should have gurneys for transporting dogs that size. When the receptionist saw Big Boy, she took us right back to an exam room. Big Boy's vet is a female, but the one who saw my dog at the animal ER was an old man with a bald head on top and a long gray ponytail in back. He poked around Big Boy, took a look at his incision, and announced, "This dog is dehydrated. I'll want to keep him overnight and give him fluid by IV. Do you have insurance for him?"

My mouth must have dropped open because Daddy handed him a Platinum American Express card and said, "Will this do?"

"Are you coming for New Year's Day dinner tomorrow?" Daddy asked on the way back to St. Mary.

"Am I invited?" I asked as though I didn't know the answer.

"Of course, and bring Jane, too. You girls need some good luck in the coming year, and I'll be cooking the foods that will bring it to you."

"Besides," Frankie interrupted, "you'll get to see me before I go off to school Thursday."

"What kind of school?" I asked.

"Not gonna tell you. It'll be a surprise, but I'll get my license after that."

"Is your driver's license suspended?"

"No, it's not that. I . . ."

"It's not a license; it's a permit," Mike butted in.

"Tell me," I said, but the three men refused to say anything else about this school Frankie was going to attend on Thursday.

By the time we were back in St. Mary, the clock was ticking past twelve. I called Otis and explained I would be there soon.

"Do you want us to drop you off?" Frankie asked.

"If we did that, how would you get back to my place for your truck? Go to my apartment and pick up the truck. I'll drive the van back to Middleton's."

"You need to change clothes," Mike suggested.

"I'm wearing work clothes," I answered.

"But they're covered with dog hair."

"Big Boy's in the hospital," I told Odell first thing when I walked into work—an hour late, but wearing a clean black dress with no dog hairs on it.

"I thought you brought him home."

"I did, but he's got IVs because he's dehydrated. I don't understand it. He hasn't been throwing up or running off and he's been drinking plenty."

"Well, I understand why you're late, but I've got something for you to do right way. I showed that Patterson man his wife's paperwork on the computer and offered to print them out for him, but he's adamant he must see the actual papers his wife's first husband signed for the prepaid funeral."

"You showed him everything about the prepay on the computer? I scanned the full documents into electronic records."

"He says his lawyer says he has the right to see the actual signed documents. I doubt he even has a lawyer, but I put several boxes of old records in your office for you to search and see if you can find them. I doubt you will. Doofus and I went through them last night."

"Anything else?" I asked, knowing he was irritated because he only calls Otis "Doofus" when he's annoyed.

"Mrs. Corley is bringing Miss Patsy's clothes and wants to talk to you while she's here. Otis has gone to Charleston to pick up Amber Buchanan."

"Will you be prepping Mrs. Buchanan when she arrives?"

"Not right away. She'll go in the cooler until the sheriff locates next-of-kin." We don't embalm anyone without permission from the legally responsible person. A lot of people in South Carolina think embalming is required by law, but it's actually a choice though public viewing is forbidden without it.

Yes, I was tempted, but I didn't say, "I know that."

The next several hours bored me—I almost said "to death" —but while we have our dark humor in this business, that's an expression I don't use. I was surprised at how many people had prepaid for funeral services way back ten to fifteen years ago. Most of them had already been buried, but I found Emma Lou Riley's papers filed in the wrong folder. I could say that doesn't happen with computers, but as everyone knows, errors persist in the computer world, too.

"I found it!" I said to Odell waving the folder in front of him.

He harrumphed, which is a sound he makes frequently. "Must have been in one of the boxes Doofus went through. I'm positive I wouldn't have missed it." He took the folder to his office, where I hoped he wouldn't lose it again.

I'd hardly had time to consider what to do next when the

telephone rang.

"Middleton's Mortuary. Callie Parrish speaking. How may I help you?"

"This is the medical examiner's office in Charleston. Mr. Middleton just left here with the Buchanan case. I didn't know then that the pathologist had finished with Miss Corley and Mr. Rodgers. According to my paperwork, they both go back to Middleton's until the sheriff releases them to next-of-kin for final disposition. I'm sorry I didn't know until after Mr. Middleton left in the hearse. You might want to stop him and send him back for Corley and Rodgers. He hasn't been gone long."

"Thank you very much. I'll call and send him back." Good grief! Middleton's serves as the morgue for Jade County and has the contract to transport bodies for the county, but we'd never before had *three* murder fatalities on the premises at once. Some folks might say we only had two, but I consider suicide a very sad form of homicide also.

Otis didn't complain at all when I called and asked him if he'd go back and pick up the other two victims. In fact, he said he was only about ten miles out of Charleston and would much rather go back then than have to return once he was all the way to St. Mary.

"Do you have room for three bodies in the hearse?" I asked without thinking.

"You should know by now that it's called the funeral coach, and of course there's plenty of room. It's not like they're in caskets."

I apologized and hung up before I made some other *Duh* comment. Usually, Otis is sweet as candy and Odell is a little rough around the edges. Maybe, like me, Otis was feeling lonely at the thought of no date for New Year's Eve. Or maybe he had gas again. Who knows?

Even without a single client on the premises, I stayed busy all afternoon. Mrs. Corley didn't bring Patsy's clothes. Surprisingly, she sent Walter with them. I don't know if he wadded them up on the way or what, but the hot pink pants suit and pretty pale pink and white flowered blouse were crushed. I took them into my workroom and steamed the wrinkles out. Officially, my title is cosmetician, but I do a little of whatever needs to be done around

Middleton's.

New Year's Eve—all dressed up and nowhere to go. Well, I was dressed in my usual black and would be planning to wear something else if I had a date for the evening. But I didn't have any plans. I didn't even expect to hear from Patel. My feelings about him were swinging like the pendulum in Edgar Allan Poe's story. Back and forth between anger and worry. If he'd changed his mind about our relationship—well, really just a friendship at that point—the polite thing to do would be to tell me. That thought brought out the angry feelings. But what if something had happened to him? What if he were unable to communicate with me? Just that notion brought tears to my eyes.

I was swabbing my face with a tissue when Odell walked up to me.

"Callie, are you crying?"

"Just allergies," I lied, hating myself for doing it, but mentally justifying it with the thought that it would make Odell sad to know I was feeling so low that I wept.

"You can go on home. I'm sure you're going somewhere exciting tonight. I'll stay here and help Otis."

"You're sure you won't need me?"

"We'll be fine. You get outta here, and I'll see you day after tomorrow."

I put on my coat and headed toward the back door. As it closed, I heard him call, "Happy New Year," to me.

Magazines and television shows talk about exercise releasing endorphins that make people feel good. Sometimes I get the same benefit from driving my Mustang. It's a blue 1966 ragtop and was my ex-husband Donnie's pride and joy. Since we divorced not long after he finished his medical internship, no alimony was granted because I'd been the main breadwinner and supported him through medical school. The judge thought Donnie should forfeit something though and awarded me the Mustang. My first reaction was pleasure that the court recognized my contribution to Donnie's future and that my getting it made Donnie furious. After I began driving the car, I understood how Donnie felt about that piece of blue metal. I don't speed—just drive around—and it makes me feel better, especially this early evening when I drove along Highway 17 and could see the ocean through the rain.

I called Jane before I headed home. "I know Roxanne is probably working tonight, but would you like to go somewhere early and have dinner before Roxanne starts?"

She giggled. She *actually* giggled, and Jane's not usually a giggler though I am sometimes. I realize that's a lot of giggling, but a lot of giggling was going on.

"Sorry, but I have a date."

"Ohhhhhhhhhhh, who?"

"Your brother Frankie called. He misses me. I miss him. We don't know if we're going to renew our relationship or just be friends, but we're going out together tonight."

That was a surprise. They'd been engaged and their parting hadn't been pleasant. Jane and Frankie had pointedly avoided each other when I took her with me to Daddy's on Christmas day.

"Oh," I said, "Daddy said to remind you that he's cooking the traditional New Year's Day dinner tomorrow, and you're invited."

"I know. Frankie told me. Listen, I'd love to keep talking, but I've got to get ready." I could hear excitement in her voice, but then, maybe she'd been feeling sorry for herself at the thought of spending New Year's Eve alone—like me.

I speed-dialed Daddy's house. Mike answered.

"What are you guys doing tonight?" I asked.

"I've got a date and Frankie's got a date, and you won't believe this—Pa's got *two* dates."

"What? I figured Daddy would be home washing collards and prepping for dinner tomorrow." That was a poor choice of words. "Prepping" means one thing to a cook, another to a mortuary worker.

"Daddy's going over to Miss Lettie's and have dinner with her and Miss Ellen. He and Miss Ellen think it might lift Miss Lettie's spirits a little."

It certainly didn't lift mine. I'd been almost ready to offer to help Daddy clean collards on New Year's Eve!

With no one, not even Big Boy, to share dinner or New

Year's Eve with me, I decided to pick up a to-go plate from Rizzie. I might be home alone, but I could eat well.

Gee Three was packed, and Tyrone had several extra servers helping him. I assumed Rizzie was in the kitchen. Even Pork Chop Higgins was there drinking a cup of coffee. He sat in his favorite booth—the one with a movable table that could be pushed over to allow him to fit from front to back. It took almost the whole bench seat to accommodate his width. He had on his usual bib overalls over an orange T-shirt. I looked around and saw no other vacant seats, so I squeezed myself into the cramped space across from him.

"Hi, do you mind if I sit with you?" I asked. "Been delivering any babies lately?"

"No to both questions. I'm happy for you to sit with me, and I haven't delivered a baby since the one you helped me with. Did you know Misty and Billy Wayne named the baby for me?"

It took a minute for that to register. I couldn't picture that little infant being called "Pork Chop." The huge man seemed to read my mind. He laughed.

"They named him Edward. That's my middle name. Full name is Richard Edward Higgins. Before I started raising hogs, people called me Rick—Rick Higgins, but I told Billy Wayne I'd rather they name the baby Edward. He liked that and said they'll call him Eddie."

"Nice to meet you, Rick," I said and reached across the table to shake his hand.

"Same here." His handshake was surprisingly gentle.

We both looked up when Rizzie spoke, though I don't think either of us had noticed her approaching our table bringing me a glass of sweet iced tea.

"Some of us are going over to Kenny B's when I close," she said. "Would either of you like to go with us? Nobody's dating, just a group of friends celebrating the beginning of a new year."

My mind immediately bounced to Jeff Morgan. "Rizzie, please don't go out and drink tonight. You know I've worked on people in my work room because they drank and drove, and it's raining. The roads are wet."

"We're just going to dance and celebrate. Nobody's planning

to get drunk, but just in case, we're not letting anyone who's had even *one* beer drive. We're taking Ty as the designated driver."

"Tyrone doesn't have a driver's license. He's only fifteen."

"Callie, Callie, Callie, Ty's my brother. I know how old he is, but I also know he's been driving on Surcie Island since he was ten years old, and he's a better driver than most of us are when we're sober—and certainly a safer choice than anyone who's been drinking." Rizzie chuckled. "We'll be safe. Do either of you want to go?"

Pork Chop spoke up. "Thanks for the invite, but I'm going to bed early. Gotta get up at dawn and do all the farm chores since my kids went to their Mee Maw's with my wife."

I almost agreed to go with Rizzie, but considering the mood I was in, I'd probably put a damper on everyone's spirits. Maybe, just maybe, Patel would call.

"No, thanks, I have plans for later." Okay, I told another lie—two in one day. Sometimes so-called white lies are kindnesses. Knowing Rizzie, if she'd realized how sorry for myself I felt, she'd have worried about me, and I would have ruined her evening. One of my talents is rationalizing.

"Okay," Rizzie answered, "if either of you change your minds, just come on to Kenny B's. What do you want to eat, Callie? I've got to get back to the kitchen."

"Surprise me, but pack it to go. I'm taking it with me." Seeing the look of sympathy on her face, I added, "Make it two." I could always put one of the plates in the freezer for another time, and Rizzie wouldn't feel sorry for me being alone on New Year's Eve.

"I'll pack you two dinners to go, but I'm trying something new—Gee Three Shrimp Sliders. I'll bring you a sample to eat here while I get your plates together. I'm checking out a new cook, too."

"Sure." I turned my attention back to Pork Chop. "Did you say your whole family's out of town?"

"Yes, my wife took all the kids to see her mom in Georgia. My mother-in-law hasn't been feeling well, and those nine grandchildren always lift her spirits."

"I don't see how you do it. I taught kindergarten and had about fifteen in my class, but nine at home all the time sounds like a busy, busy household."

"It is busy and it's fun. The older ones help out taking care of the younger ones as well as lending lots of hands with chores. You'll have to come over to our house when my wife is home. When you see how great a big family is, you'll be wanting to get married and have a house full of kids yourself."

"No, thanks." He looked puzzled at my response. "Oh, I don't mean no thanks on the visit. Just on getting married and having children, and my family isn't exactly small. I have five brothers."

"Why don't you want to be married?"

"I tried it once and it didn't work out. I don't think I'll ever meet the right man."

"You will, and when you meet him, you'll recognize he's the right one."

Just then, Tyrone set plates in front of both of us. Pork Chop's was a platter full of rolls with a side of sweet potato fries and a side of bacon. Mine was a smaller dish with one roll and a scoop of Rizzie's pasta salad that I like so much.

"These are Rizzie's new Gee Three Shrimp Sliders," Tyrone said. "Look inside."

I lifted the top part of the roll and saw fried shrimp topped with lettuce, tomato, onion, and remoulade sauce. Now, part of my love for po boys is that crusty sub loaf bread they're made on, but this slider was perfect, just perfect, on that soft dinner roll.

"What do you think?" Pork Chop asked.

"Scrumptious!"

"They were my idea. Little hamburgers made on rolls sell well in the chain restaurants. They call them hamburger sliders. I suggested shrimp sliders to Rizzie, and here we are eating the first batch of them. My wife's been cooking those hamburger sliders for years. She calls 'em baby burgers and fixes them for our little ones. Of course, at my house, we use ground pork instead of beef for hamburgers." He noticed my staring at his plate, picked up a slice of bacon, and said, "Bacon—definitely not good for the heart, but sometimes it's good for the soul."

"I like to hear you tell about your family. Your eyes light up, and you look happy when you talk about them. Doesn't it make you sad that they're all gone and not with you on New Year's Eve?"

"Every day is a new day of life, so it's always New Year's for me. I miss my family, but it pleases me for the ones I love to be happy and to bring joy to the ones they love, and believe you me, my young'uns love their Mee Maw in Georgia." His expression changed to slight embarrassment. "I hope that doesn't make you think of me as sappy."

"Not at all. I think it makes you wonderful, and I'm glad to get to know you, Mr. Rick Higgins." Perfect timing. Ty set a plastic bag with two Styrofoam food trays inside on the table.

"What's in them?" I asked him.

"Yahd bud." He grinned as if I wouldn't understand, but I'm well aware that "yard bird" is Gullah for chicken.

"Happy New Year, Callie," Pork Chop said and winked. "Trust me. When the right man comes along, you'll know it."

The rain had stopped when I put the bag of food on the passenger seat and slid under the steering wheel. It wasn't late, and I wasn't in any particular hurry to go home. The thought of my apartment without Big Boy saddened me and gave me an idea. I called the animal ER in Beaufort.

"Kirk's Animal Emergency Medical Services," a young female voice answered.

"Is this an answering service?" I asked.

"No, I'm here at the vet's."

"This is Callie Parrish. I brought my dog in this morning and the vet said he has to spend the night. I was wondering how he's doing."

"The black and white Great Dane?"

"Yes, ma'am."

"He's resting, but the doctor has added antibiotics to his IV fluids."

"When can I see him?"

"You can see your dog any time you come here. We're open twenty-four hours a day."

"Then I'm coming to see him now."

"We'll be right here."

The drive into Beaufort took less than twenty minutes. The young lady I'd spoken to on the telephone asked, "Are you the Great Dane's owner?" when I walked in.

"Yes, I'm Callie Parrish."

"Doctor Kirk wants to speak with you, but I'll take you back to see your dog first."

Big Boy was sleeping, but he looked comfortable even with the IV needle in him. I petted his back for a while before the veterinarian came to my side.

"Beautiful animal, Ms. Parrish, absolutely beautiful."

"Do you know what's wrong with him?"

"He has an infection and an electrolyte imbalance, but we're taking care of both of those problems."

"He looks peaceful."

"He became a little agitated, probably missing you, and since I'd already inserted the IV for fluids and antibiotics, I added a little something to keep him calm and comfortable. He should sleep all night, and if he doesn't, someone will be here to care for him. Why don't you call in the morning? We can tell you then how he does through the night."

On my way out, both Dr. Kirk and the young lady called, "Happy New Year's."

I left the vet's with a smile on my face. I'd still be alone at home on New Year's Eve, but I felt so much better knowing that Big Boy was resting well and receiving good treatment.

During the ride from Beaufort to St. Mary, James Brown blasted out of my bra singing "I Feel Good," and for a moment, I was positive, absolutely sure that it would be Patel. I hope Otis didn't hear my sigh when he said, "Hello, Callie. I'm sorry to interrupt your festivities, and I know we told you to take all day off tomorrow, but could you come in for a few hours late tomorrow afternoon?"

"No problem. Do we have someone new?"

"Not really new. Odell and I examined Patsy Corley carefully, and we think with some extreme reconstruction that can be covered with cosmetic hair, we can make her look presentable for her mother. Mrs. Corley was very upset thinking that the casket would have to be closed. Odell and I will do the rebuilding, but we want you here on makeup."

"I can come in. Daddy usually serves holiday dinners later than regular lunches, so we'll probably eat between one and two. What if I come over around four o'clock?"

"I think that will be fine, but phone first. If what Odell and I think we can do doesn't work, we won't need you."

"What about Amber Buchanan and Snake Rodgers?"

"They're here, but we won't be doing any prepping until law enforcement releases those bodies. Mrs. Rodgers called and said she'd talk with the sheriff and see when she can make arrangements for Eugene."

"I'll call you tomorrow."

Before he said, "goodbye," Odell said, "Happy New Year."

Dalmation! I knew people meant well, but I was sick and tired of hearing those three words.

Heavy rain began again about the time I reached home, but the dinners were in a plastic bag, so I ran to the front porch without worrying about the trays getting wet. That Gee Three Shrimp Slider had tasted great, but I was really hungry after going to Beaufort. I put one of the dinners in the fridge and set the other on my kitchen table.

Rizzie—or her new cook, whoever had prepared my plates—had outdone herself. The "yard bird" was yummy pan-fried chicken smothered in spicy gravy. The sides were sweet potato pone and a special okra dish Rizzie created.

Once more, I pressed the key to speed-dial Patel. This time there was an answer, but it wasn't his voice.

"The voice mail for the number you've reached is full."

My emotions rocked from anger to worry and back again. Why was he ignoring me? Was it by choice or had something happened to him?

What should I do? I definitely didn't want to watch any New Year's Eve shows and I had no interest in seeing the ball drop in New York. I love to read, especially mysteries. That used to be all I read. They're like puzzles and I enjoy trying to figure out who-done-it before the end of the books. Recently, I've read some sci fi and fantasy as well as a ghost anthology, but bottom line is that mysteries are still my favorites. I'll read anything by Janet Evanovich or Mary Higgins Clark as soon as it's available. I like Ann Rule's true crime books, too, but I hadn't thought to buy a book on my way home.

My spare bedroom is piled high with books on the floor, on the bed, and on every other piece of furniture in there. I went looking for a novel that had been so good I wanted to read it again. The sight of my rumpled laundry where I'd found Big Boy so sick that morning made me sad. I finally chose Beth Groundwater's *Fatal Descent.* I considered gathering up the clothes Big Boy had slept on. I'd thrown them on the bed planning to fold them later. Now they'd have to be rewashed, but my daddy always said, "Don't wash on New Year's Eve or New Year's Day. It's bad luck."

I'm not overly superstitious, but that sounded like an excellent reason not to bother with laundry that night. I noticed a box of candles beside the bed. I'd bought them in case the power went off sometime. Now I had a better idea. I took them into the kitchen and lit one. I dripped candle wax on half a dozen saucers and stuck a candle in each puddle. Then I carried all seven candles to the bathroom, set them around, and turned out the light. I'm normally a shower person who uses peach scented body wash and shampoo, but a package of Japanese Milky White Rose bath salts that my niece Megan gave me for my birthday had been in the cabinet for six months. I emptied the whole thing into my tub of almost hot water.

Many things in life give me pleasure, and reading in the bathtub is one of them. The candles gave me just enough light. I dropped my clothes on the floor and climbed into the tub, carefully holding my book above my head until I was settled into the silky, smooth water. Every time it cooled off, I added more hot water. I thought about what Pork Chop said. For the first time that day, instead of feeling sorry for myself and a little jealous of everyone else, I was glad that my family and friends were having good times. I said a little prayer for their safety and went back to reading my book. A man in my life wasn't necessary for my world to be good.

Deep into the book, I was startled when James Brown shouted from the counter. I didn't plan to answer—just let whoever was calling talk to the machine. The phone made that sound it makes to let me know a message was left just as I heard loud beating on the front door.

I reached out the dry hand holding the book, and laid *Fatal Descent* on the pile of clothing on the floor. I clutched my phone and retrieved the message.

"Callie, I'm on your porch. Your car is here and your lights are on. Why don't you answer your telephone? I can only see you for a few minutes, and if you have company, I'll certainly go away, but I'm worried about you. Please come to the door or call my cell if you're all right."

That message was something my daddy or my brothers or the sheriff might leave right before they broke down my door to be sure I wasn't sick or injured, but the caller was none of the above. It was Dean Robinson.

I climbed out of the tub and wrapped a towel around me. The pounding increased in intensity and volume. At the door, I peeped through the little hole and saw Dean with a very worried, very frantic look on his face.

"I'm all right. I was in the tub," I shouted through the door.

"Can I come in and see you for a few minutes?" he asked.

"I thought you had to work tonight," I answered, and the sheriff's cautioning words to me about not telling *anyone* I wasn't dressed when they showed up at my door crossed my mind. What did I really know about Dean Robinson? He was a homicide detective, but I've read a true crime story about a trooper raping and killing a woman on I-95. It had happened in Florida, and Dean said he'd come to South Carolina from Florida. I remembered that creep who'd told me about tying his wife to a tree and shooting over her head. I remembered the women at Safe Sister and their tales of how men who'd seemed nice turning violent. Those thoughts flew through my mind like migrating geese.

"I am working, but even on duty, we get a break occasionally. I want to see you. Will you open the door?"

He'd been the perfect gentleman on our date, and I was sure Wayne had checked Dean out before hiring him.

"You'll have to wait until I'm dressed. Can you do that?" I

did exactly what Wayne had cautioned me not to do.

"Yes, I'll wait."

I don't know what I was thinking then—I must not have been thinking at all—because I ran to the bathroom and pulled on the clothes I'd dropped on the floor before my bath. Dirty clothes on a clean body? That's too weird. It just shows I wasn't thinking.

Car horns blew and firecrackers shot off like bombs just as I opened the door. All the noise startled me.

Dean Robinson stood there holding a piece of mistletoe over his head. He dropped the mistletoe, took me in his arms, and gave me the kiss I'd wanted the night we went out to eat. The man was a wonderful kisser, and when we parted, I saw that he was as impressed with that smooch as I was.

"Wow! Happy New Year!" he said. "May I come in for a few minutes?"

I hadn't caught my breath yet, so I nodded. He stepped inside and pulled the door closed. That night he was wearing a uniform, and the khaki clothing set off his light hair and blue eyes.

"I get a meal break when I'm on duty. I decided I'd rather be here with you at midnight, so I skipped dinner, but I can't stay long. Some of the partygoers will be on the roads soon now. The joke is that New Year's Eve releases all the amateur drunks, but any drunk on the roads is murder waiting to happen."

"It's midnight?" The question must have made me sound senseless after all the noise we'd heard. Honestly, I *felt* senseless after that kiss.

"Midnight's over. Now tonight's work really begins for law enforcement."

"Did you say you skipped your dinner?"

"That kiss was worth missing a meal."

"Sit there at the table. I'll have dinner for you in no time."

I spooned food from the Styrofoam tray I'd saved in the fridge onto a plate and microwaved it.

Dean seemed to enjoy the chicken as much as he had all the sampling we'd done at the Brazilian steak house. When he finished, he wiped his mouth on his napkin and stood. "That was fantastic. Did you cook it?"

I laughed. "Didn't you see me dip it out of a to-go tray? I

brought it home from Gee Three." Embarrassment swept across his face as he asked, "Did I just eat your dinner?"

"No, I've already eaten."

Looking back, it seems strange that I would tell him all about my frustrated day and buying an extra meal so my friend wouldn't know I would be alone on New Year's Eve, but Dean was easy to talk to, and when he left, we shared another of those magnificent kisses.

Lying in bed, I thought about how lucky I am to have a good job, real friends, and a loving family. I considered making a New Year's resolution, but the next thing I knew, my alarm clock was ringing.

★ ON THE EIGHTH DAY OF CHRISTMAS MY TRUE LOVE GAVE TO ME

EIGHT COLLARDS COOKING

"Whew! The house smells awful. That's the stinkingest food in the world!" Mike's words as he stepped out the door and walked over to my Mustang in Daddy's front yard didn't surprise me. He's the only one of Daddy's six kids who doesn't love collards. Sprinkle them with hot pepper vinegar and give me a big spoon full of chowchow, and I can eat a mess of collard greens.

The odor wafted across the porch and into the yard even with the doors closed. I won't deny the aroma of collards cooking isn't as appetizing as the taste of them. Rizzie told Daddy a long time ago that if the cook puts a whole, raw, unshelled pecan in the pot, the collards wouldn't smell. Daddy's answer was, "I *like* how collards smell."

"Will you help me get a couple of folding tables and some chairs out of the shed?" Mike continued. "Pa sent Frankie and Jane to the store for something. I don't know what. Pa's invited company for dinner today, and I swear he's acting like a chicken with its head cut off."

"Company? Who'd he invite?"

"Wayne, Pork Chop Higgins, Miss Lettie, and Miss Ellen plus him, you, me, Frankie, and Jane. That's nine, and we may have Bill and Molly. Don't know about them yet. Bill said he'd call back when their plans are made. They seem to be having the holiday problem married folks suffer."

"What's that?"

"Husband wants to go to his family's house and wife wants to go to her mom's home for holiday meals. My wife's mama and daddy were divorced. One year, we ate Thanksgiving dinner three times—her mama's, her daddy's, and Pa's. Thought I'd bust wide open that night. Don't guess you had that problem since your in-laws were in Columbia and we were down here."

"Not exactly, but there were a few times we had holiday brunch at Donnie's and drove down here for dinner."

"If I ever marry again, I'm gonna make my wife cook all the holiday meals and invite every one of the family members from all sides. If they come, okay. If they don't, okay, but I'm going to eat my Thanksgiving, Christmas, and New Year's meals in my own home." I noticed he said he'd *make* his wife cook and *my* meals in *my* home. I hoped that wasn't indicative of his real feelings. If so, no wonder his first marriage failed.

"How many tables do we need?" I asked as Mike unlocked the shed door.

"He said bring in two—one for overflow for eating and one for him to spread out the food."

When we had the tables and chairs set up, I went back to my car and brought in a black outfit to change into before I headed to work. I hung it in Daddy's closet and went into the kitchen to ask if I could help.

Daddy had a big old Cheshire grin plastered across his face. "How's Big Boy?"

"I went by and saw him last night. They're still treating the infection, but he's improving. I called this morning, and the vet said he may be able to come home tomorrow."

"Good," Daddy said, then added, "I want your dog to be well, Calamine, but don't leave him any longer than is medically necessary since I left an open charge card there for his care."

"Yes, sir, and I promise to pay you back no matter how much the bill is."

"So far as helping, you know I don't like people getting in my way when I'm cooking."

Mike began singing, "Paw don't allow no helping in here, Paw don't allow no helping in here. I don't care what Paw don't allow, I'm gonna help him anyhow . . ."

Daddy snorted, "That boy's a singing fool."

"No kidding, Daddy, what do you want me to do?" What I wanted to do was change the subject before Mike got smart alecky with Daddy. Instead of mouthing back, Mike left the room. In a minute, I heard the shower running.

"I don't have tablecloths, so get some sheets out of the closet and put them on the tables. Then, set the main table with the china out of the breakfront and use those fancy napkins over there. You can use our regular dishes on the overflow table."

Daddy is not one to bother with tablecloths, and I can't remember ever using the china out of the big, mahogany dish cabinet he calls the breakfront. It was Mama's china—wedding gifts when she married him—and Daddy was too afraid one of us would break a piece to ever use it until now.

Just then, Frankie and Jane came in the back door. He carried several green tissue cones of mixed hothouse flowers—red carnations, yellow mums, and lacy green fern—which he handed to me and said, "Find a vase to put these in. I don't know nothing about flower arrangements."

A vase? Daddy's idea of a vase is a fruit jar, or, if we're being fancy, a glass or pitcher. Frankie took Jane by the hand and led her into the living room. Soon I could hear him playing guitar and singing to her. Jane likes old music. She's a big Patsy Cline fan, and she *loves* Elvis songs, undoubtedly because her mother sang them before she died about the time Jane and I graduated from high school. Frankie was singing "Love Me Tender," and if a visually handicapped person can gaze at someone lovingly, Jane was doing it. I guess in reality, it was her body language, not really her eyes that shouted her feelings for my brother. *Oh, Lord, here we go again,* I thought.

Frankie had bought so many flowers that I separated them into two containers—Daddy's biggest, best drinking glasses. "Will these do?" I asked, holding up an arrangement in each hand.

He turned and looked at the arrangements. "Yeah, put that one on the main table," he said, pointing to one of them. "It's the prettiest. Put the other one on the spare table. We won't need that table if Bill and Molly don't come. We can add a chair and sit nine without it, but eleven would be too crowded." He hooted a happy laugh. "I invited Pork Chop Higgins to eat with us, so we might need both tables with or without Bill and Molly."

"What made you invite Pork Chop?" I asked.

"Now, Calamine, I can add a few people any time I cook, but with Pork Chop's wife and nine kids, that's eleven people, so I've never invited all of them for an inside sit-down meal. When I heard his wife took the children to see her mama, I called and invited him. He said he'd love to come, asked what he could bring, and told me he'd talked to you at Rizzie's grill yesterday."

"We did talk. He's a nice man."

"That he is. I don't like to think of any man being alone on a holiday. I don't know what I would have done after your mama died if I hadn't had six kids to keep me so busy I couldn't spend much time alone."

"What are we having today?" I asked him.

"Calamine, what do we always have on New Year's Day? Collards, Hoppin' John, sweet potatoes, coleslaw, deviled eggs, mixed winter vegetables, corn bread, biscuits, whole smoked pork ham, coconut pie, pound cake, and all kinds of cookies. If I have time, I may fry a chicken or two, also."

"I can't wait. What time did you invite the others to come?"

"Told 'em to come any time they want, but we'll eat between one and two. I promised we'd do some pickin' and have a sing-along after dinner."

"Sounds good, but I have to go to work this afternoon. Otis and Odell are prepping Patsy Corley this morning and expect to be ready for me later today."

"I didn't think about the Middletons. They could have come here to eat."

"They're planning to eat at Bubba's Bodacious BBQ Barn. They'll have all the New Year's Day fixings on the buffet."

Daddy grinned and stirred the Hoppin' John as he bragged, "None of it will be as good as my cooking. I wish you'd be here for Miss Lettie and Ellen to hear you sing."

"Maybe another time." I pinched a taste off the pound cake.

"Don't worry 'bout it. I'm sure Mike will sing enough for everyone. Sometimes that boy spends all day sitting around making up songs, but most of the time, they're silly songs."

"What does Frankie do?" I asked.

"He spends too much time mooning over Jane and fixing up that old van. I told him the best way to win that woman back is to get a job and pull his own load in the relationship."

I really didn't want to get into discussing Frankie and Jane, so I asked, "What do you want me to do now?"

"You can start carrying those desserts in and put them on the food table."

Before I'd completed that assignment, Wayne came in. He helped me finish with dessert trays. "What did your father do?" he asked. "Cook everything he knows?"

"Looks like it. Wonder if anyone would miss some of these Peanut Butter Blossom cookies if we take them out on the porch?"

"I doubt it. Hey, Mr. Parrish, do you have anything else for Callie and me to do?"

"Not right now. I'll call you when I need you."

Wayne and I put on our jackets, grabbed cookies, and went out to the swing on the front porch. The day was cold but cloudless with dazzling sunshine.

"Did you find Norman Spires?" I asked, pumping my feet to make us swing high and fast.

"You never give up, do you, Callie? Sometimes I think you should quit your job with Middleton's and get a degree in criminal justice. I'd hire you. Your nosiness would make you an extremely persistent deputy."

"I have no interest in going to morticians' school to please the Middletons or to the police academy to become a deputy. I just want to know what's happening with Amber Buchanan's case. After all, whoever killed her left her on my porch. I realize you're not supposed to tell me, but don't forget, I was a deputy for a few days."

"It won't hurt to tell you about Norman Spires anyway because we haven't found him. We located the abandoned hunting lodge, but he wasn't there. We did find evidence that someone had spent time in the cabin recently, but there's no proof that it was Spires."

"What kind of evidence?"

"Opened canned foods that looked like someone used a knife

for a can opener."

"There wasn't a can opener at the lodge?"

"A nice electric one, but the power is off."

"How do you know the cans were recent?"

"Just like determining how long a corpse has been dead—amount of decomposition of the remains."

"Do you have any idea where he might have gone from there?"

"Not really, but the fact that he's on the run does indicate he's the perp in Amber Buchanan's murder."

"Her body has been brought back to Middleton's. Do you know when you'll release it?"

"For evidence, we should have what we need from Charleston's postmortem exam, but the problem is I don't know her next-of-kin. To release Mrs. Buchanan, I need to know that. Can't release a body to a blank line on a form."

Before I'd had time to process that news, Pork Chop arrived, carrying a huge covered roasting pan. He panted, short of breath, as he climbed the steps. Wayne stepped up and relieved him of the roaster. "What's this, Mr. Higgins?" Wayne asked. "I didn't know we were supposed to bring anything."

"Parrish said it's not necessary, but I never go to eat empty-handed." Pork Chop stopped at the top of the steps to catch his breath.

"What is it?" I asked.

"Can't you guess?" the huge man asked with a chuckle. "It's pork chops. I grilled 'em. I like 'em best chicken-fried like my wife cooks them sometimes, but I'm making a resolution. This year, I'm going to cut back, not really go on a diet, but try to eat healthier and lose some of this fat." He patted his wide girth. "I'm like that old commercial Terry Bradshaw used to be on. Feelin' old and fat and ugly."

"Rick," I said, "you're one of the most beautiful men I've ever known."

"Remember she said that," Pork Chop said to Wayne. "If my wife ever gets tired of me and takes off, I'm going to come courtin' Callie."

"You'll have to get in line," Wayne answered. "My new homicide detective seems to have taken a liking to Callie."

"Hush that talk and come on in," I told them and held the front door open. I figured Pork Chop needed to sit down, and there wasn't enough space on the swing for him. Wayne carried the pan to the kitchen and stayed in there with Daddy.

Pork Chop sat on the couch. Mike came from the bedroom, welcomed him, and sat beside him. Mike called Pork Chop Mr. Higgins and seemed to know him pretty well.

Frankie scowled as though he resented our interrupting his private serenade and invited Jane to go for a walk. He helped her with her coat, and they left hand in hand.

Mike and Pork Chop were talking about what time the ball games would start on television when Bill arrived alone. I could tell from his expression that he wasn't in a good mood.

"So Molly went to her house and you came here?" I asked. "That might be a solution to where to go, but it doesn't sound like a happy newlyweds' decision."

"Why are women so nosy?" Bill demanded as though I'd have an answer to that.

"Wayne says he's glad I'm nosy and that I'd make a good investigator because of it." I moved to a different chair. "What did she catch you doing, Bill? I told you when you got married not to tie the knot if you couldn't stop womanizing."

"I haven't been cheating on Molly. I promise I haven't."

"Then why are you complaining that women are nosy?" Mike asked.

"I might be complaining about our nosy sister, always asking questions, but I'm griping about my wife this time."

"What did she ask you?" Mike questioned.

"She didn't ask me. That's the problem. While I was in the shower, she took it upon herself to look at all the calls and messages on my cell phone. An old friend has been calling me for advice about a problem she's having. Molly found her number and some texts from her in my telephone. She didn't bother to ask me about them. She called my friend and told her off and then lit into me like I'd done something wrong."

"What's the name of your old friend?" I asked.

"Lucy, but it's not like you think. She just needs someone to talk to."

"Isn't Lucy the woman you were making out with at the vigil where Molly caught you that time?" I accused, though I knew the answer.

"Yes, Molly was right about me and Lucy back then, but now we're not *doing* anything, just talking."

I couldn't help scolding my brother. "Bill, you're *married*. Of course Molly's going to be jealous and angry if you're talking to a woman you cheated with before."

"We weren't married then, and I'm not cheating now. All I've been doing is *talking* to her." Bill looked like a little boy who's been falsely accused of breaking a window when he wasn't even one of the kids playing ball.

Mike apparently couldn't keep quiet any longer either. He broke into song: "Here comes divorce" to the tune of "Here comes the bride."

Nobody laughed, so he did his high-pitched Tammy Wynette imitation of "D-I-V-O-R-C-E," which brought Daddy and Wayne out of the kitchen at the same time Frankie and Jane returned.

"Dinner's almost ready, so you can stop that, Michael. I'm gonna call and see if Miss Lettie and Ellen are on the way or if they need a ride. I'd appreciate it if you kids would be quiet while I'm on the phone." He went to his bedroom and closed the door behind him.

"What's that all about?" Bill asked.

"I don't know," Mike answered. "Pa doesn't usually need silence to make a telephone call, and he uses his cell phone, not the house phone behind closed doors."

"Calamine, didn't you say you have to go to work after dinner?" Daddy asked when he came out of his room.

"Yes, sir," I replied.

"Miss Lettie isn't feeling well, so they aren't coming. I told Ellen you'll bring them two plates this afternoon."

"No problem," I answered.

With only eight of us, we didn't need the extra table to seat everyone, so Daddy filled both of the folding tables with food. We served ourselves and sat at what's always been called the "eating table" at our house with Daddy on one end and Pork Chop on the other. I'd be hard-pressed to identify the best food at that dinner. Everything was excellent, and Pork Chop's grilled chops were superb, but Daddy was quieter than usual and seemed a little gloomy.

"This is a magnificent feed, Parrish," Pork Chop said to Daddy. "Last night, Callie and I previewed Rizzie Profit's new sandwich. It was fantastic, but these collards are even better."

"What's Rizzie's new dish?" Jane asked.

"Gee Three Shrimp Sliders made like miniature Shrimp Po Boys, on dinner rolls," Pork Chop told her.

"Like hamburger sliders," Frankie commented, and then added, "I'm surprised you didn't invite Rizzie and Tyrone for dinner, Pa."

"I did, but they're working today," Daddy answered.

An idea popped into my head. "May I be excused for a moment?" I asked.

"Aren't you going to have dessert?" Jane was clearly surprised. She knows how much I love sweets.

"I'll be right back. Don't eat up all the good stuff." Considering that we had one entire table covered with cakes and pies, that was a ridiculous statement.

In Daddy's bedroom, I called Rizzie at the restaurant.

"Gee Three, Gastric Gullah Grill," Rizzie answered.

"Callie here. Do you still have that makeshift stand you used at the bluegrass festival?" I asked.

"It wasn't much more than a table with a sign on it," she answered, "but I can set it up again. What's happening?"

"Mrs. Corley read about a man whose funeral procession went through a fast-food drive-in where everyone received one of his favorite burgers. She wants to do the same thing for her daughter Patsy. Her favorite food was shrimp, and I thought you might be interested in setting up some kind of drive-through by the road in front of the grill and serving them your new Shrimp Sliders. The service is at Middleton's and the interment is at St. Mary Cemetery, so the procession could go right by your place."

"Patsy Corley would have loved my Shrimp Sliders." Rizzie's nostalgic tone sounded sad. "Patsy and Snake came here often for Shrimp Po Boys. I hated to hear what happened, but it's not surprising. Patsy and Snake left here arguing every time they came in. I wondered why they didn't split up and get it over with, but I never expected them to end the way they did. I'll be glad to do that if Mrs. Corley wants me to."

I promised to get back to her after I talked to the Middletons and Mrs. Corley, then we said goodbye. I went ahead and changed into my work clothes while I was in Daddy's room.

"Would you look at that?" Mike laughed when I sat down at the table again. "Callie's dressed for dessert—even wearing her pearls." Everyone got a laugh from that.

Daddy doesn't like help when he's cooking, but he's turned the clean-up over to us kids as long as I can remember. I used to stand on a stool to wash dishes. Though the dinner was delicious, he'd made his usual chaos in the kitchen. I don't cook much, but I'd noticed a big difference between Daddy and Jane, who's also a first-class chef. She always washes each bowl, pan, or utensil when she finishes with it. Daddy just piles them up for the clean-up crew.

After everyone had consumed at least sample servings of several desserts, Daddy said, "Calamine, dip up two big plates of dinner and two more of desserts. Wrap them good and keep them level so Miss Lettie and Ellen can enjoy my cooking without everything sloshing together. Pork Chop, you and I will visit in the living room while the boys clean up everything."

"What about me?" Jane asked. "Is it all right if I stay in the kitchen and help?" She's been around Daddy since we were teenagers, but she always asks permission to do anything at the Parrish house. I've never really understood that because Daddy wasn't that hard on us girls, though he made the boys tow the line.

"You can sit in here with me and Pork Chop or you can work in the kitchen—your choice. I'm about to run Calamine out of here so those two ladies get their food before suppertime. After everything's put away and cleaned up, we'll do some pickin' and singing."

Happily cruising down the road to Miss Lettie's with four big plates wrapped in aluminum foil on the seat beside me, I was singing "Once in a While" to myself." I didn't see any other vehicles on the road and thought most folks were either sleeping off a big dinner in front of the TV or still sleeping off last night's celebration.

The deer appeared with no warning.

I slammed on the brakes. Even wearing my seat belt, I lunged forward, barely missing the windshield, which I fully expected to shatter. For a moment, I thought the deer had leapt onto the hood of my car, but he ran off into the woods on the other side of the road. My heart felt like it dropped to the pit of my stomach and was trying to pound its way out of my body. I couldn't tell much about the deer's true size because directly in front of my eyes, he looked gigantic. I say he, but it was impossible to tell the gender of the animal. Male white-tailed deer around here lose their antlers during the colder months, and I certainly hadn't seen between its legs.

Trying to catch my breath and stop shaking, I pulled over to the side of the road. That's when I saw that the plates I'd fixed for Miss Lettie and Miss Ellen had fallen upside down on the floor in front of my passenger seat. Daddy's New Year's dinner had been beautiful and delicious, but all slopped together on the floor of the car, it was a mess and so were my floor mats.

What now? The two elderly ladies were waiting for their lunch, and Daddy would be disappointed if I didn't provide them with their collards and black-eyed peas to assure them of prosperity in the New Year.

I don't mind the smell of collards, but I wasn't happy at the thought of my car smelling like a green vegetable forevermore. I'd stopped fairly close to Gee Three. I headed there.

Surprisingly, the parking lot wasn't full, and when I went inside, there were only a few people at the tables and booths though Rizzie had extra serving staff working. Tyrone sat at the counter doing something on his iPad. If I asked, he'd probably say he was doing homework even though school was out for winter break, but I'd bet he was playing a game.

"Want to earn some extra money?" I asked him.

"Sure," he answered without even looking up from the screen. "What do you need?"

"I spilled a lot of food onto the floor in my car. I'll pay you to clean it up."

Tyrone didn't answer me. He put the iPad behind the counter and went out the front door.

I slid onto a stool and spun it around to look at the restaurant. I never get tired of the beautiful Gullah arts displayed on the walls—sweetgrass baskets, brightly colored paintings, and intricate weavings. One of the servers approached, but I asked to see Rizzie. She came out of the kitchen smiling and stepped behind the counter. I turned around to face her. "What are you doing here? I know your dad cooked a feast today."

"He sure did, but he sent me to take plates to Miss Lettie and her friend, and I've spilled them all over my car. Do you have enough traditional Southern New Year's Day dinner left to make me two generous plates and separate desserts?"

"I have plenty, and I'll dip them for you myself. Did you have your dad's dinners in Styrofoam go trays?"

"No, plates wrapped in foil."

"You can buy the trays at the dollar store, and they sure make carrying food easier. I buy them by the case from my supplier. I'll give you some for future use."

She walked back to the kitchen. I twirled my stool around to face the other customers again. I couldn't believe she didn't have more diners. Then I realized it was late for lunch and early for supper. A man sitting in a booth by himself caught my eye. No, not because he was that hot, though he wasn't ugly either. He was big, not fat, but tall and broad-shouldered with fairly slim waist and hips. He leaned forward with his face close to his plate. I wondered if his vision was so poor that even with his eye glasses, he couldn't see his food from a normal distance.

When his server brought him the ticket, he put a wrinkled ten-dollar bill on the check tray and waited for her to return. When she brought back his change, she asked, "Will there be anything else, sir?"

"Could I get a glass of iced tea to go?" he mumbled.

"I'll get it for you."

While she was gone, he carefully picked up the ones and left only the silver on the tray. *Kind of cheap tipper,* I thought, but he redeemed himself.

"Sorry not to be more generous," he told the woman. "I just got hired on this morning by a pig farmer. He said starting tomorrow when his wife comes home, my meals will come with the job, but he'd been invited to dinner and a music jam this afternoon. I'll be back here to eat again when I get paid, and I'll tip you better then."

"Oh, that's okay," the server responded. "I understand how it is. It took me a while to find *this* job."

Dalmation! Pork Chop was probably the pig farmer who'd hired the man. If Daddy had known that, he would have invited the new hired hand to dinner, too.

Rizzie loaded me up with two plastic bags of food trays and I went outside. Tyrone was hosing off my floor mats. "I'm washing both of the front mats. I've got the passenger side so clean that I didn't want to make your side look shabby in comparison."

I peeked in the car. It was impossible to see where that tremendous mess had been. He put the mats back in, then carefully placed the plastic bags of food on the floor.

"Great job, Tyrone!" I said and pulled my wallet from my jeans pocket. "How much do I owe you?"

"Not a dime, not a dime," he said. "I'm just glad I could help you out. Did you eat your share of collards and black-eyed peas today?"

"I sure did. Did you?"

"No, Rizzie threatened to kill me if I didn't eat collards and Hoppin' John, but I cooked myself a frozen pizza, I ate Tomato Pie, too. I *love* Tomato Pie even when it's made with those tomatoes they ship into the supermarket this time of year."

Daddy created chaos in his kitchen. I spilled a mess in my car. Neither of those could compete with the bedlam I found at Miss Lettie's. When Miss Ellen opened the door, I could hear Miss Lettie crying. No, not crying. She wailed.

"Bad day?" I asked Miss Ellen.

"Yes, come on in. Let me take one of those bags for you. Your father must think we've got an army to feed over here instead of only two old ladies."

I didn't respond and hoped neither Miss Ellen nor Miss Lettie mentioned to Daddy that the food arrived in Styrofoam trays. Some things are better left alone, and I had a sneaky feeling that my dad was sending food to these ladies not so much to see they were fed as to impress one of them with his culinary skills.

"What's wrong with Miss Lettie? Is she still just grieving?" I asked as I handed a sack to her.

"Lettie took it upon herself to climb up into the attic and pull down all the boxes of Junior's toys and baby clothes. Now she's grieving over every piece as she looks at it. Come on into the dining room and see for yourself."

I followed Miss Ellen to a large room with an enormous oval dining table piled high with children's clothes and toys—from infant items to tricycles and even a bicycle leaning against a wall. Miss Lettie sat at the head of the table, blubbering and occasionally yelling out her anguish.

"Lettie," Miss Ellen said gently, "here's Callie Parrish from Middleton's. She knows all about mourning someone you love. Maybe she can help you get through this."

Shih tzu! I can color a person's hair any shade desired. I sometimes work miracles with makeup. Either way—I can use cosmetics to beautify or to create an ugly face like mine was when I went to Safe Sister. I was a good teacher before I changed professions. I can do lots of things, but I can't counsel the grief-stricken. Otis and Odell are better at that than I am, but even they don't get really involved in it. I did what I've heard my bosses do in the past—made a suggestion.

"There are several grief support groups here in St. Mary to help you get through this. I can give you a list of them if you want to come by or I can drop one in the mail to you," I told Miss Lettie.

"No piece of paper or bunch of people can help me," Miss Lettie sobbed. "My heart is broken. Both of my Jeffreys have left me here all alone. Look at this." She held up a small camouflage suit that would fit a child about three years old. It was the old darker print with a lot of green like military camouflage was before the fighting moved to deserts. "My boy Jeffrey Junior wore this when he was little. Now he'll never use any of this stuff again."

That puzzled me. The grown, bald-headed man we'd buried wouldn't have ever used those baby clothes and toys again even if he were alive. Maybe she meant he wouldn't have kids to use his childhood possessions.

"I even saved his crib in the basement for my grandchildren," she added. One minute, she talked like her son might have used his childhood things again, and the next minute, she made sense and spoke of using Jeffrey Junior's belongings with a grandchild.

"Miss Parrish has brought us dinner, Lettie." Ellen's chipper voice sounded similar to one I'd used when speaking to my kindergarten students. "Let's go into the kitchen and eat at the little table in there." She turned to me. "Would you like to join us?"

"No, ma'am. I've already eaten."

"How about a glass of tea or a cup of coffee?" Her tone was normal, but her look was pleading.

"I can't stay long. I have to work this afternoon, but I'll have a glass of tea."

I remembered the kitchen from when I'd carried the Brunswick stew and food register to Miss Lettie's, but it looked very different from then. Someone had been shopping. The counters were covered with snack foods—bags and bags of chips, cookies, and candy. Miss Ellen waved her arm at the clutter. "Lettie got confused and bought all this stuff for Junior. Said it's stuff he begged her to buy when he was little, but she wouldn't back then. Now she wants him to have what he wants. She didn't remember he isn't a little boy anymore, and he won't be back."

"Don't be ridiculous, Ellen," Miss Lettie spoke up as she lowered herself into one of the chrome and plastic kitchen chairs. "I certainly have enough sense to know what's happened. We buried my Jeffrey Junior the day the Lord sent that beautiful white blanket of snow in his honor. I didn't buy all this junk. You must have."

Ellen didn't say anything. She didn't have to. Her eyes said it all.

I sat while they ate in silence. When they started on the rice pudding, I excused myself, explaining, "Oops! I've got to get to work."

"Are you just on duty or did someone die?" Miss Ellen asked.
"Patsy Corley," I answered.
"I heard about that. Do you know when the service will be?"
"Not yet."

I drove carefully, possibly overly cautious because I wasn't fully over my shock and fear from when that deer leapt in front of me. Hitting a deer, a horse, or a cow can wreck a car and kill people. Most persons wouldn't say they were happy to arrive at a funeral home, but I was. Sometimes, Middleton's Mortuary is comforting to me. It's beautifully furnished and decorated. When we don't have a planning session or funeral, it's quiet and peaceful, even when I'm working.

Odell's door was open when I passed his office. He looked up. "Oh, you're here already. I was about to call you. I think you'll be surprised and pleased with how Miss Patsy looks. Try not to move her head, and most of the hair is a wig, so don't do much styling to it, but her face looks good, and I believe Mrs. Corley will be pleased with what we've done, especially since she saw her after the gunshot." He burped. "Excuse me. Too much lunch at the barbecue place."

"Where's Miss Patsy?"

"Otis and I put her in your workroom. Let me know if you need help. As soon as you're finished, we'll call Mrs. Corley and tell her she can come see her daughter. She's already checked with us several times today."

"Where's Otis?" I asked.

"In the prep room." Odell and I both knew what he was doing in there when we didn't have a decedent needing prepping. Otis has a tanning bed in the prep room, and he uses it whenever he gets the chance. He's invited both me and Odell to use it, but the thought of lying in there with something over my face creeps me out. Odell could care less about that bed. He'd rather eat than tan any day.

I *was* both pleased and surprised with the restoration Otis and Odell had performed on Miss Patsy. There really wasn't much for me to do because one of them had already made up her face. I gave her a nice manicure, then using the lift, dressed her in the pink pantsuit and flowered blouse. I stepped back and admired her. No one could look at her and tell she'd died of a gunshot wound through her mouth and out the back of her head. She looked pretty much like she did back when Middleton's buried her father June Bug.

I buzzed Odell and let him know that I was ready. He wheeled in the bier, and we casketed Miss Patsy without disturbing any of the work that had been done to change her mother's memory to a better one than what she'd seen at that mobile home.

Barely back into my office, I'd just begun reading a Charlotte Hughes book when an instrumental version of "The Old Rugged Cross" played softly over the sound system, announcing that the public entrance was open.

I met the Corley family in the front hall and led them into Slumber Room A where Odell and I had placed Miss Patsy. Odell joined us. Mrs. Corley had eleven people with her. I counted them—eleven. I recognized some of them as her kids. The others might have been nieces and nephews because all of them were younger than Patsy's mother.

Otis said, "Mrs. Corley, I think you'll be very pleased, but I have to ask you not to touch Miss Patsy's face. Those who want to touch her should pat her hands."

"I understand." Mrs. Corley turned and faced the others. "Did everyone hear that? Don't touch Patsy anywhere except on her hands."

Their "Yes, ma'am" was so together that it sounded like bluegrass harmony.

People ask me how I can stand to do my job—to work at a funeral home with dead bodies. The Corley family reaffirmed my satisfaction with my job. They all *oohed* and *ahhed* about how good Miss Patsy looked. At a horrific time when people face their worst fears, my work tries to give them some comfort. I was thinking about that when I remembered the Gee Three Shrimp Sliders.

I asked Otis and Mrs. Corley to step over to the side and told them about Rizzie's offer to set up a road-side stand and serve miniature Shrimp Po Boys to the people in Patsy's funeral procession. Mrs. Corley glowed, and Otis beamed.

"Can we have the funeral day after tomorrow?" Mrs. Corley asked. "I want to use your chapel, but have my pastor and our church organist. I called both of them before we came over here, and each of them can do the service on January third."

"What time?" Odell asked.

"About eleven?" Mrs. Corley said. "That way we'll be passing Gastric Gullah around noon. Tell the owner I'd like each person served a soda also."

"Would you like to have a visitation? We could do that at ten if you like."

"That will be fine. Do I need to go by there and pay Gastric Gullah in advance?"

"Not necessary," Odell assured her. "We'll pay Miss Profit and add it to your funeral bill. I'll call her and work out the details. The insurance policy you showed me will cover everything."

The Corley family left with what passes for smiles on the faces of people who've lost someone they love.

★ ON THE NINTH DAY OF CHRISTMAS MY TRUE LOVE GAVE TO ME

NINE GUNS A'SMOKING

"Callie, didn't you say you've got today off?" I was in no mood to answer Frankie's question. He'd called while I was in the shower, and, thinking it might be Patel or Dean, I'd jumped out and tracked water from the bathroom to my phone on the nightstand.

"Yes, but I'm not doing anything for you today. I'm taking the day for myself. There are things I need to do, and I'll be working tomorrow at Patsy Corley's funeral."

"I don't want you to do anything *for* me. I want to *give* you something."

"What?"

"Remember I said I'm going to school today?"

"Yes, and then you acted like a jerk and wouldn't tell me what kind of school."

"Well, I've been worried about you and Jane finding a dead body on your porch, and even before that, it seems like you get into trouble all the time." The hair on the back of my neck hackled at that comment, but I didn't say anything. "Well, I knew you nor Jane would want me staying overnight with you, even though I'm hoping Jane and I will wind up back together. I've been rigging up a hammock in the back of that old van Pa has down by the barn."

"What does that have to do with me?"

"I'm going to sleep in the hammock in your front yard, so if anybody comes to bother you or Jane, I'll be there to protect you."

"I don't think Jane will like that, but I still don't know what it has to do with school."

"Well, I figure I need to be able to carry a gun to protect you and Jane, so I'm taking the class to get a CWP."

"What's that?"

"Concealed Weapon Permit. South Carolina requires a day-long class before anyone gets a permit. My friend Ralph and I signed up and paid to take the class."

"So what does that have to do with me being off today?"

"Ralph got arrested for DUI Tuesday night. Nobody's bailed him out, so he can't take the class."

"I doubt they'd let him take it with a DUI hanging over his head even if someone got him out of jail, but I still don't know what that has to do with me."

"The class we paid for requires ten people to be signed up or they put it off. The instructor called and said our class would be postponed unless we find someone to take Ralph's place. It cost a hundred dollars, and Ralph says if you'll go, you won't have to pay him back. In fact, he said if you'd take his place, he'll treat you to dinner one night when he's out of jail."

"Oh, no!" I knew Frankie's buddy Ralph. He'd asked me out before, and I'd always declined. Adding a DUI to his previous list of accomplishments did nothing to change my mind about dating him.

"Think about it, Callie. I don't know what you did for the day or so you were working with Wayne, but as much as you stick your nose into the sheriff's business, it might be to your advantage to have a Concealed Weapon Permit. What else did you have planned for today?"

"I need to clean the apartment."

"And you'd rather do that than go shooting at the indoor shooting range with everything already paid? Ralph even ordered the catered lunch, so you'll eat free, too. Besides, you'd be doing a really big favor for your favorite brother."

That was an outright lie. Frankie is closest to me in age, but my favorite has always been my oldest brother John. I didn't agree until after some real bribery in the form of Frankie promising to take down my Christmas tree and clean my apartment.

We had to be at the indoor shooting range by nine o'clock, so I told him, "If I don't get off the telephone, I won't be ready."

"You have to wear pants with loops and a wide belt so the holster will fit. I'll bring everything you need—gun, holster, and ammo."

Frankie showed up driving the beat-up van from Daddy's yard. I didn't even know it would run. He'd made some efforts to turn it into a camper with a portable gas stove, an ice chest, a lantern, and that hammock he'd told me about.

When I got in, Frankie handed me a brochure. "Read this." I began looking it over silently. "Read what we get for our money out loud," he instructed.

"What do you mean *our* money? I'm not spending any."

"I told Ralph that after you saw what a good day this will be, you might decide to reimburse him, but you don't have to."

"I'm not. Here's what it says we'll be learning: *firearm construction and operation; ammunition construction, identification and ballistics; safety rules; fundamentals of firearm shooting and storage; South Carolina firearm laws and use of deadly force restrictions; range instruction and demonstrations.* Then they offer assistance in filling out the application for the permit."

"All that and free lunch. What more could you ask for on your day off? Besides, this will be a breeze for you."

Frankie was probably right. I'd been brought up around guns in a family of hunters, and though I hadn't been hunting since the first time I'd seen a deer killed, I enjoy target shooting.

When we pulled into Hoyt's Indoor Shooting Range's parking lot, Frankie and I locked our holsters, guns, and ammunition in the truck and joined a group of people just inside the door. I silently counted them—one, two, three, four, five, six, seven, eight, nine. I thought they had to have ten. Then I realized that I was number ten. *Duh.*

I was surprised to see Walter Corley in the group. I waved at him. He waved back and then stepped over to where Frankie and I stood.

"Guess you might think it's a little unusual for me to be here taking this class the day before my sister's funeral, but I'd signed up before any of that happened. It's probably a good idea anyway. I keep wondering if Snake's family is going to come after any of us Corleys since Patsy killed him."

"I wouldn't think so," I answered. "It's not like Patsy shot Snake and she's out dancing and having a good time now. She's dead, too."

"Yeah, it's hard to believe she's gone forever. Maw was so afraid we was gonna have to have a closed casket, but you fixed Patsy up fine."

"Otis and Odell always do their best."

"Her pink suit looked fine, too. Maw let me pick out what Patsy would wear, but, of course, when I picked it, we didn't know anyone would get to see her."

"You did a good job. The outfit's very pretty on her."

The instructor called us into a classroom. I was kind of glad that Walter didn't sit near Frankie and me. I didn't want to think about the reconstruction of his sister's head anymore. In fact, I'd like to think about it less. Classes filled the morning and ended with a written test. As we finished our answer sheets, we dropped them off with the teacher and went back into the lobby where those who'd ordered them picked up box lunches. Some folks had brought their own meals, and I was envious of those with fried chicken when I opened the box and found we had an apple, a bag of baked chips, and a sliced turkey sandwich. I like turkey okay, but we'd just eaten a whole lot of it at Christmas. I wondered if these sandwiches were made out of somebody's Christmas left-overs.

The afternoon raced by like Dale Earnhardt on a Nascar track. First, we received our scores on the written test. Only one person had failed and couldn't continue with the course. Everyone went to their vehicles and returned with weapons. The instructor inspected each gun and ammunition before we were allowed back into the facility. Individual firing evaluations followed range demonstrations and instruction. Both Frankie and I passed. I declined the offer of help with the CWP application. I spend a lot of time at work completing applications for death certificates and filling out insurance forms, and I didn't really think I cared to spend fifty dollars to actually get a permit anyway.

I saw Walter Corley across the lot as Frankie and I walked to the van. Walter speed-walked over to me.

"Callie," he said, "was Jeff Morgan's funeral handled by Middleton's?"

"Yes, it was last Saturday, the day it snowed."

"I don't read the newspapers much, and I didn't know about it until yesterday. That's sad that Jeff and Patsy died so close together."

"Were they connected in some way?"

"Yes, Jeff dated Patsy while he dated Amber Clark. Patsy was heartbroken when she found out she wasn't the only one he was seeing then."

"You know Amber's dead, too, don't you?"

"My sister Penny told me she was found dead on your front porch. Reckon whoever killed her put her there so you'd see that she got to the funeral home?"

"I don't know why she was on my porch. So Jeff dated both of them at the same time?"

"Yes, but I don't know if Amber knew about Patsy. I doubt my sister even knew Jeff Morgan had died. That business with Jeff was years ago, and, irregardless of how it turned out, Patsy was better off not to get tied up with Jeff Morgan. He drank too much, and me and my sisters and brothers had enough of that from Paw."

"I guess so," I said and cringed at his use of the non-word *irregardless.*

I stuck my foot in my mouth big time with my next question. "How did Patsy and Snake get along?" The words were barely out of my mouth before I realized what a ridiculous question that was. She shot the man, killed him. That sure didn't mean they had a peaceful, loving relationship.

"They fought all the time. I don't mean like hitting each other, but fussed and argued about everything. Patsy was always a little round, but she was a pretty woman with a sweet personality. Back when Paw had the club open, Patsy worked there on weekends and met tons of men. She dated a lot of them. I don't know for sure if she and Snake hooked up back then and got back together after her divorce or ran into each other when she was here visiting and started something new. After they began staying together, I hated to go to family dinners and reunions because no matter where they were, they'd wind up screaming at each other. To be honest wid'ja, I wasn't surprised one of them murdered the other. I just never figured Patsy would kill him. I thought Snake would get fed up with the hollering and do something to my sister one day. I used to worry about that sometimes."

I said what I've been trained to say: "I'm sorry for your loss."

"You people at Middleton's did a good job. Maw was really afraid there was no way to fix Patsy decent enough to be seen."

"We always try. No matter how much somebody talks about closure, there's no real closure when someone dies a violent death, but Otis and Odell feel strongly that seeing their loved ones looking peaceful helps survivors through the ordeal." I sounded like a grief brochure. Probably because I'd learned that from one of them.

Frankie interrupted with, "We've gotta go. Pa's expecting us to eat leftovers from yesterday tonight."

Normally, I'd object when one of my brothers intruded when I was talking, but I was glad Frankie's interruption gave me an excuse to leave Walter. Being with him made me so sad.

I called the animal ER as we left Hoyt's and asked about Big Boy.

"He's much better. Dr. Kirk said you can pick him up whenever you want."

Now it was my turn to plead. "Come on, Frankie, I gave you my day off. Take me to Beaufort to pick up Big Boy. He'll be more comfortable in this van than in my car."

"I told you Pa wants us home by six to eat leftovers before he goes over to Miss Lettie's house."

"Back to Miss Lettie's?"

"Yep, back to Miss Lettie's."

"Frankie, that woman's mentally disturbed, and I don't understand how she got that way in these few days since her son's death. I feel sorry for her, but Daddy doesn't need to get mixed up with Miss Lettie."

"Fine, you tell Pa that. He doesn't listen to me or Mike."

We both knew Daddy wouldn't listen to me either.

"Speaking of getting involved, has Jane been seeing anyone since we broke up?" I'd known Frankie would ask me that sooner or later.

"It's not fair for you to ask me that, and if she was, I don't know that I'd tell you, but the answer is no. She hasn't dated anyone since you moved out." I faked a yawn to show him I wasn't interested in pursuing that conversation.

"I didn't move out. She threw me out." He blinked several times. Good grief! Was my brother going to burst into tears?

"Same difference," I said and yawned even bigger.

"Is she still working that phone job?" He faked a yawn back at me. I didn't know what that was supposed to show, maybe to diminish how important that question was to him.

"She's still Roxanne." My big sister impulses took over even though I'm younger than Frankie, and I began to lecture. "You're living with Daddy and you occasionally pick up day work here and there. Jane can't do that. Don't you remember all the times she tried to get work and no one would hire her because she's blind? Don't you remember the times she got jobs and lost them because she had problems getting to and from work? Roxanne pays the bills and keeps Jane in the apartment, safe and sound."

"I worry that some kook she talks to will come looking for her."

"She assures me that the Roxanne phone is in the name of the company she works for and can't be traced to our building. If you're serious about making up with her, you need to back off about Roxanne until you have a job that will support the two of you."

"I understand a phone job has advantages for her, but I'd rather she do surveys or be a telemarketer, something like that."

Uncontrollable laughter gushed out of me. "She *is* a telemarketer," I protested. "You just don't like what she's selling."

"Oh, I like what she's selling all right. I just don't want her selling what she gives me for free."

I wanted to hit him, but he was driving and besides, I'm too old to keep swatting my brothers when they make me mad.

Instead I screamed, "How dare you insinuate that Jane does

anything wrong! Roxanne talks on the telephone. That's all. What people do while she talks to them is nobody's business."

I'd been so involved in our conversation that I hadn't been paying a lot of attention to where Frankie had driven until he pulled into Dr. Kirk's animal ER and let me out at the door.

"Thanks!" I gushed in a pseudo-Southern magnolia voice, hopped out of the van, and ran inside. There was no one behind the desk, but several people sat in the waiting room, including a man and a little girl with a gigantic, absolutely colossal, light brown dog with wide-set eyes and a wrinkled forehead. Long ropes of slobber dangled from its jowls. I'm nosier than I am shy, so I asked, "What kind of dog is that?"

"He's an English Mastiff," the man said and stroked the huge dog's back. "He weighs over three hundred pounds and is far from the largest English Mastiff on record."

"He's my dog," the child said. "His name is Duke. He likes to play. Watch." She reached into a Dora the Explorer bag beside her and pulled out a fuzzy, stuffed Rudolph, the Red-Nosed Reindeer. She held it out toward Duke, almost poked it at him. When she squeezed the toy's sides, its nose blinked. Duke moved his head closer to her and licked the toy.

"Miss Parrish, good to see you," the receptionist said when she came back to her desk. She took a large medicine container from the shelf and handed it to me. "This is an antibiotic the doctor wants you to give the dog one each morning and one at night." I opened the cap and looked at the capsules. They were humongous.

"Excuse me," Frankie said when he stepped inside, "may I use the restroom?"

"Certainly," the receptionist said and pointed toward a door behind her desk. She turned back to me. "I'll get your dog, be right back."

She didn't lie. She returned in no time with Big Boy on a leash. He looked at me and I swear, he grinned. I know some people don't believe dogs have facial expressions, but mine does. Sometimes he even rolls his eyes.

Just then, Big Boy saw Duke. He stiffened and barked angrily. If I hadn't been holding the leash tight enough to restrain him, he would have attacked the larger dog. As I apologized, Big Boy snarled and pulled against the leash, trying to get to Duke. I looked around for Frankie. I wanted to get out of there, but I didn't know where he'd parked the van.

"You can bring Duke back now," the receptionist told the man.

"I don't want to see the doctor give Duke a shot," the little girl said.

"You can wait for me here then," the man told her and took the dog through the door.

I restrained Big Boy close to me and sat down waiting for Frankie to come out of the restroom.

"I'm sorry my dog acted like that," I told the child.

The little girl brought the toy Rudolph around and thrust it at Big Boy just the way she had pushed it toward her own dog.

Big Boy went bonkers. He screamed. Yes, he did. It wasn't a bark nor a howl. It was a terrified yelp as my dog tried desperately to climb into my lap. Frankie hooted a long, loud, snorting guffaw. I hadn't even noticed his return from the restroom. The little girl snickered a high-pitched, joyful giggle. I yanked as much of Big Boy as possible up onto my lap and rubbed his head. The child put the stuffed animal back into her Dora the Explorer bag, but she still laughed softly. Frankie gently lowered Big Boy from my lap and led him outdoors by the leash.

The past few minutes must have really upset Big Boy because the minute we cleared out of the vet's office, he squatted like he always did to relieve himself. My dog was over a year old and had never lifted his leg. He *always* hunkered down like a girl dog.

I can't say Big Boy stopped mid-stream because he hadn't begun yet, just assumed his usual position. He crouched there a moment, then stood, legs fully extended.

"What's he doing now?" Frankie demanded.

I couldn't answer because it was my turn to laugh, and I couldn't stop. Big Boy hiked his leg like a boy dog and shot a sizable stream directly onto my brother's leg.

Frankie didn't say a word to me or Big Boy all the way back to St. Mary. He let us out at my apartment without asking to go in or inviting us to eat leftovers at Daddy's. My brother was not just pissed on, he was pissed off.

Big Boy had learned to lift his leg like a male dog, but other than that, he was back to normal. He brought his leash to me from the front door knob where I'd put it and nudged his nose into the book I was reading.

"Want a walk?" I asked and clipped the leash to his collar.

The sky had clouded over between the time we reached home and went for the walk. I'm not much on meteorology and couldn't tell what kind of clouds they were. I wondered if we were going to get a little more snow or rain. I hoped not. Especially not the following day—the day of Patsy Corley's funeral. Sure, there's rain on lots of funerals, and Middleton's provides big, expensive umbrellas when that happens, but I really hoped the day would be bright and sunny for the services of the girl I now felt guilty for thinking of as Fatsy Patsy a few years back.

I was hoping we'd be back from our jaunt around the block before the rain or snow began when a tall man approached me. His pulled-up hoodie shadowed his face, and I didn't recognize him at first.

"Excuse me," he said in a low voice, "can you tell me if this is Oak Street?"

"Yes, I can, and it is." Big Boy and I continued walking, and the man fell into step with us.

"Looks like rain." The man looked up at the sky, and his face became more visible. He was the fellow I'd seen in Gee Three the day before, the one who'd said he was working for a pig farmer whom I'd assumed was Pork Chop.

"Sure does. Hope it's not snow again. This whole town grinds to a screeching halt when it snows." Big Boy had decided to trot, and the man and I began jogging to keep up with the dog.

"Won't matter to me. I'm headed out of town anyway, but before I go, I wanted to see where they found that Buchanan woman on Christmas Day. I read about it in the newspaper and want to see where it happened. Do you know which house it is?"

Coincidence or did this man know I lived where the body had been found? The sheriff tells me that he doesn't believe in coincidence. I decided to ask a few questions of my own.

"Yes, it's in the block behind us, the building with the big Christmas tree on the porch."

"Are you going back that way?"

"We'll pass it again. I usually walk Big Boy around the block a few times."

"Mind if I walk with you?"

I wanted to say, "Yes, I mind. I don't like a stranger walking with me uninvited and if Pork Chop hired you and was going to start feeding you today, why aren't you at work?" That's what I wanted to say, but the curious part of me thought I might get better answers by not asking those questions directly.

Catch more flies with honey than a fly swatter. My daddy used to say that, and I guess the bottom line is that I tend to believe the things Daddy told me when I was a little girl.

"My name's Callie—Callie Parrish." I transferred the leash from my right hand to my left and reached out for a handshake.

"Ned—Ned Shives." His handshake was firm, too firm, and the squeeze was tight enough to hurt my fingers.

"Good-looking dog you've got." Ned attempted a smile, but it was more of a smirk, the self-satisfied sneer of a liar. I learned that from watching a body language expert on HLN television. Sometimes liars have a slight leer when they lie. What had the man lied about? Big Boy is not just a good-looking dog. He's a *beautiful* animal.

Before I'd had time to think that through, Big Boy slowed down and stepped off the sidewalk to a grassy area. He squatted. *Dalmation! He's going to tee tee like a girl again.* I was wrong. As my students used to say, he had to poop, make a doo-doo. I waited for Big Boy to finish his business, and Ned stopped beside me. As we stood there, Wayne Harmon drove by in a squad car and waved. I raised my hand in reply. Ned turned his head toward me and began talking animatedly about dogs, describing some hound he'd had when he was a boy. As soon as the sheriff had passed, he finished the story and asked, "Did you know that Buchanan woman?"

"No. I'd never met her, but my brother went to school with her."

"Got any idea why someone would want to kill her?"

"No. I heard she'd had an argument with someone not long before Christmas, but I don't know any details." I used my plastic bag to pick up Big Boy's deposit and drop it into another bag.

"I understand they're looking to talk to that man. I believe his name is Norman Spires." Ned said. "But I don't see why they assume someone would kill a woman just because he shoved her."

"I don't know." I didn't want to confirm or deny anything the man said. Big Boy bounded back to the sidewalk and took off at a brisk pace. We followed him.

"That's the problem," Ned continued. "Any time somebody gets into trouble for one thing, the law wants to blame everything on them."

I didn't answer, which was just as well because the man began whistling. He whistled an intricate, beautiful version of "Winter Wonderland," as we walked on around the block and arrived in front of my apartment. Something about his whistle nudged my mind, but I didn't have a real thought about it. It bothered me, but I wasn't sure why. The man didn't seem threatening in any way, but a spine-chilling eerie feeling crept over me. It certainly wasn't caused by his whistling. It was exquisite.

What should I do? I didn't want to continue walking with Ned Shives, but I didn't want him to see me go into the place where a body had been found on the porch. Some people are creepy. Otis and Odell have told me about disturbed people who have bizarre attraction to the deceased, and I've read enough mysteries and watched enough on television to know that some weirdos have peculiar interests in crimes and death, even collect mementos associated with them.

As I considered how to get myself away from the man without letting him know my connection with where Amber Buchanan's body was found, Wayne's Jade County Sheriff's Department cruiser drove past us in the opposite direction and pulled over to a stop. The sheriff stepped out of his car and walked toward us. Ned said, "Nice to meet you, Callie. I'll see you later," and continued walking. Big Boy lay down and rolled over for Wayne to scratch his belly. I noticed that smudges of blood had seeped through the dog's bandage.

"Who's your friend?" Wayne asked as he gently rubbed Big Boy's abdomen, making it a point to avoid the bandaged area.

"Some character who wanted to know if I could tell him where Amber Buchanan's body was found."

Big Boy stood, turned around, and began walking toward my apartment.

"Is that all you know about him?" Wayne asked and followed Big Boy.

"If you want to know more, call Rick Higgins," I offered. "I saw that man in Rizzie's restaurant yesterday and overheard him tell the waitress that he'd been hired by a pig farmer who was going to dinner and a bluegrass jam."

"I assume Rick is what you call Pork Chop."

"Yes, I like him a lot, and I don't want to make fun of him by calling him Pork Chop."

"Did you know Pork Chop himself is who started that nickname?"

"No, I figured it had to do with his appetite and raising pigs."

"Pork Chop was named for his alcoholic uncle Richard. When Pork Chop's daddy was injured in a farm accident, he became addicted to prescription painkillers. His brother Richard had been in the Army and would go to the VA doctors and get free prescription narcotics. He sold them to Pork Chop's father at ridiculous street prices, and Mr. Higgins wound up losing over half of their farm acreage. I understand that when Richard died, Pork Chop went to the funeral and claims he wanted to laugh when he looked in the casket. Pork Chop Higgins is a kindhearted man, but I've heard him say the only person he's ever hated was his uncle Richard. He chose to be called Pork Chop rather than by the name his father gave him."

"Whew! I had no idea! I thought I was showing him respect by not calling him Pork Chop."

"Trust me. He'd rather be called Pork Chop."

"That explains why when Billy Wayne and Misty wanted to name their baby after Pork Chop, he told them to use his middle name, Edward. You might want to call Pork Chop and ask him about the man he hired yesterday morning before he went to Daddy's. He'll know more about him than I do."

"I will. You didn't tell him Amber Buchanan's body was left on your porch, did you?"

"No. I didn't want him questioning me about finding the body."

"Did you tell him your name?"

"Yes."

"I wish you hadn't. Your name was in the newspaper article about Amber's death."

Dalmation and a hundred and one dalmations!

The sheriff drove away. Big Boy and I went indoors immediately.

Decisions. Decisions. Should I call Big Boy's usual vet, the one who removed his tumor, or should I call Dr. Kirk at the animal emergency clinic? I finally decided to call Dr. Kirk rather than call our regular veterinarian and have to explain everything that had happened since she released Big Boy. It wasn't that I doubted her professionally. She's well qualified and highly respected. She'd taken care of my dog since he was a puppy, but she wasn't the one who'd be most up-to-date with what might be happening.

Dr. Kirk said, "The infection that developed would cause some seepage of blood, but that should clear up with the antibiotics we gave your dog in his IV and the pills you're to give him each day. Watch the bandage and if it becomes bloody instead of just showing some seepage, bring the dog back to me."

In a way, I wished I'd gone by Rizzie's and picked up something to eat or called Daddy and invited myself to get a plate of leftovers, but I didn't want to leave Big Boy when he might begin bleeding again nor on the first day he was home from the doggie hospital. I filled Big Boy's dish with his preferred Kibbles 'n Bits, picked out his favorite red pieces, and placed them at the top of the bowl. For myself, I warmed a can of chicken noodle soup I found in the back of the cabinet.

Not finding a book I wanted to read again at the moment, I put my TV table between the couch and the television—where better?—sat on the sofa and pressed the power button on my remote control.

The program was a crime show about a man who'd committed a murder, moved, and created a whole new life under a new name. He married, though not divorced from the wife in his previous life, and even had another family. What caught my attention were the names. The man's moniker in his new life was very similar to his original name. The commentator noted that this is frequently true. Criminals will change their names, but not their initials.

I remembered a show I saw long ago about a woman who'd scammed people out of money and savings in not just many states, but also several countries. Every pseudonym had the same initials.

Like that feeling I'd had when walking Big Boy with that man by my side whistling "Winter Wonderland," something tickled my mind. The feeling was similar to when I try to remember the name of a person or a movie and it's "right on the tip of my tongue," but eludes my brain. Taking a clue from my Sue Grafton books where Kinsey Millhone sometimes writes out her facts in search of clues, I moved to my computer and keyed in:

Ned Shives is same initials as Norman Spires
Wants to see where Amber Buchanan's body was found
May have known who I was before approaching me
Seemed shifty
Appeared to be lying
Should have been working for Pork Chop
Criminals frequently return to the scenes of their crimes
Whistles

My brain slid into gear as I wrote the last word. Whistles? Someone mentioned whistling to me not long before. Click, click, click. My brain jumped into fourth gear. I sprang up and exclaimed *Shih tzu!* Big Boy came running. First and last notes: Ned Shives whistles. N. S. Same initials as Norman Spires. Who'd mentioned whistling? Naomi Spires. She'd said Norman whistled all the time and that he whistled beautifully.

I couldn't stand still as I pulled my cell phone from my bra and speed-dialed Wayne Harmon. I almost tripped over Big Boy as I paced around the room waiting for the sheriff to answer.

Finally, I heard the words: "Callie, do you need me?"

"No!" My voice squeaked far louder than I meant for it to. "*You* need *me*. I think that the man who came to check out where Amber Buchanan was found is Norman Spires."

"Why?"

"Because the name he gave me has the same initials and he whistled like Naomi Spires told me Norman does. Also, sometimes criminals return to the scene of their crime."

"Your porch was a secondary scene. The site where Amber Buchanan was killed is the primary scene and that wasn't at your place."

"I still think he was back here to revisit where he dumped her body. He saw me, and wanted to pick me for information."

"What else?"

"Female intuition."

ON THE TENTH DAY OF CHRISTMAS MY TRUE LOVE GAVE TO ME

TEN TURKEYS TROTTING

"I told Odell that I'd be glad to bring the sliders and drinks to Middleton's. I know they've served catered refreshments there before, but he said Mrs. Corley wants a drive-through because she read about something like that in one of those tabloids they sell at the grocery store." Rizzie was busy draping cloth over a long table in front of Gee Three while Tyrone brought out equipment and coolers.

A detour by the grill on the way to work to be sure Otis and Odell had completed the arrangements with Rizzie had seemed like a good idea, but it proved to be totally unnecessary. They were setting up before nine a.m., and the projected arrival of the funeral procession was at eleven forty-five a.m.

"I'm leaving Tyrone and some employees here to take care of business until I get back. I want to speak to Mrs. Corley before the service, so I'll be over there as soon as I change clothes." Rizzie and I both looked down at the jeans and Gee Three sweatshirt she wore—definitely not suitable for a visitation or funeral, though in these parts, sometimes people show up dressed even less appropriately.

"Okay, I'll see you there," I answered and turned to go back to the Mustang.

"Wait, how's Big Boy?"

"He seemed fine this morning. I took him for a walk and left him home watching TV."

"Doing *what*?"

"He likes television, so I leave it on for him now when I go off. He likes the animal channel with the sound turned down." I waved goodbye to the Profits and took off for Middleton's.

Otis and Odell were both in the chapel when I arrived. Identical twins or not, it's hard to believe they once looked so much alike that people could only tell them apart by the fact that one always wore black suits and the other always wore midnight blue.

Several part-timers were carrying floral tributes from the florists' receiving room to the chapel. If everyone who'd sent flowers showed up for the service, the chapel would be full, and we might have to set folding chairs in the aisles.

My mind bounced back to the first time I'd seen Patsy Corley when her father, June Bug Corley, was buried. Patsy's mother had insisted on very specific clothing and grooming for her deceased husband, allowed the family to see June Bug, and then had him cremated with no memorial service. Everyone in town had known June Bug, who ran a nightclub where several generations had partied. Maybe the wreaths, baskets, and pot plants were from people who'd known Patsy's father and would have sent memorials to his service if there had been one. Then again, Patsy had worked in the club and probably knew most of the folks her daddy had known.

By ten o'clock, Middleton's was packed with locals. I caught a glimpse of Rizzie across the room. She'd changed into a long black outfit that I'd love to have for work and even though I think of black as work clothes, her dress was such a knock-out that I would have worn it on a dinner date—if Dean called again or Patel showed up in town.

I watched Rizzie go through the receiving line and give Mrs. Corley and all her kinfolk hugs. I'm sure Patsy's brothers enjoyed Rizzie's tight embraces because they squeezed back, smashing her more than ample bosom.

Eager to talk to Wayne Harmon when I saw him come in, I made a beeline over to his side of the room and intercepted him.

"Did you arrest Norman Spires?" I asked.

"No, we have nothing to arrest him for yet."

"What? Don't you think he killed Amber Buchanan?"

"I believe he did, but there's no direct evidence until I can question him and hope I get him to confess."

"You didn't even interrogate him?" I'm not sure if my expression was more surprise or outrage.

"No, because he left Pork Chop's yesterday morning. Said the smells of pig farming didn't suit him or his sinuses. I showed Pork Chop a mug shot though, and you were right. The man hired as Ned Shives is Norman Spires. I want you to look at it, too, and confirm this is the man who was snooping over on Oak Street." The sheriff pulled out his wallet and unfolded a piece of paper. He handed it over, and I immediately recognized the photo as the man who'd walked part of the way 'round the block with me.

"What happens now?" I asked.

"I attend this funeral and then go back to work. Detective Robinson is investigating some possibilities, but I knew both Patsy and Snake. I'm here out of respect for the Corleys." He looked at his watch. "Can you slip out of here for a few minutes?"

"I'm working, but if you only need a few minutes, I suppose anyone who misses me will assume I've gone to the ladies' room. What do you want?"

"I want to take a look at Amber Buchanan's body. Isn't it here until I find out who can legally claim her?"

Standing beside Amber Buchanan's corpse on the stretcher we'd pulled from the drawer-like compartment of what we call the cooler, I was again impressed with the work that the Middletons and I do. When I'd opened the body bag, I immediately remembered that Ms. Buchanan's body hadn't been prepped. Her skin was not the pinkish flesh tone I was used to working on after embalming fluid not only stopped deterioration but also tinted skin to a more natural flesh tone than the dark shades of death. Her eyes and mouth were both slightly open. Before I work on restoring beauty to loved ones, Otis or Odell secure eyelids closed and the lips into a slight smile.

Don't get me wrong. Amber Buchanan was not the horror that movies and television choose to show dead people. She just looked like most bodies did when I'd gone on pickup calls for

Middleton's.

"Can you tip her head back a little bit?" the sheriff asked.

"Let me glove up first." I pulled on a pair of gloves from the dispenser on the wall and gently angled Ms. Buchanan's head. Wayne leaned in close, but not quite near enough to touch her.

"What do these look like to you?" he asked and pointed to darker spots of skin on the obvious strangulation marks around the neck. "The autopsy report states there are contusions or discolorations in a regular configuration on the ligature pattern around her neck. What do you think?"

"What I see doesn't involve all those long words." I leaned closer and almost bumped heads with the sheriff. "I see Christmas lights."

"What?"

"It looks to me like she was strangled with a string of Christmas lights—not those tiny ones most people use on inside trees, but the slightly larger bulbs some folks use outside. Look." I pointed to the spots. "They're about four inches apart and go all the way around. If the lights had been on for a while, the bulbs would have made those marks. A contusion is another word for a bruise, but those look like slight burns to me."

Wayne eyes lit up. "I believe you're right, and if you are, we know where the primary murder scene is, and we've walked all over it."

"Her front porch?" I asked.

"You've got it. She wasn't taken from her house and killed. She was murdered right there on her porch. That's why one end of the string of lights over the door was hanging loose."

"That explains why someone who kept her house so neat inside would have left those candy canes scattered all over."

"Zip it up." For just a moment I thought Wayne was being rude and telling me to hush, but he motioned toward the body bag. "Let's get back to the visitation. I'll call Detective Robinson and tell him what we think. He'll take care of a closer examination of that porch."

Wayne received an emergency call and didn't go back into the chapel, but I did. Everything went well until Snake Rodgers's brother Gordon walked in.

Could have heard a pin drop? A deaf man could have heard a tear drop fall in that silence. With a determined manner, head held high, Gordon Rodgers moved through the crowd to the pulpit at the front behind the casket. He picked up the microphone and flipped the switch to turn it on.

I've been to weddings and funerals where fights erupt. It's always tragic for something like that to happen at what should be a solemn affair, but it wouldn't be the first time. I saw that Otis, Odell, and the part-timers all began moving quietly toward the podium.

"Ladies and gentlemen," the voice rang out loud and clear. "For those of you who don't know me, I'm Gordon Rodgers. Until a few days ago, my brother lived with Patsy Corley here, God rest her soul." He gestured toward the casket. "I've heard rumors around this town that the Rodgers and the Corleys are going to have a feud like the Hatfields and McCoys or that one of my brothers is going to challenge one of Patsy's brothers to a duel." He stopped and looked around, as close to eye to eye as was possible in that crowded room.

"Well, I'm here to tell you that's not what the Rodgers family wants. None of us could understand why my brother and Patsy stayed together, but they must have cared about each other, no matter how much they fussed and yelled all the time. Everybody knew the two of them were a catastrophe waiting to happen. If Patsy hadn't pulled the trigger, sooner or later, my brother would have done it. Now two families are grieving about losing kinfolks they loved. Two mothers mourning the loss of their children. My mama is out in the car. She wants to come in and pay her respects to Mrs. Corley and the Corley family, but I told her I'd better check first to see if it would be all right."

Mrs. Corley rose from the chair she'd been sitting in and walked to the podium. She was a tiny woman but strong and determined. *Dalmation!* I hoped she wasn't going up there to slap Gordon Rodgers. No need to fear. She reached up and put her arms around Gordon in a motherly hug. Then she took the microphone from him, held it to her mouth, and said, "You go out there and tell your mama to come on in. This tragedy is enough of a disaster for both our families without any hate starting up."

Applause broke out. The pastor stepped forward and called for blessings on everyone who was there.

Mrs. Corley looked down and then added, "I know it's about time for the service, but I'd like to wait a few minutes for Mrs. Rodgers to come in and set beside me. We'll share our grief over losing our children."

And so it was that the mother of the man that Patsy Corley shot sat beside Patsy's mama at the funeral in the chapel and rode with her in one of the family cars right by Rizzie's grill to receive a Gee Three Shrimp Slider and soda.

Odell and a couple of part-timers drove the family cars back to the Corley home. I rode from the cemetery to Middleton's in the funeral coach with Otis. He's positively wild about Mumford and Sons and played their new CD until I said, "Otis, I've been thinking about Mr. Patterson and the Field of Flowers."

Otis turned the volume down and asked, "What about him?"

"That prepayment was over a decade ago. Wouldn't it be cheaper to refund the money than to supply the casket and everything in the contract?"

A grin spread across Otis's face. "It would be, and I'll tell Odell that, but we won't give him any money until after his wife dies and he's her legal heir." He turned Mumford and Sons back up until I spoke again.

"Otis, what's going to happen to Amber Buchanan?"

Once more, Otis turned the volume down and this time, he answered my question with one of his own. "What do you mean?"

"Sheriff Harmon said he hasn't located a next-of-kin for her. Will we just keep her in the refrigeration unit indefinitely like Spaghetti in North Carolina and Deaf Bill in Alton, Illinois?" I remembered tales he'd told me about them. They'd both been embalmed and held for decades by mortuaries waiting for relatives to pay for funeral services.

"No, I don't see us keeping a body over fifty years. There are legal ways to avoid things like that these days."

"I'm glad. That seems disrespectful to me. When I Googled Deaf Bill, I read that some people believe his ghost haunts the building where that funeral home was."

"You don't believe in ghosts, do you, Callie?"

"Not really. It's like Odell says, if ghosts haunted the places where they died, you wouldn't be able to turn around in hospitals and nursing homes. They'd be full of ghosts."

"So you know about Spaghetti and Deaf Bill. Sometime when you're not working or reading, Google 'Unburied bodies.' I'm not saying it's common, but not as rare as you might think."

I shuddered, hating to even think of such disrespect toward decedents.

"Those aren't the only cases like that," Otis continued, "and not all of them were years ago. As recently as 2004, an elderly lady named Ada in Texas died and went unburied at least five years because the family didn't pay for the service in the funeral home chapel nor interment, so the mortuary kept her all dressed up and resting in her casket. They even moved Ada when the funeral home relocated."

"Would you and Odell do that?"

"No, we wouldn't do that. Most morticians perform their responsibilities in respectful, honorable ways, but sometimes awful things happen in this business. One incident occurred right here in South Carolina when a funeral home quoted a price to bury a minister who was six feet, five inches tall. After the interment, rumors circulated around town that when his legs hadn't fit inside the coffin, an employee had cut off his feet to get the man in his casket. The gossip was so bad that the family demanded the preacher be exhumed. Sure enough, his feet and lower legs were in the casket, but they were no longer attached to the man."

I trembled with disgust. Reverence for decedents and their families is one of the first policies the Middletons taught me.

"So what will we do with Amber Buchanan if no one claims the body?" I swung the conversation back to my original question.

"We can petition the court for permission to cremate or bury an unclaimed body in Potter's Field."

The thought of that woman being murdered and lying six feet under in an unmarked grave brought the quick sting of tears to my eyes. I hadn't known Amber Buchanan before her death, but I felt like I had. Sometimes I thought of her as simply "Amber." The women at Safe Sister had seemed to care deeply about her. I remembered the unopened presents under their Christmas tree. I wondered if they'd be willing to contribute to some kind of memorial service for her. As quickly as that thought popped into my mind, I rejected it. Those ladies were in no position to do anything about Amber.

Otis didn't offer me a penny for my thoughts. Perhaps he didn't figure they were worth that much. He adjusted the sound, and Mumford and Sons filled the hearse—I mean the funeral coach—the rest of the way.

Two people sat in the rocking chairs on the verandah when Otis pulled into Middleton's Mortuary parking lot. I was surprised to see Frankie and Jane. I asked Otis to let me out before he parked the funeral coach.

"Why are you here?" I called.

"Came to see if you want to go to a turkey trot with us," Jane answered. She tugged at the orange and red tie-dyed T-shirt she wore beneath a suede fringed jacket. Jane loves to wear her mother's old clothes, but since her mom was shorter than Jane, sometimes the lengths are a big short. In the summertime, a bare belly button wouldn't matter these days, but in the cold winter, that shirt was probably freezing her middle.

"You must mean a turkey shoot, but most of those closed right after Christmas."

"No, we're going to a turkey trot. It's all over town that Buster Gwyn's having a turkey trot. Frankie's taking me. I've never been to one." Jane brushed her hand across the suede fringe on her mother's old hippie jacket.

"Jane, I don't mean to hurt your feelings, but there's no way anyone's going to let you shoot a gun."

Frankie laughed. "You're wrong."

"You plan to let her shoot?"

"No, I mean you're wrong about where we're going. It really is a turkey trot, not a turkey shoot."

"A turkey trot is a footrace. They're held in November, and the people who started them used to say that they were running to work off the calories eaten at Thanksgiving."

Frankie turned to Jane. "That's my sister, the encyclopedia.

Daddy should have named her Wikipedia instead of Calamine. She thinks she knows everything." He looked at me when he continued, "I might look like I fell off a turnip truck, but it wasn't last night. I know all that, but this is something different." He only said that bit about the turnip truck because he knows I despise that expression. Otis joined us and pulled two more chairs over to where Jane and Frankie sat.

I seated myself and said, "Then tell us about it."

"There's a place in Texas where a turkey trot is different. They line up domesticated turkeys and hold them back with a gate. Then they fire a starting pistol and lift the gate. All these gobblers go trotting down the street."

"What's the point of that?"

"I guess they do it for fun in Texas. Buster Gwyn got the idea that we could put numbers on tags around the turkeys' necks and see which one crosses the finish line first. He has more turkeys than usual left after the holiday season."

"So?" That was a childish response, about like when kids used to say, "Psych," but I saw no point in watching turkeys race.

"Jane and I are going to place bets and win some money. Thought you might want to come along."

"Are you sure that's not against the law like cock fighting and dog fighting?"

"No more than betting on anything is against the law. People are arrested for fighting dogs and roosters because it's cruel to the animals. This won't injure the turkeys at all." He laughed. "Unless somebody steals one and eats it."

Everyone knows Buster raises turkeys and is proud that his operation's a sideline, not industrialized. He claims his turkeys are free-range, which means they aren't crowded into small spaces and fed chemicals. Daddy buys his turkeys for Thanksgiving and Christmas from Buster because he likes to cook fresh, not frozen, birds. He also likes that Buster's birds are brown-feathered, not white like commercial turkeys usually are. I have no idea if the color has any effect on the taste, but my daddy has his own ideas about most things. All of that meant that I didn't think Buster would even consider an activity that would hurt the turkeys.

"You can go if you want, Callie," Otis said. "I'll be here the rest of the day and Odell should be back soon."

"Why don't I stay here and you go to this turkey trot?" I suggested.

"Because I'm not a betting man. Go ahead. You might win."

I've never been to a dogfight or cockfight in my life, and I never want to see animals made to hurt or kill each other, but if I ever get the chance to go to another turkey trot, I will. It was as much fun as watching the pigs race at the fair and wound up being far more exciting.

We left the van at Middleton's and took my Mustang to Buster Gwyn's farm. I thought that most of St. Mary's residents had been at Fatsy Patsy's funeral—oops! I didn't mean to call her that anymore. Like I said, I thought everyone was there, but a lot of them must have left the cemetery and headed over to Buster's because parked cars and trucks covered two fields and some of the people we saw getting out of them were, like me, dressed more suitably for a funeral than a turkey race. We had to walk at least half a mile following arrows from where we parked to the area designated by hand-lettered signs as the "Trotting Track."

Card tables manned by Buster's teenaged kids were labeled *$5*, *$1*, and *50¢*. Lined up beside those were more of his children and their friends with big washtubs of ice filled with sodas and beer.

"I don't know if we'll win any money here," I said, "but Buster Gwyn's sure to come out ahead."

We found out how much ahead Buster would be when we discovered there was a charge to get inside the makeshift fence surrounding the track.

Someone had rigged up a sound system, and a voice reverberated telling everyone: "Place your bets at the tables, buy yourself a drink, and pay just five dollars to have a place up close to see the first ever St. Mary's Turkey Trot."

A man yelled, "What if I want another beer after I pay to get in?"

The amplified words broke up and crackled this time, but their meaning came across. "We're gone stamp . . . hand . . . pay . . .

like they do at clubs."

Frankie bought Jane and me a beer and then steered us into the betting lines. He grumbled that he wanted to get a close look at the turkeys before placing a bet. The kid told us there were ten turkeys in the race, so we'd bet by number—anything between one and ten. Frankie put down five dollars on turkey three for every race. I put a couple of two-dollar bets on different numbers for each race. Jane decided to wait and bet later.

We paid our way into the fenced area and one of Buster's kids stamped our hands like they do at Kenny B's. The turkeys strutted around, gobbling loudly, in a separate pen at the beginning of the track. Just as the starting pistol fired for the first race and the gate opened in front of the turkeys, Frankie snaked us right up to the fence surrounding the track.

Across the way a pretty blond woman leaned against the fence, looking like she'd fall down without the support. Obviously totally intoxicated, she looked familiar. I recognized her just as she slumped to the ground. The drunk lady was Bill's old friend Lucy, the one I used to call Loose Lucy, the one his wife Molly had discovered texting him on his cell phone. Lucy's khaki cargo pants turned a darker color, and I realized she'd wet herself when she passed out. Another reason to feel sorry for her and grateful that I don't have an alcohol problem. I considered trying to get over to her. The crowd was big and boisterous. I didn't want to think about her getting stepped on or crushed, but there was no way to cross the track.

Just then, a man bent over her and tried to rouse her. The minute I saw him I glanced away quickly, hoping he hadn't noticed me. I didn't think he had because when he couldn't wake her, he stood and turned his attention back to the race, screaming, "Nine! Nine!" which must have been the turkey he'd bet on.

Sometimes I've wondered if I should have done what I did next. It got Buster Gwyn in a world of trouble, but I didn't hesitate then. I called Sheriff Harmon on my cell without considering the consequences. Most of the time, I'm glad I did. That man betting on nine needed to be questioned.

"Wayne," I screamed into my cell phone, trying to be heard over the yelling of turkey numbers all around me. "Norman Spires is here. I'm looking straight at him right now."

"Where are you?"

"I'm out at Buster Gwyn's farm with Jane and Frankie."

"What's going on?"

"Buster's having a turkey trot."

"Don't you mean a turkey shoot?"

"Nobody's shooting anything. Not a turkey nor a target."

"Has Buster got turkeys fighting?"

"No, they aren't fighting. They're racing. Come Highway 17 to the Gwyn farm and then follow the turkey trot signs. I don't know for sure how many races they're running, but I'll try to keep an eye on Spires until you get here."

"Don't dare talk to him or try to detain him if he starts to leave. Consider him armed and dangerous."

At the end of the first race, Jane squealed with excitement when Frankie told her he'd won fifteen dollars. I didn't win anything. Turkey number nine didn't win or place, and I sneaked a peek at Norman Spires. Mean and ugly sums up his expression, but he was standing protectively behind Lucy, kind of blocking her from the spectators.

Turkeys aren't the most domesticated bird. Daddy had never bothered to have any turkeys on his farm since he considered them more trouble than they were worth when he could buy a fresh one, alive or dressed out, from Buster. He didn't keep geese either, because, according to him, geese can be mean and he wasn't fond of the meat, preferring chicken or turkey.

I anticipated Wayne or Dean would slip up to Norman Spires and arrest him. My call to the sheriff had summoned law enforcement to Buster's farm, but I wasn't any more prepared than anyone else when it happened.

Sirens screamed and Jade County Sheriff's Department cars surrounded the turkey trot area all at once. People took off running in all directions, but deputies detained them.

"What's going on?" Jane demanded.

"This place is being raided, deputies all over," Frankie said. "Drop your beers and, Callie, give me the tickets for your bets." I handed him my stubs and he threw them on the ground and nudged us to step over, away from the evidence.

"I thought you said this wasn't illegal," I complained.

"I told you no animals would be hurt, but you need to put your big girl panties on and grow up. You know as well as I do that gambling's against the law in Jade County."

"Then why did you say there are deputies all over?" Jane asked.

"Because betting is against the law, and I'd bet you Buster didn't get a license to sell alcoholic beverages out here today. Even if he did, there's no way he'll get by with letting his kids sell beer and take bets."

"Will he go to jail?" Jane asked and then laughed. "If the charge is the same no matter what kind of alcohol, he should have been selling Wild Turkey shots in coffee. It's turning colder."

"Buster will probably get hauled into town, and anyone who's caught with a betting stub or beer will get a ticket and have to go to court. I don't think Wayne will try to book this many people," Frankie assured her.

Just then I saw a big, burly deputy tackle a man who was running across the field away from the track. I recognized the officer as a former football player on St. Mary High School's team. Another guy jumped on top of them, and it looked like a Friday night football pile up. They stood and handcuffed the man who'd been on the bottom—Norman Spires.

Other deputies climbed inside the track and chased turkeys. Now, full-grown turkeys can't fly because of their weight, but those gobblers ran faster from the deputies than they had during the race. The sky opened up and dumped freezing-cold rain on us.

"I heard that domesticated turkeys have to be taken inside the roosting house when it rains because they're so stupid that they'll look up at the rain until they drown from the water rushing down their throats," Jane said.

"Old wives' tale," Frankie answered. "Think about it. Their eyes are on the sides of their heads. To look at rain coming from the sky, they'd have to turn their heads sideways, not directly upward."

"Are we going to just stand here and watch it rain ourselves?" I asked.

"I think it's better if we don't try to walk away. We might

wind up like that guy the deputies just tackled and hauled over to the paddy wagon in handcuffs."

Not bothering to explain that the tackled man hadn't been arrested just for being there, I stood beside Frankie and Jane while we got drenched.

When an officer finally got around to us, Frankie talked to him. He didn't actually lie, but we all emptied out our pockets, showing we had no betting stubs, and the deputy told us to get out of there. We were walking back to the Mustang when I saw EMTs carrying a stretcher toward an ambulance. I never liked Loose Lucy, but I was glad she was getting medical attention. What if she wasn't just passed out?

The ride back to town was quiet. Jane and Frankie both seemed to be in pouty moods while I was just glad I hadn't been arrested.

"Where are you going now?" Jane asked when we pulled into Middleton's parking lot and Frankie parked my car beside his van.

"I thought we'd go back to your place," Frankie answered.

"Not talking to you," Jane said with sadness in her voice. "I'm asking Callie."

"I'm going to stop by the grocery store and then head on home." All that excitement had worn me out.

"I need some things from the grocery, too." Jane.

"I'll take you by the store," Frankie offered.

"No, you go on home. I'll ride with Callie. Call me in the morning." Jane again.

Frankie got his, *Oh, no, what have I done now?* hurt expression, but he didn't try to talk her into changing her mind. He got out of the car and into the van. He drove off without even waving.

Jane said nothing on the way to the store. Once we were in the grocery produce department, she asked, "Are you buying a lot of stuff?"

"No, just the basics. MoonPies and Diet Coke, plus I need dog food."

Jane suggested, "You help me round up the ingredients, and I'll cook dinner for us. What would you like?"

Now, that's a great suggestion because Jane's a good cook,

but she hadn't been cooking much for me since she started dating Frankie. I thought of all the wonderful dishes I hadn't had lately, but the one that sounded so good in my mind that I could almost smell it there in the grocery store was lasagna.

"What I want may take too long." I hesitated. "Is it too late to start lasagna?"

"Do you have a hot date for tonight?" Jane grinned.

"No."

"Well, I don't either, so lasagna will be fine. There are some things I want to discuss with you, and we can talk while I cook. Go get me some hot Italian sausage. I've got noodles, sauce, and some parmesan cheese, but we'll need ricotta cheese and a loaf of French bread. I want some fresh mushrooms as well, but I'll get those. I think I have everything else."

"Be right back," I said.

"And buy Big Boy some dog bones or that fake bacon for dogs they advertise on television," Jane called after me. I left her standing by the cart, feeling tomatoes and other salad ingredients, which I knew from the past that she didn't trust me to choose.

I returned to Jane with arms full of sausage, cheese, Moon-Pies, and doggy treats. Just as I placed the items in the cart basket, I heard someone calling, "Callie, Callie." I looked up and saw Miss Ellen and Miss Lettie hurrying toward us.

"I *told* Lettie it was you," Miss Ellen gushed.

"I didn't know you were talking about her. I thought you meant the red-haired one." Miss Lettie poked her hand out at Jane, and I said, "Jane, she wants to shake with you."

Jane laughed and wiggled her hips suggestively.

"What's she doing?" Miss Lettie asked.

"She's shaking with you, but she can't see that you're not shaking." Miss Ellen giggled and began gyrating her own derriere. Miss Lettie laughed and started doing the twist. Jane must have guessed what was going on because she guffawed.

"I'm Jane Baker, Callie's friend," Jane said and extended her right hand when she stopped jiggling her behind.

"Miss Lettie Morgan and her friend Miss Ellen," I introduced them and they shook hands.

"We came out to pick up some canned pineapple and a

banana to make my cousin Gloria's version of banana nut bread for tonight," Ellen said while Miss Lettie tittered like a teenaged girl. "Mr. Parrish has fed us so many wonderful dishes that we decided to cook something to have with coffee tonight. Gloria adapted the recipe and gave it to me right before she passed away last year."

Before I could comment, Jane asked, "Mr. Parrish? Which one?"

"What do you mean which one?" Miss Lettie looked puzzled.

"Callie's daddy or one of his brothers?" Jane clarified.

"Oh, her father," Miss Ellen answered. "Lettie and I are going to make two of them—one for us to eat tonight when Mr. Parrish comes over and one to send home with him to his sons."

"Would you two like to come by and have coffee and banana nut bread with us this evening?" Miss Lettie invited.

"No, thank you," Jane responded quickly, "maybe another time."

Jane didn't say anything else until we'd checked out and were on the drive home. "I want to tell you that I've decided Frankie and I should split for good. I know this is difficult because he's your brother. You love him, and I don't want to offend you by hurting him." She paused. "Actually, I love him, too, and I don't want to hurt him either, but I can't deal with the tension. He talks about taking care of me and then takes us somewhere we could get arrested, and he's so bossy that it scares me to think he might turn into a control freak. Lately, when I'm with him, I spend the whole time worrying about what he's going to say or do to make *me* do what he says."

My mind shot back to Safe Sisters. "Are you telling me he's abusive?" I asked. "What do you mean? Has Frankie ever hit you or shoved you?"

"Oh, no. Never, but sometimes I wonder if I could accidentally make him mad enough to do something to me."

"You know I'd never want you to stay with Frankie because of me," I said. "Actually, there have been times I was jealous of all the time you spent with him."

"Well, I'm getting ready to make some major changes in my

life, and I think I'll have to go away from Frankie for a while. We can't even be friends for a while. When that woman sounded so warm about 'Mr. Parrish,' I got jealous thinking Frankie had been going to see them."

"Jane, those women are in their sixties or seventies, and neither of them looks like a cougar to me."

"I'm considering moving away from St. Mary, Callie. I'll miss you so much, but it's not like I'd have to find a new job or anything. I can work from anywhere. Would you be interested in moving? Not necessarily across country. Maybe somewhere close like Charleston or Columbia?"

"But I can't take my job with me," I protested. "Many funeral homes have their embalmers do makeup. That's part of their training. I don't think I want to teach anymore and I know I don't want to *ever* work in a beauty parlor again."

Jane broke into tears. I couldn't think of anything else to say, so I turned the radio on. It happened to be on the old station, not oldie goldies, but *old* music from before either of us was born. I recognized Ella Fitzgerald's voice. She's not bluegrass or country, but Daddy has some of her old LP records that he listens to on the ancient record turntable in his room. I keep telling him he can buy CDs of everything these days, but he likes to play those old vinyl records.

"How I wish I had someone to watch over me," Ella Fitzgerald sang in a pure, beautiful voice.

Jane joined in and they finished the Gershwin tune as a duet.

"How do you know that song?" I asked. "It was way before our time."

"Amy Winehouse did a cover of it and so did lots of other singers, including Linda Ronstadt. I've done it when I used to go out and sing Karaoke when you lived in Columbia."

"Don't they still do Karaoke some places?" I asked, and then continued before giving her time to answer. "You and I could go out sometime and sing at those venues."

"Maybe. Let's not talk about it anymore. When we get home, take Big Boy for a walk and then bring him over to visit while I cook, but I've said what I had to say. I don't want to talk about anything serious."

"Fine, but I want you to know that our friendship isn't dependent on your dating my brother. I'll always be your friend, no matter who you hook up with."

"And I'll be yours."

"If I ever meet anyone who doesn't run out on me," I lamented. "Everyone I get interested in seems to like me, and then they drop out of my life. What's wrong with me?"

"Maybe you're attracted to men who are commitment-shy or it could be your creepy job."

"Maybe so. You attract men who want to watch over you, but then you complain when a man tells you what to do."

"No offense, Callie, but I want someone who won't think watching over me means telling me what to do without making any effort to help me."

"And I want someone who will hang around more than a few weeks."

When we reached our building, I carried the groceries in and took Big Boy for his walk. By the time we returned, Jane's apartment smelled like Italian sausage. Big Boy loved the dog treats, and I loved the lasagna. Jane and I spent the evening having our own Karaoke night—singing along with the radio until I went home to bed and she went to work as Roxanne.

★

ON THE ELEVENTH DAY OF CHRISTMAS MY TRUE LOVE GAVE TO ME

ELEVEN AXES GRINDING

Jane's scream pierced my mind and wrenched me from a wonderful erotic dream. I shot out of bed, grabbed my keys, and raced next door, nightgown flapping against my knees and my heart pounding like it would burst out of my chest. I didn't need the key. The apartment was wide open with the front door dangling from one hinge.

I dashed in screaming, "What's wrong?"

In that horrible moment, I saw Jane cowered against the far wall, still wearing her jeans and tie-dyed orange T-shirt. Terrified, she screamed and wildly whipped her white metal-tipped mobility cane back and forth, but there was no one in front of her.

A heavy fist crashed into the back of my head. I buckled to my knees, disoriented in a world of blackness. I was in Jane's universe—sightless. I crumpled to the floor.

I tried to sit up. "Oh, no, you don't!" a voice growled. It sounded far away. My vision cleared a little. A tall form in a hooded brown overcoat appeared in front of me—arms uplifted, holding Jane's ceramic Christmas tree. A flash of bright light blasted through my head, and I collapsed in agony. I may have lost consciousness or I might not have. I'm not sure. I lay limp while Jane screamed, "Callie! Callie! Say something so I can find you!"

I must have moaned because I don't remember speaking or moving. I felt Jane leaning over me, pressing her hands against my head, whispering, "Are you all right?"

"No, I'm not all right." The words seemed to stick in my

throat. "Someone broke your ceramic Christmas tree over my head. Who was it?"

"I don't know. I'd just finished working and was putting my hair in a French braid when whoever it was bashed the door in and rushed at me. I grabbed my mobility cane and tried to hit the person while I screamed for help. Then you came in." She mashed even harder on my head.

"Where's the intruder now?" I managed to get the words out.

"Ran out the front door. Hold on, Callie, I'm calling 911. Your head's bleeding, and I'll get a cloth to hold against it."

I can't say that I heard Jane make the call, nor that I remember the sirens, but I was vaguely aware when a male voice assured me, "Callie, they're taking you to the hospital to be checked out. You probably have a concussion and you definitely need stitches."

Shih tzu! I thought, *If I keep getting concussions, I'll be like those boxers with the cauliflower ears and football players after they've had so many head injuries.*

A male voice barked toward a direction away from me, "Don't touch anything you don't have to. I'm calling in the forensics team. They may be able to get prints off the broken glass pieces." A pause. "Take the red-haired lady with you in the front of the ambulance and let her stay with the victim at the hospital. I'll call the Middletons, too."

That's when I recognized the voice—Dean Robinson. I wanted to sit up and tell him, "I don't need a homicide detective *or* a funeral home. I'm *not dead*!" That's what I wanted to do, but my hands wouldn't move and I'd lost the ability to talk again.

Paralysis, I thought. *I'm paralyzed.* I tried to lift my arms and realized they were strapped down. I wasn't paralyzed. I was on a body board. I opened my eyes and saw Dean, Jane, and two emergency technicians around me.

"Don't struggle," one of the EMTs said. "We've got you stabilized to carry you to the hospital."

My mind went to Fields of Flowers and their webpage stating they would transport a body for one hundred dollars plus mileage. *Bet this ride will cost a whole lot more than that,* I thought. *Good thing Otis and Odell have hospitalization insurance on me.* Then, even with my muddled mind, I realized how ridiculous it was to be thinking silly ideas about Fields of Flowers. I should have been grateful I wasn't headed to a real cemetery.

I opened my mouth and found that I could finally speak once more, "Is Jane okay? Did the thief hurt her?"

"I'm fine, Callie," Jane said. "You're the one who was hurt, but I'm going with you to the hospital."

"I broke your ceramic tree." I knew that was irrelevant when I said it, but my brain was even less capable than usual of controlling my mouth.

"You've got a hard head," Jane laughed.

I first met Dr. Donald Walters, my used-to-be sometimes boyfriend, when I went to the ER a couple of years ago. I didn't expect to see him this time because he has his own practice now and doesn't work emergency anymore, but he met us as the EMTs wheeled me into the hospital.

"What are you doing here in the middle of the night?" I managed to whisper to Donald.

"When they reported the ambulance was on the way with you, hospital admissions pulled your records and saw I'm listed as your doctor. They paged me, and since I was checking on another patient here, I came down to ER." He patted my hand, which was still strapped to the body board below the IV needle the EMTs had inserted.

"Seems like you're here almost every time I'm hit on the head," I said.

"Callie, head injuries shouldn't be taken lightly. You know the routine. I want tests, and then I may want you here overnight for observation. Open your mouth."

I stretched my jaws wide and he looked inside with a little flashlight.

"You've bitten your tongue. Chances are you have a concussion and were unconscious." Donald loosened the restraints, and the paramedics moved me from their stretcher to a hospital gurney and left.

"I don't think I lost consciousness," I said. "I was hit and then Jane was looking for me."

"*Looking* for you?"

"You know as well as I do that Jane *looks* by touch. I remember her calling my name, telling me to make noise so she could find me."

"Could still have been out of it for a few minutes. Doesn't matter now. The tests will show me what I need to know, and from the looks of your head, we'll need to stitch some of those cuts."

"Then sew me up and let me go home. I don't want to spend the night here."

"Tough. I'll make that decision, but I won't make you stay unless I think it's necessary. The bleeding's stopped. We'll get a CT scan first."

Two nurses, one on each end of the gurney, took me for the scan. I hate, positively *hate* when they put my head in those machines. I always get these terrifying thoughts that the metal will fail and the machine will crush me.

When it was over, they took me back to Emergency, which I thought might mean I was going home. Jane was sitting in a chair by the bed. A nurse helped me out of my bloody nightgown and into one of those hospital thingies that tie in the back but leave the patient's behind open for all the world to see. I'd just leaned back when Dr. Donald came in with another nurse carrying a tray. He bent over and examined my head.

He reached up and turned on the brightest lights I've ever seen and directed them toward me. "Best shave the cuts after you clean them," he told the nurse.

"*Shave?*" I shrieked. "You're going to shave my head?"

"Not your whole head. Just where you need stitches. You won't feel a thing after I get a couple of shots of local anesthetic into the wounds."

He lied. Of course, that's not the first time a man has ever lied to me, but I was still disappointed in him. When he injected the numbing medication directly into the cuts, I definitely felt it and moaned.

After Dr. Donald was satisfied that the assistant had cleaned and shaved the appropriate spots on my head, I felt the stitches go in, though, to be honest, it didn't feel like he was sewing my head.

More like he was pinching me, and the shots must have taken effect because I didn't much care. I didn't object to what they were doing to my head, but my mind took off in peculiar directions. There I lay—head partially shaved, wearing my backless hospital gown with no boobs because I wasn't wearing inflatable underwear, actually no underwear at all. Light green cloths draped all around me. I felt like I was drifting in and out of reality.

By the time the attendants pushed me out of the trauma room, down the hall, into the patient elevator, and up to my room, most of the reality was gone, and all I wanted to do was sleep. After what might have been a few minutes or much longer, I forced myself to open my eyes and saw that Daddy and Mike had joined Jane in my room. She was the only one who didn't look completely shocked. I guess because she couldn't see me.

I was vaguely aware when the sheriff came in. He took a statement from Jane about her intruder right there with my father and brother listening. Then he apologized for not arriving sooner. "I would have been here before, but we've got a kidnapping."

"Kidnapping?" Jane said. "Is there an Amber Alert?"

"Technically, it's not an Amber Alert because we have no vehicle description, but I've put out an APB as well as media releases."

"Who is it?" Daddy asked.

"The baby." Wayne said it matter-of-factly in his official cop voice.

I sat up the best I could and demanded, "Betsy? Naomi's baby? Did her daddy get her?" I knew, just *knew* that's what had happened.

"No," Wayne replied, "the kidnapped baby isn't the Spires child. It's Misty and Billy Wayne Bledsoe's newborn son."

"Did they take him from the hospital?" Mike asked.

"No, the hospital had already released mother and son. The infant was abducted from his bassinet when Misty took a nap while the baby was asleep. Billy Wayne had gone to the store. Both of them are hysterical with fear, and I've got search parties combing the land around the Bledsoe's trailer. Pork Chop Higgins is heading a civilian hunt."

I couldn't help but wonder if and how there was a connection between what had happened at Jane's apartment and the kidnapping.

They were still talking when Dr. Donald returned.

"I know you're concerned about Callie, but she needs rest. Why don't you all go home and come back this afternoon when she's feeling better?"

"Why are you keeping her?" I had closed my eyes, but I recognized Daddy's voice. "Does she have any brain damage?"

"Not that we know of. Her skull isn't fractured anywhere, and the scan shows only one minuscule spot of bleeding. The cuts and abrasions aren't life-threatening. Some doctors might not even have stitched them, but if I hadn't, they could heal with scars that keep her hair from growing back in normally." He glanced at me and grinned. "She's too pretty to have bald spots." Everyone smiled as though they agreed, but I had an idea that at that moment I wasn't anywhere near pretty.

"I'm going to order neurological checks every two hours," Dr. Donald guaranteed Daddy. "I promise you the hospital staff will take good care of her."

"I'm. Not. Leaving." Jane spoke emphatically—one word at a time.

"You need rest, too," Dr. Donald told her.

"Then I'll rest right here in this chair. Callie got hurt trying to help me. Whoever did this was after me. I'm staying with her until she's better."

"I don't think her condition is as serious as it seems from her appearance," Dr. Donald assured her.

Jane was in no mood to be soothed.

"If you don't let me stay, I'll talk Callie's family into asking the hospital to call in another doctor and get you off her case."

"Now, Jane, that's a bit severe," Mike interrupted. "Dr. Walters has taken good care of Callie every time she gets hurt." His words didn't calm Jane at all.

"I don't care. I'm not leaving her." Jane's posture stiffened.

"Now, Michael," Daddy interjected. "We can all be reasonable. Jane, do you have your cell phone?"

"Yes, I put it in my pocket when I called 911."

"Then we'll leave Jane with Callie while we close up the front of her apartment. We'll come back this afternoon after both of them have had some rest. If anything changes, Jane will call me."

As much as I love my family, I was relieved when everyone except Jane left, leaving me to sleep without hearing their voices. Knowing Roxanne had worked until late in the night and Jane hadn't been to bed at all, I assumed she was heavy-eyed, too. She was, because soon I heard her snoring.

"I hate to wake you."

He might have hated it, but Wayne Harmon's voice did jar me from sleep. "I talked to Jane earlier, but as soon as you can, I need a description of who attacked you."

"I didn't see much," I mumbled. "He was tall and had on a brown coat with the hood pulled up around his face. I assume it was Norman Spires. Why didn't you keep him in jail after you picked him up from the Turkey Trot?"

"No way did Spires assault you. He's been in the county jail since yesterday afternoon."

"Oh."

That was all I could say. If not Spires, who broke into Jane's apartment? Who broke her ceramic Christmas tree over my head? Could it have been theft gone bad? That didn't make sense. What did Jane or I have that anyone would want to steal? Did whoever came there take the Bledsoe baby?

"So you can't tell me anything about what the intruder looked like?"

"Not really. Taller than I am but covered in that brown overcoat."

Wayne laughed. "Taller than you are? How tall are you, Callie? About five feet, two inches?"

"I'll have you know I'm five feet, four." I said defensively, and then added, "What about the baby?"

"I doubt he's over eighteen or nineteen inches tall." Wayne tried to sound humorous, but his expression was filled with worry.

"You know what I mean," I retorted. "Do you know anything yet?"

"Nothing yet." He added, "You girls get some sleep and rest. I've gotta get going."

Though Jane and I aren't known for always following directions, we did exactly what the sheriff told us. We went back to sleep. I'm not sure about her, but I slept right through breakfast and lunch. I vaguely remember an attendant telling Jane to eat my lunch and that I'd be okay with the IVs.

Nurses kept rousing me slightly from sleep, having me follow simple directions that didn't require much effort or thought. When I finally woke up for real, Jane was sitting by my bed French braiding her hair into one long pigtail on the left side. I remembered she'd said that's what she was doing when the assailant broke in. She still wore the same clothes from yesterday.

"Why don't you call Daddy and get one of The Boys to bring us both some clothes?" I asked before adding, "Is Dr. Donald going to let us go home this afternoon?"

"He left not long ago, said he's keeping you one more night. I'll call your father and let him know you're wide awake. He's checked on you a couple of times, but I didn't want to interrupt your nap."

"I'd really like something besides the nightgown they brought me in or one of these thingies to wear home." I smoothed my hand down the flat front of the hospital gown I wore.

"I'm going to show my tush when I go to the bathroom in this thing, and I need to go *now*."

"If I could see, I'd have seen your butt more times than I care to remember." She laughed, "Actually, a person doesn't have to be sighted to see you when you show your ass, and you don't seem to mind doing that every so often. How are you going to the bathroom with that IV?"

"I'll roll it with me." I managed to get myself off the bed and drag the IV pole behind me, feeling the breeze across my backside. I felt better after using the bathroom—until I looked in the mirror above the sink.

My eyes looked out at me from darkened eye sockets that were impossible to describe as black, blue, or purple. The color mottled from one shade to another. Above those horrible eyes, my head was a hot mess of shaved spots, bandages, and tufts of blondish hair shooting out in all directions. I felt like crying. Instead I laughed.

"Are you all right?" Jane called.

"No, I'm so bad that it's funny," I answered.

I shoved the IV pole in front of me and made it to the bed. Once I'd climbed back in place, I looked around the room. While I slept, someone had left a dozen roses of all different colors arranged beautifully with baby's breath in a vase. "Who brought the flowers?" I asked Jane.

"Don't know. Must have come while we were asleep. I didn't even know there were any flowers here, but now that you mention it, I smell them." She coughed. "I called your father and told him Dr. Donald is keeping you another night. He said he'll get Frankie to bring us some clothes and he'll be back later. Instead of just nailing plywood over the opening, they're replacing the door with a metal one. They took Big Boy to your dad's house, too."

A Certified Nursing Assistant came in and assisted me in taking a bed bath while Jane listened to a soap opera on the television. The earphones for the television reached far enough from the bed for her to wear them while sitting in the recliner beside me.

A knock on the door elicited, "Wait a minute," from the CNA. When I had on a fresh hospital gown, she tucked the sheet around me and opened the door. Frankie stood there holding a small piece of Jane's hot pink luggage. He set it on the foot of my bed.

"Pa sent me to bring each of you fresh clothes—night things and outer clothing to wear home when they let you out of here." He turned to Jane and asked, "Are you okay?"

"Of course, I'm okay. It's Callie who always gets hurt."

"I worry about both of you."

Jane couldn't see the expression in my brother's eyes, but I could. His love for her showed in his concerned, caring expression when he looked at her.

"Where are Mike and Daddy?" I asked.

"Finishing up with the doors. They decided to replace all four of them, front and back at both apartments. If Pa has his way, he'll put bars on the windows, too."

"Has he talked to the landlord about all this?" I asked.

"Certainly not. You know Pa. He'll do whatever he wants now and clear it later."

"Our leases say we have to get permission to make structural changes."

"Do you think anyone's going to argue with Pa making the place safer after you've been injured like this?" Frankie waved his hand at me, and I knew he was telling me how bad I looked without spelling it out for Jane. "We're installing dead bolt locks, too."

He looked around. The room had two seats—the recliner Jane sat in and a straight back wooden chair on the other side of the bed. I figured he'd sit in the wooden one, but he remained standing.

"Would either of you like something to eat or drink?" he asked after a few minutes. "I didn't have lunch, and I'm going down to the cafeteria and get something."

"Chocolate," Jane said. "Pudding, pie, cookies, or a brownie. Just bring me something chocolate. What about you, Callie? Want Frankie to see if they have any MoonPies?"

"Actually, I'd like chocolate, too, but I'd rather have something warm to drink—maybe hot chocolate with marshmallows in it."

After Frankie left, Jane asked, "Do you want me to help you get dressed?"

"No, it will be difficult with this IV in my arm. I'm clean and all covered up. I'll just wait."

Frankie returned with what must have been one of everything chocolate the hospital cafeteria carried along with a cheeseburger, fries, and a Coke for himself.

"Wow!" I said. "What'd you do, rob a bank?"

He grinned. "Pa gave me some money to buy you whatever you want."

My brother didn't seem to notice the slightly annoyed look that flickered across Jane's face. One of their problems from the beginning has been that Frankie won't hold a job and sometimes lives hand to mouth. That's why he stays with Daddy. Jane didn't like hearing Frankie, a full-grown man, had to get money from his father to buy snacks.

We settled in, watching afternoon television, which isn't really fascinating, and eating. The only thing better than chocolate is chocolate *with* chocolate, which is what I had with my hot cocoa and devil's food Swiss Miss rolls.

I fully expected Mike to return with Daddy, but he didn't. When my dad announced, "Look who I brought to see you," he had Miss Lettie and Miss Ellen with him. He did the gentlemanly thing and helped both with their coats.

Since there were only two chairs in the room, Frankie saw this as an excuse to tell us he was going home to take Big Boy for a walk. Jane got up and sat on the edge of my bed, and Daddy stood at my foot, leaving both seats for the two elderly ladies. Miss Lettie set her big crocheted tote bag on the floor beside the recliner and sat there.

To be honest, I would have been happier if everyone had just left me alone. Since I couldn't go home until the next day, I would have been contented if someone found me a book and let me read it in silence. I can block out radio or television while I read but not people talking. Daddy and the ladies went on and on about how horrible it was that I'd been hurt. Daddy raved about everything he'd eaten at Miss Lettie's the night before, and then went into detail about the wonderful doors he and The Boys had installed.

"But I'd still prefer you girls come live with me until Sheriff Harmon has this situation solved," he suggested. "I'm taking these lovely ladies over to Rizzie's for dinner. That banana nut bread with pineapple in it was so delicious that I invited them both out tonight. Jane, you come with us and then spend the night at my house."

"I'm not going *anywhere*," Jane answered. "It's my fault Callie was injured, and I'm st-st-staying with her. I don't know why anyone would think I have anything worth st-st-stealing, but Callie got hurt when she came to rescue me from the burglar. I'm going to sit up with her tonight and every night until whoever attacked her is in jail." She stuttered on the *st* sounds, which she'd done a lot when we were teenagers, but hardly ever in the years since.

Just then Dr. Donald walked in. He looked at Jane, who was

slumped across my bed, gave his head a negative shake, and said to Daddy, "I'll order up a cot for Jane. One night in that chair is too much, but she's not going to be satisfied anywhere except right here with Callie. I suggest the rest of you go home. Callie should be able to check out of here in the morning, but I want someone to be with her for a few days." He turned toward me. "Callie," he added, "it wouldn't be a bad idea for you and Jane both to stay with your dad."

"An even better idea is for them to move in with me for good," Daddy insisted.

"It's a three-bedroom house and three of you already live there," I said, though that wasn't my real reason for not wanting to occupy my dad's house. Not only would staying there mean Mike and Frankie had to share a room, Jane and I would, too. We're the best of friends, but every time we've lived together, it's brought chaos. Besides, Daddy would treat us both like we were ten years old.

"I raised six kids in that house," he said. "Three bedrooms should be enough for any family—a room for parents, one for the boys, and another for the girls."

I couldn't help giggling. "That's Daddy's idea about bedrooms. It's why I always had my own room and The Boys were all piled up on bunk beds together. He also believes that one bathroom is enough for a family of any size."

"A family of seven?" Miss Ellen asked.

"All of us," Daddy said and nodded. "I was one of nine children, and we grew up with just one bathroom. When the children wanted me to add another, I didn't see the need for it with just me and my kids." He winked at me. "You'd better be glad you're your age, not mine. When I was growing up, my grandmother still had an outhouse instead of indoor toilets."

Dr. Donald looked a little irritated by the continuing bathroom discussion. Surely he wasn't offended. After all, don't doctors deal with all kinds of bodily functions? He interrupted, "You can figure out where everyone's sleeping tomorrow, but I don't want Callie staying by herself for a few more days." He gestured toward the top of the IV pole. "I'll tell the nurse to remove that when this bag of fluid is empty."

After he left, Miss Lettie looked at me and almost purred, "He's certainly a nice young man. You should try to get a date with him."

"She's already dated him several times," Daddy informed her.

"What was wrong? Too busy with his career?" Miss Ellen asked, but she was smiling.

"No, he's a womanizer," Jane said in a matter-of-fact tone. She slid off the bed and found her way to our chocolate stash. "Anybody want something?" she asked as the felt the cellophane-wrapped goodies and settled on a brownie. She stood there and ate it.

"Maybe you could tame that doctor," Miss Lettie suggested.

"Like Sheriff Harmon says, 'If it walks like a duck, looks like a duck, and quacks like a duck, it probably *is* a duck.' Dr. Donald says he's ready to settle down, but he can't take his eyes off any good-looking woman he sees, and he's got that smooth-talking charm that comes with lots of practice," I responded.

Miss Ellen laughed. "They don't cheat with their eyes, honey. If all he does is look, he might be a good catch anyway."

I lay back, trying to give Daddy and the ladies the idea that I wanted to rest. They took the hint and remained silent for a while. Jane gathered several more chocolate treats, put them on the bed, and then sat and examined them with her fingers.

"I believe you're right not to try to change that doctor," Miss Lettie commented as though she'd been seriously thinking about it the whole time. I peeked through the bottoms of my almost closed eyes and noticed she was staring at Jane. "People who run around don't ever change. I was lucky that my Jeffrey Senior was a faithful husband and never stepped out on me. Some of those girls that Jeffrey Junior fooled around with in high school cheated and lied all the time."

Personally, I couldn't think of any response to that, but Miss Ellen objected, "All of that's water under the bridge, Lettie. Most people don't settle down with their high school sweethearts like you and Jeffrey did. Junior got a rough start what with his daddy dying before he was born, but he was a good boy. You were blessed to have him. I'd give anything if my Leland and I could have had children, but the good Lord didn't see fit to send any to us."

Bored. It was obvious to me that we were all bored out of our minds sitting there. I couldn't understand why Daddy had brought Miss Lettie and Miss Ellen to see me. I didn't know them that well, and I certainly didn't look nor feel like receiving visitors. Apparently, Miss Ellen picked up on my thoughts because she stood, patted my hand, and said, "Is there anything we can get you before we go—maybe some munchies or something?"

I waved my arm toward the top of the cabinet where Frankie had left all the chocolate snacks and pointed toward Jane and her pile of food. "We have plenty to eat," I answered, "but before you leave, I'd really like for someone to go down to the gift shop and buy me a paperback book." Maybe my headache would ease up enough for me to escape into the world of fiction.

"What do you read?" Miss Ellen said.

"Mysteries," I answered. "Sometimes I read Stephen King or sci fi, but what I really like are mysteries."

"I don't know how to pick a book for a girl," Daddy grumbled.

"I'll go with you." Miss Ellen continued patting my hand, but her words were for Daddy. "I read mysteries, too. We'll buy the newest one they have and hope Callie hasn't already seen it." She looked at Miss Lettie. "Do you want to come with us, Lettie?"

"No, I'd rather wait here. I certainly don't want to pick out a mystery book, something about a homicide, when my own dear boy Jeffrey Junior was murdered."

"Lettie, I've told you over and over. Junior's death was an accident. It wasn't anyone's fault." For the first time, I detected a bit of irritation in Miss Ellen's voice.

"It was *so* that woman's fault. If she'd kept dating Jeffrey Junior, they could have settled down right here in St. Mary and made me grandbabies."

"That was years ago, Lettie. You've gotta let it go."

Daddy looked uncomfortable, which isn't normal for him. Most of the time, he ignores things that would be embarrassing to other folks.

Obviously ready to get out of there, he asked, "Jane, can we get you anything?"

"No, just buy a book for Callie. I'll listen to the radio or television through her earphones. This is a great hospital room. The earphones reach to the chairs as well as the bed, and when you push the call button, it activates a signal at the nurses' desk and they ask what you want through an intercom above the bed. That way, they can bring what you need when they come. Back when Mommy was in the hospital, the call button just turned on a light in the hall. The nurse had to see the light, come ask what Mommy wanted, and then go get it." She slid off the bed and sat in the wooden straight-back chair where Miss Ellen had been.

When Daddy and Miss Ellen left the room, Miss Lettie babbled on about her deceased son. She started loud and fast but soon reduced her words to mumbling as she opened the tote bag beside her. She pulled out a tiny, unfinished blue sweater, skeins of yarn, knitting needles, and a gigantic pair of scissors. It's not unusual to see ladies knit or crochet in public around St. Mary, and I've read Maggie Sefton's Kelly Flinn Knitting Mysteries, but I'm not into needlework of any kind.

With my eyes closed, I wondered why Miss Lettie's scissors were so big. My aching brain jumped to Little Red Riding Hood telling the wolf, "My, what big teeth you have," and the wolf answering, "The better to eat you with." That thought didn't come from my years of teaching kindergarten. I'd edited the fairy tales I told my students. The bad people (or animals like the poor beleaguered wolf in so many stories) always died in such gruesome ways that I changed the endings for the boys and girls in my class. I mean, get real. Do five-year-olds need to hear about the wolf falling through the chimney into a fire at the third little pig's house?

I wanted to tell Miss Lettie, "My, what big scissors you have," but I didn't. I was afraid that she'd answer, "The better to cut you with."

Silly, silly, silly. Too many ridiculous thoughts. My head hurt, and I didn't really care what Miss Lettie was doing.

Jane started humming—not one of the Christmas songs she'd been singing since Halloween. This was an old Patsy Cline song—one of Jane's favorites—"Crazy."

We used that trick in high school. When we wanted to tell each other something we didn't want anyone else to know, we'd hum the melody to a song with words we wanted the other to think. It generally worked. Was Jane telling me that Miss Lettie acted crazy?

Why not? The whole world seemed insane. My mother had six children and died before she raised them while Miss Ellen never had any kids and lived to old age. Amber Buchanan, a good woman who devoted her life to helping other females out of abusive situations, lost her life. Whoever killed Ms. Buchanan dumped her body on *my* front porch under the huge Christmas tree that celebrated the birth of Christ. Then someone attacked Jane and hurt me. Senseless, too, that anyone would steal an infant who was only a few days old and needed his mom and dad.

Wayne says that police officers don't believe in coincidences. It seemed way too coincidental that the home where someone dumped a dead body was the same house where a tall stranger tried to make a corpse out of me—unless the person was one and the same. Unreasonable that the man most likely to have killed Amber Buchanan was locked in jail when Jane and I were attacked. One person violating our home by leaving a corpse and later attacking Jane and me seemed possible. Was someone after me because of my involvement in solving previous murders? Could the corpse under our Christmas tree have been a warning, a threat? But separate, unrelated events? I didn't think so. The whole thing was—yep, crazy.

I lay back, agreeing with Jane that Miss Lettie seemed to be more and more irrational. I didn't like her being here with Jane and me, and her constant talking was maddening. I wished Daddy and Miss Ellen would hurry back. If Miss Lettie kept mumbling and Jane didn't stop humming, I'd soon be crazy myself.

I looked over and saw Miss Lettie drop her yarn and needles on the floor beside the bag. I closed my eyes again and thought about pressing the call button for a nurse. I could ask for something for the throbbing pain in my head, but I was afraid Dr. Donald would want to keep me hospitalized longer if I complained. When would Daddy and Miss Ellen be back? Despite the noise, or maybe to escape it, I dozed off for a few minutes.

"What are you *doing*?" Jane's gasp woke me.

Miss Lettie stood behind my friend, holding Jane's waist-length red pigtail in one hand and those huge scissors in the other. She forced Jane into a headlock and *chop*! The scissors hacked off ten years' growth of Jane's hair—prized locks that had seldom been cut and never artificially colored.

Jane swatted her hand at Miss Lettie and hit the point of the scissors. Blood dripped. I jammed my finger against the call button for the nurse over and over. No one answered on the intercom. I bounded off the bed, bringing my IV pole crashing down to the floor and pulling the needle from my arm. I yanked the tape away, releasing the tubing that held me to the pole. This time, blood didn't drip, it flowed.

Miss Lettie rushed toward me, holding the scissors over her head and cackling as she swung the pointed end at me. I sidestepped her and knocked her off balance onto the floor. As I tried to move away, Miss Lettie locked her teeth into my ankle. I howled in pain. She unclenched her jaws, dropped the scissors, jumped up, and seized me.

She tossed me across the room—literally hurled me through the air like those wrestlers Daddy likes to watch on television. I landed on the recliner. Jane's pillow softened the blow, but my head blurred—dizzy and dazed.

Miss Lettie caught Jane and headlocked her again. She lifted the red braid from the floor and grasped each end of it. She wrapped it around Jane's neck like a garrote, and then twisted, pulling the ends so hard that the muscles stood out in her sinewy arms. Jane thrashed in every direction, trying to pull away. The crazy lady was strong, but Jane's adrenaline must have been sky-high because she snapped her arm straight up and pried one of Miss Lettie's hands off the noose just as I reached them. Jane's elbow hit the old woman's face, and blood gushed from her nose all the way down to her wrinkled chin and throat. Weird thoughts popped into my mind. All three of us were bleeding. Would we create a DNA puzzle for forensics if Miss Lettie succeeded in killing Jane and me?

No time for such ridiculous thoughts. I'd like to say I jumped from the recliner. The truth is that I got up as quickly as possible, but I certainly didn't leap. My head felt like it was turning round and round like that possessed girl in that old movie, *The Exorcist*.

Excruciating pain across the back of my skull didn't stop my weird thoughts. Was I going crazy? Or was the concussion causing these ideas?

Miss Lettie's voice dropped to a whispered growl. "I gotta bone to pick with you, Amber Clark, an axe to grind. My boy would never have left St. Mary if it hadn't been for you. He wouldn't have wrecked his car. He's lying in a box in a cold graveyard, and it's *your* fault."

She reached for Jane, but Jane had positioned herself as far as possible from the sound of the old woman's voice.

"No! No!" Jane wept as she quickly circled the bed, finding her way by clutching the edge of the mattress like an infant holding onto the sides of a playpen.

I managed to get from the recliner to the bed and reach the call button—smacked it as hard as I could.

Miss Lettie walked methodically behind Jane like a wild animal stalking its prey. Her words became slower and more precise.

"You lied to me on your porch and told me it was his idea to break up." Miss Lettie lifted the scissors over her head, ready to stab. Jane turned around and struck out wildly at Miss Lettie. She knocked the scissors to the floor.

"What porch?" Jane sobbed. "I didn't talk to you on the porch, and I never even knew your son."

Miss Lettie seized Jane by the shoulders and spit in her face. She squeezed her arms around Jane as I struggled to pull them apart.

Hate spilled from Miss Lettie's mouth—still slow and particular. "I'm going to kill you, Amber Clark. You couldn't hide from me when you came out your door with that Santa Claus disguise. I knew who you were even before I snatched off your beard and hat. You're the slut who made my Jeffrey Junior so unhappy that he moved away from me."

She managed to hold Jane with one arm while she reached for the braid. "You thought you'd get me when you snatched that string of lights loose from over your door, threatening to tie me up and call the cops, but I fooled you when I took that cord from you. I might be old, but farm work all those years made me strong. You've come back after I choked you with those Christmas lights around your neck, but now I'm going to strangle you to death forever."

I struggled with Miss Lettie, but I couldn't pull her away from Jane. Hair! I grasped a handful of gray hair and yanked as hard as I could. Miss Lettie released her hold on Jane and shoved me across the room like a rag doll. I thrust my arms out and cushioned myself with my hands. No telling what might have happened if my head had hit the wall. Breathless—I couldn't move.

Miss Lettie gripped Jane and wrapped the braid around her throat again. She pulled it tighter and tighter. Jane's face went from bright red to bluish. Miss Lettie released the pigtail and let it drop. Jane collapsed into a limp pile on the floor beside it.

"I howled with laughter when I saw that giant Christmas tree." Miss Lettie's speech changed again—now fast and loud. "I was taking you to Jeffrey Junior at the cemetery, but I couldn't resist leaving you at that house. Nobody was around, so I carried you to the porch. Under the Christmas tree—the perfect place to leave a dead Santa Claus."

She broke into a long peal of maniacal laughter.

"You were just pretending then," she persisted, "but I've killed you for good this time, and now I'm going to stab your friend."

She grabbed the scissors once more and charged me.

The door opened.

Nurses rushed in.

But they weren't at the front of the line.

Daddy was.

★

ON THE TWELFTH DAY OF CHRISTMAS MY TRUE LOVE GAVE TO ME

TWELVE EGGS A'NOGGING

"Have a holly, jolly Christmas." Daddy's voice rang out so loud I could hear him before I went inside and headed toward the delicious smells of the kitchen.

He stood at the table, sounding like Burl Ives and looking like a gray-haired Larry the Cable Guy wearing his bright red "Rudolph the Red-Nosed Reindeer" apron over jeans and a flannel shirt. Years ago, when John gave him the apron, Rudolph's nose lit up, but no one had replaced the battery since it burned out a few years ago.

"Christmas is over," I said as I pulled off my jacket and draped it on the coat rack by the back door.

"It doesn't have to be," Daddy answered. He'd arranged a carton of jumbo brown eggs, a bag of granulated sugar, a quart of whole milk, one of heavy cream, a little bottle of genuine vanilla extract, and a small brown nut in a line beside the large punch bowl that had always been at our house. As a little girl, I'd wondered if that bowl had belonged to my mother.

I simply stood and watched him as silent as that proverbial creature, the mouse who wasn't stirring in "The Night Before Christmas." He placed two medium mixing bowls beside the egg carton and carefully cracked one egg at a time. He visually examined each of them and held it up to his nose, sniffed, then separated the white from the yolk into the two dishes.

"What'cha making?" I asked.

Daddy looked up with a puzzled expression. "What does it

look like I'm making? Eggnog, of course."

"Where's the rum? I've never known you to make eggnog without rum."

"I sent Mike to the red dot store to get a liter of spiced rum." He put the bowl of egg whites on the mixer stand, flipped the switch, and beat them to stiff peaks.

"You don't usually make eggnog except at Christmas. What happened? You just didn't get enough of it then?" I looked around for the bowl of peanuts he usually has in the kitchen, but it was gone. There was, however, a dish of Christmas hard candy.

"No, the truth is that the last dozen days have been terrible. I'm gonna start over—have a new twelve days of Christmas—and I'm beginning with today, which is my new Christmas Day."

He measured one and a half cups of sugar into the punch bowl, then stopped and looked me over, head to toe. "Aside from those black eyes and that hairdo, you look pretty good, considering all things." My new hairstyle could have been called whacked off. I'd tried to trim it, but I hadn't improved it much.

Daddy poured the egg yolks into the sugar and beat them together with a wire whisk. "Where's Frankie? Didn't he come in with you?" he asked.

"He and Jane are outside, talking on the porch. He's so relieved that Jane had fainted and wasn't dead like you thought when you came in the hospital room that he's making all kinds of promises to get a job and rent his own place. I was surprised you sent Frankie to pick us up, knowing how he and Jane have been lately, but he says he's going to prove himself to her." Words poured out of me, but I wasn't thinking about anything except the holly-shaped bowl of hard Christmas candy on the counter. It looked mighty tempting.

"Frankie was out of his mind when he learned what happened yesterday," Daddy said. "He insisted on picking you girls up from the hospital when you called while ago and said you'd been dismissed."

"You could have sent Mike for us."

"I told you. I sent him for rum, and he's gone to get Ellen. She's mighty upset over Miss Lettie's meltdown." He added the milk and heavy cream to the punch bowl, then slowly stirred it into the yolk and sugar mixture with a whisk.

"Meltdown? It's a whole lot more than that. I keep thinking what a waste it is for Amber Buchanan to be dead. She worked so hard to help lots of women, and from what I understand, she didn't dump Jeff Morgan in high school. He dropped her for someone else." I popped a piece of hard candy into my mouth. "Last night I lay in bed thinking about everything and wondering if maybe Patsy Corley was Amber's replacement, but I don't guess we'll ever know that."

"Finding out is as easy as calling your brother John or even asking Wayne. Those three knew everything about each other back then." Daddy measured a tablespoon of vanilla into the bowl, stirred again, and then reached below the cabinet for a tiny metal grater. The nut that had been lying beside the ingredients was exactly what I'd thought it was—nutmeg. The scent of it wafted over the other appetizing aromas as he grated a tiny bit directly into the punch bowl and stirred again. He folded the beaten egg whites into the concoction gently with a spatula.

"Did you know the sheriff learned the rings you found in Amber Buchanan's house were fake? Not even high-quality imitations. They were what we used to call dime store jewelry, but she valued them because they'd belonged to her mother. Amber must have been afraid someone might steal them."

"Wayne hadn't told me that. Amber was probably afraid her husband would take them," I said before adding, "Are you going to add cinnamon?"

"No, I'll put some beside the bowl. Ellen doesn't care for cinnamon."

He dipped a ladle into the punch bowl, spooned some eggnog into a cup, and handed it to me. I took a sip.

"Delicious," I said, "and it will be even better when you add the rum."

"You know I don't like you drinking alcohol. That stuff's smooth and creamy just as it is." I didn't argue with him. I knew, and he probably did too, that I'd sneak more of it after Mike came back.

"I owe you a great big thank-you, Daddy." I stepped forward and hugged him. My daddy isn't very demonstrative and sometimes kind of shrugs out of hugs, but he hugged me back. A big, tight hug.

"You don't owe me anything, Calamine. When I heard you scream, I just about knocked the nurses down rushing to your room. My heart almost stopped when I saw what was happening. I don't know what I would do if I lost you. I might even turn out as crazy as Miss Lettie did."

He poured himself a small cup of eggnog and drank it down like a shooter. "I know I was more frightened than you were." He smiled.

"What makes you think that?" I asked. "I was terrified." I held my cup out for more.

"You didn't throw up like you've always done when you're scared." He filled both of our cups. Good thing it didn't have the rum in it yet.

I took another sip and explained, "I was about to upchuck all over when you came through the door, and then I knew I'd be safe."

"I always swore I'd never hit a female," he said after he swallowed, "and that's the first and only time in my life I ever struck a woman, but I'd a' killed her to save you."

"I know it was hard on you, Daddy. You were kind of sweet on Miss Lettie, weren't you? It seemed like that to me when you were so disappointed she didn't come for New Year's dinner."

"Miss Lettie? You thought I was interested in Miss Lettie?" He guffawed. "It's not Miss Lettie that attracts me. It's her friend, Ellen. That sweet little woman is kind and thoughtful and everything I like in a female. Besides, she's about the only woman I've talked to since your mama died who didn't seem jealous. I told her I'd be making my first wife's Sunday cake today. Know what she said? She smiled and said she'd look forward to it."

"Did you say *first* wife?" I asked.

"Oh, you know what I mean. You never can tell, but I've invited Ellen over for dinner tonight because she's so distraught about her friend. She agreed to stay for music, too. She likes both country and bluegrass."

That's about all Daddy plays, though he'll throw in a folk tune once in a while, and sometimes he shuts himself up in his room and listens to old jazz records on his turntable.

"At least Miss Lettie's not in jail. Maybe they really can help her in that mental hospital." I couldn't resist another piece of candy. This one tasted strawberry.

"Let's hope so. Meanwhile, I've got to get busy cooking up some treats to go with this eggnog tonight and finishing up dinner."

"I'm sorry it all turned out like it did anyway."

"Why should you be unhappy that you closed another case?"

"I didn't solve it. I'd realized that Miss Lettie was unstable, and I may have put it all together in time if she hadn't attacked Jane again when she did, but I hadn't realized how disturbed she was until she chopped off Jane's hair."

"You weren't thinking straight after Lettie cracked that tree over your head. It's sad that Amber Buchanan died, but did you know Otis and Odell are donating a casket and service for her, and Safe Sister is contributing a grave site?"

"No, I didn't know that. I can understand Safe Sister, but why the Middletons? They didn't know her before."

"Otis said it had something to do with you being worried that Amber Buchanan would be like some carnival man in North Carolina. Is he talking about that fellow you met at the fair?"

I chuckled. "No, he's talking about a body that was kept for years because no one paid for services."

"I'm just glad Lettie will get the help she's probably needed for years." Daddy filled his cup again. His turn to chuckle. "How's Jane dealing with having that long hair she's grown for years chopped off?"

"I shaped it for her. She actually looks cute, kind of pixieish. You act like Miss Lettie getting help solves everything, but there's still a baby missing."

"No, there isn't. After they arrested Miss Lettie, the sheriff got a search warrant for her house to look for evidence. They found the Bledsoe infant in a crib in Lettie's basement."

He lifted the lid off a pot on the stove and stirred the butter beans.

"Was the little boy all right?"

"She hadn't hurt him, but she'd neglected him and finally

forgot he was there. The pediatrician says he'll be fine, but much more time alone and neglected would have been bad, really bad."

Whew! The word gusted out of my mouth like a hurricane wind. "I'd hate for anything to happen to that little fellow. I was there when he was born."

"I know. Pork Chop told us all about it. His wife's so proud of him that she says she'll start feeding him breakfast again."

"You still haven't explained why you're making eggnog."

"I'm making a whole Christmas dinner. Got one of Buster Gwyn's turkeys in the oven. I told him I wanted one that won a race, but he probably sold me a loser."

"I don't understand."

"Have you ever seen that old movie *City Slickers*? One of the men says his life is a 'do-over.' That's what I've decided to do. We're having a Christmas do-over."

I was about to ask him if that meant we'd all be receiving more gifts from him when my ringtone sounded.

"Callie Parrish here," I answered.

"It's so good to hear you." No mistaking the smooth tone of Jetendre Patel. I needed a minute to think of a response. My heart sped up, but I wondered if he'd called to say goodbye.

"Good to hear you, too." I said. Daddy kept right on cooking.

"As Ricky Ricardo would say, 'I got some 'splainin' to do.'"

"Go right ahead. Did you meet someone else, or did you think we were moving too fast?" Okay, I said it in a snarky tone, but sometimes my feelings control my mouth. That's not all bad because my brain certainly doesn't always do a good job of it.

"The last time we spoke, I planned to call you back after closing the restaurant when I got home that night. I haven't gotten there yet."

"What do you mean?"

"I was mugged while making the night deposit at the bank. I'm in the hospital. Been here since then. I was in a medically induced coma some of the time, but I'm alert and thinking straight now—thinking about you. I hope you didn't run off and marry someone else while I was unconscious."

"No," I laughed, "but I was worried about you." I didn't add that I'd been as angry as I'd been concerned.

"I want to come see you as soon as I'm out of here." His voice was *so* smooth. "I hope things have been better. The last time we talked, you'd found a corpse under your Christmas tree."

"It was interesting," I answered, "very interesting."

"May I call you later?" he asked. "My doctor just came in."

"Yes, call me tonight." I felt like I was grinning all over when I disconnected.

"Who was that?" Daddy asked. I know that's rude and he knows it's rude, but my dad thinks my business is his business no matter how old I am.

"J. T. Patel, that man I met at the fair."

"The one who owns the curry place in Florida?"

"It's not just a curry restaurant, and he also owns a major food concession with Middleton's Midway." For some reason, Daddy's question made me jump to the defensive.

"He's not one of those people who think cows are sacred, is he?"

"I've never asked him that, but he serves all-beef frankfurters in his corn dogs, and he wished me a Merry Christmas." I picked one of the green and white swirly pieces out of the candy dish and slipped it in my mouth.

"Well, ask him next time you talk to him, and don't eat all that candy. I bought it for Ellen. She likes it."

"Then why did you put it out here where everyone can get to it?"

"I didn't know you'd gobble it up." He slipped two oven mitts over his hands and pulled a steaming roaster pan from the oven. I love the smell of roasted turkey.

"I can't believe it." I sounded like a little girl who'd just found the doll she wanted under her Christmas tree instead of a grown woman who'd found a corpse there. "I didn't have plans for New Year's Eve, and now I have three men who want to date me. My life is raining men." I pondered that for a moment. "That would be a good song title. Maybe Mike will make up a song called 'It's Raining Men' for me."

"No need." Daddy grinned. "There's already an old song named that. Look it up on YouTube."

"Is it bluegrass or country?" I asked. Daddy just laughed.

I went to Daddy's computer in his room and listened to "It's Raining Men" on YouTube. Buh-leeve me, I love that song, and it's definitely not country or bluegrass.

When I returned to the kitchen, Mike and Miss Ellen were coming through the back door.

She wasn't carrying a casserole dish. For years Daddy's friends have teased him about the "Casserole Parade" after my mother died. Around here, widowed and divorced ladies carry peach cobblers, homemade fudge, and especially chicken casseroles to men whose wives die. It's an indication they want to become friends—better friends, maybe even more than friends. My three older brothers say Daddy didn't cook a meal for his first year of widowhood because there was always some woman over at the house babying us kids and feeding the whole family. My personal thought is that they must have been desperate to chase a man with six kids all under twelve years old. Or, who knows? Maybe Daddy was a hunk back then.

Mike set a liter of spiced rum on the table beside the punch bowl. I noticed Miss Ellen might not have brought a casserole, but she held a bag from the liquor store in one hand. She placed it on the counter and took out two bottles—one sherry and one top-shelf bourbon. She smiled at Daddy and said, "I hope it's all right to put these here. You said not to cook anything to go with dinner, so I brought something for the music session or you can save it for another time."

"You're one sweet lady," Daddy said and gave Miss Ellen a little hug. He grinned.

Mike rolled his eyes, but it was okay because neither Daddy nor Miss Ellen was looking at us. They were gazing at each other like two kids during their first infatuation. My brain still felt discombobulated as a result of the concussion. Poetry popped into my mind, specifically that famous line from Ogden Nash: *Candy is dandy, but liquor is quicker.*

CHAPTER THIRTEEN

Everyone who's ever read a Callie Parrish Mystery knows that I never write a Chapter Thirteen because I think the number thirteen brings bad luck. Since there are already twelve chapters, I debated skipping over thirteen and calling this chapter fourteen, but instead I'll call it:

AFTERWORD

When I decided to write about what happened when I found Santa Claus dead under my Christmas tree, it kind of worried me that everything happened *after* the body was found on Christmas night.

I went to my now favorite quick reference, Wikipedia, to check, and found that the song "The Twelve Days of Christmas" refers to the twelve days *after* Christmas, which was a lot more suited to this story than a nursery rhyme title, so I tied the chapter titles to Mike's version of the song. Mike sings it all the time. I won't write out all the lyrics, but I'll give enough for you to sing it if you want. Everyone knows the pattern. It begins with the first verse:

> On the first day of Christmas,
> My true love gave to me,
> A corpse under the Christmas tree.
> The second verse is:
> On the second day of Christmas,
> My true love gave to me,
> Two broken hearts,
> And a corpse under the Christmas tree.

Each additional verse adds a new present and then repeats all the previous gifts. At the end, it goes like this:

On the twelfth day of Christmas,
My true love gave to me,
Twelve eggs a'nogging,
Eleven axes grinding,
Ten turkeys trotting,
Nine guns a'smoking,
Eight collards cooking,
Seven doggies howling,
Six tongues a'wagging,
Five stolen rings,
Four falling flakes,
Three red wreaths,
Two broken hearts,
And a corpse under the Christmas tree.

I just heard about a scientific study that determined that carrying cell phones in bras increases chance of breast cancer. I'm moving mine right now and hope you will, too, if you've been keeping yours conveniently between the girls.

THE END

RECIPES FROM FRANKIE

By Frankie Parrish

Not being much of a reader, I never read a cozy in my life, but some folks call my sister Callie's stories that kind of books. I also understand that a lot of popular cozies include recipes. I talked to Callie about adding some throughout this book, but she flatly refused. That's not surprising because Callie's cooking is—well, it's not so good.

Pa, now, is top-notch in the kitchen. Being unemployed and dumped again by my girlfriend at the time Callie was writing *A Corpse Under the Christmas Tree*, I took it upon myself to watch and write down how Pa cooks the foods Callie wrote about in the book. Of course, Pa triples and sometimes quadruples these recipes, but I doubt that Callie's readers want to cook the quantities Pa does. Readers will notice that I seldom give a number of servings for each recipe because I never figured out the number of normal servings compared to the portions that Pa's big, strapping sons (including me) eat all the time.

PA'S RECIPES

BOURBON BALLS

I've eaten lots of these made with rum or whiskey, and they were all good, but Pa always makes them with bourbon—his good drinking bourbon. He cautions, "It's like wine. If you wouldn't drink it, don't cook with it." These Bourbon Balls aren't hard to make, but they go so fast that Pa always doubles this recipe. He also warns, "If you're gonna munch on many Bourbon Balls anywhere but at home, better get you a designated driver."

PA'S NO-BAKE BOURBON BALLS

Ingredients

12 ounces gingersnaps, completely crushed*
1 cup confectioners' sugar
1½ cups finely chopped pecans**
¼ cup light corn syrup
2 tablespoons unsweetened cocoa
½ cup bourbon
½ cup granulated sugar

Directions

Stir everything together except the granulated sugar in a large mixing bowl. Shape into one-inch balls. Pour granulated sugar in a paper plate with an edge. Roll each ball in the sugar, then store in an airtight container for up to two weeks. These are actually better a day or so after making them, but they don't freeze well.

*Pa has also made these using different kinds of cookies—vanilla wafers or animal crackers, but he prefers gingersnaps or sometimes graham crackers. Regardless, be sure to crush them real fine. The way he does it is to put the cookies in a gallon-size zipper bag. It needs to be big because the sandwich-size bags are thinner plastic. Close the bag real tight and use a rolling pin to crush the cookies inside.

**The recipe calls for pecans, which Pa usually has from his own pecan trees, but if he has to buy nuts for them, he uses walnuts because they're cheaper.

AUNT CUTIE'S PEANUT BUTTER COOKIES

Pa got this recipe from his sister who was called Cutie Pie when they were growing up. She lived in Eastover, South Carolina, and died when I was a little boy, but I do remember Aunt Cutie as we kids called her. She was a very sweet lady, and Pa makes these cookies to honor her.

PA'S PEANUT BUTTER BLOSSOMS

Ingredients

½ cup shortening
½ cup peanut butter
1 cup granulated sugar
3 tablespoons molasses
1 egg
1 teaspoon vanilla
1½ cups sifted all-purpose flour
¾ teaspoon baking soda
¼ teaspoon salt
Additional sugar for coating cookies
48 Hershey's Kisses, unwrapped

Directions

Preheat oven to 375° F. Cream shortening, peanut butter, sugar, molasses, egg and vanilla. Sift together dry ingredients. Blend into creamed mixture. Shape in 1-inch balls or use cookie press. Roll in granulated sugar if using balls, sprinkle with sugar if using press. Place 2 inches apart on ungreased cookie sheet. Bake at 375° for 10 to 12 minutes. Gently place and press a candy in the center of each cookie. Cool slightly; remove from pan. Makes 4 dozen.

PA'S VERSION OF WILLENE'S SUNDAY CAKE

Pa told Callie that this is the cake our mother, Willene, cooked for every Sunday dinner. I don't remember that and, of course, neither does Callie, but John says he remembers her cooking this cake except that she never used a cake mix while Pa does.

Ingredients

Yellow cake made from your favorite scratch recipe or from a cake mix
2 cups white granulated sugar

1 cup unsweetened cocoa powder
½ cup milk
½ cup butter or margarine
2 teaspoons vanilla extract
1 cup chopped pecan pieces
1 cup pecan halves

Directions

Bake cake in four layers as directed by recipe or on box. Set aside to cool. Combine sugar, cocoa powder, milk, butter, and vanilla in a saucepan. Stirring constantly, bring to a rolling boil over medium high heat. Cook for 1 minute continuing to stir. Remove from heat and beat icing for 3 minutes, preferably with an electric mixer. Mixture will cool to spreading consistency. Use ¾ cup frosting between first and second layers. Sprinkle with ⅓ cup chopped pecans. Repeat between second and third layers and then between third and fourth layers. This should leave about 1¾ cup frosting to spread over top and sides of cake. Place four pecan halves in an X-shape on the center of the top. Use halves to make concentric circles on top of cake.

BRUNSWICK STEW

When anybody's freezer goes out in St. Mary, you can be sure they'll be making Brunswick Stew and inviting all their friends and relatives over for a huge chow-down. That's because it can be made with any meat—deer, duck, squirrels, rabbits or with pork, beef, or chicken and is usually cooked with butter beans (tiny green lima beans), corn, and okra. These are things most people in St. Mary put in their freezers during the year. When the power's out or they forgot to pay the electric bill, they multiply the ingredients as much as they want, dump them into a huge pot and make Brunswick Stew. This thick stew is served with cornbread or biscuits.

Brunswick, Georgia, and Brunswick County, Virginia, both claim to be the home place of Brunswick Stew. You can look it up on the Internet. My Gullah friends add rice, too, but nobody in our family does.

PA'S BRUNSWICK STEW

Ingredients

3 pounds stewed and deboned meat*
1½ cups broth from meat
½ cup chopped onion
2 cups diced potatoes (with or without peelings)
2 cups butter beans (fresh, frozen or canned and drained)
2 cups corn (fresh, frozen or canned and drained)
2 cups chopped okra (fresh or frozen)
2 bay leaves optional
1 28-ounce can of chopped tomatoes including juice**
Salt and pepper

Directions

Stew the meat and onion on low heat in just enough water to cover it. When the meat begins to fall off the bones, turn off the heat and let it cool. Remove the bones and shred the meat with two forks. (This will look like pulled pork barbecue, and you can use that, too, if you have it.) Combine the meat, broth, vegetables and bay leaves in a large pot. Bring to a low boil. Reduce the heat. Cover, and simmer for at least an hour or maybe all day. After it's cooked for a while, taste, and then salt and pepper however much you like. Some cooks add a little prepared barbecue sauce, but Pa doesn't. If you see the bay leaves when serving the stew, dip them out. Otherwise, whoever finds them in their bowl can throw them away.

*Pa occasionally makes this with squirrel or rabbit, but he prefers to mix chicken, pork, and beef together.

**Pa peels and chops fresh tomatoes or uses home-canned stewed tomatoes if he has them. Squish them through your fingers when you add them, and it makes the stew a bit better than having chunks of tomato in it.

OYSTERIZERS

This is included as one of Pa's recipes because he always makes a couple of batches of them on New Year's Eve, but he got the recipe from Rizzie. She had appetizers called Rumaki at a Chinese restaurant in Charleston several years ago. Rumaki are small chicken livers (or halves of large ones) marinated six hours or overnight in the refrigerator. The marinade is drained off and discarded before you put a slice of water chestnut beside each piece of chicken liver. Wrap a half slice of bacon around the liver and water chestnut and push a wooden toothpick through it to hold the Rumaki together. These can be broiled or grilled. Make them extra Southern by frying in a beer batter.

Rizzie made up her own version of Rumaki, which she calls Oysterizers. When Pa tasted them, he insisted she give him the recipe. Rizzie adds garlic, ginger, brown sugar, and sherry to soy sauce to make the marinade. Pa just buys a bottle of prepared teriyaki sauce.

PA'S OYSTERIZERS

Ingredients

1 pound small shucked oysters
½ cup teriyaki sauce or "doctored" soy sauce
1 five-ounce can sliced water chestnuts
14 - 16 slices bacon, cut into halves
Optional:
1 cup beer
1 cup plain flour
1 beaten egg
Vegetable oil for frying

Directions

Drain the oysters and marinate them in teriyaki sauce for a half hour. Pour off the marinade and throw it away. Place a slice of water chestnut beside an oyster, then wrap it in bacon and stick a toothpick through it to hold everything in place. Repeat this until all oysters are used. Broil or grill until bacon is crispy or fry in beer batter. Make the batter by opening a can of beer and pouring one cup into a bowl. Drink the rest of the beer. Stir the flour and beaten egg into the beer and beat until smooth. Pa serves these with extra teriyaki sauce, shrimp cocktail sauce, and/or horseradish.

COLLARDS

First off, I don't understand why cookbooks call them "collard greens." They aren't like turnips, which can be cooked as greens, or turnip roots, or greens with diced roots stirred in. The only edible parts of collard plants are the green leaves. My ex-wife considered herself a gourmet cook and collected recipes from television, books, and the Internet. When she cooked collards, she put onions, garlic, vinegar, beer, molasses, and some other stuff in them. They weren't bad, but they didn't taste like collards. Different strokes for different folks, but Pa's collards are simple and the best I've ever eaten. We have them a lot when they're in season and always on New Year's Day. Except for the fact Pa likes to cook a lot of bunches at one time, here's how Pa does it:

PA'S COLLARDS

Ingredients

½ pound smoked meat (ham hocks, smoked turkey wings, or smoked pork neck bones)*
1 large bunch fresh collards
Salt and pepper
Dash of garlic powder
1 tablespoon sugar—brown or white granulated

Directions

Ham hocks are the bony ends of smoked hams. If you live up north or out west and your grocer doesn't stock them, use any smoked meat that's available. The ham bone you stuck in your freezer after Christmas dinner is also good for this. Add the meat to 3 quarts boiling water. Reduce the heat and simmer for 1 hour while cleaning the collards. When cool, take the meat out of the broth, remove all bones, and cut or tear the meat into bite-sized pieces. Return the meat to broth.

Wash the collards several times in salted cold water, being

careful to rinse away all dirt or sand. Leave the salt out of the last rinse. Remove the stems that run down the center of each leaf by holding the leaf in one hand and stripping both sides with the other hand. Discard the stems.

Stack six leaves on top of each other. Roll them into a tight roll, and then cut each roll into ½ to 1 inch-thick slices. Place greens into a pot with the meat and broth. Cover and cook 45 to 60 minutes, stirring off and on. Taste before adding salt and pepper to suit yourself. Be sure to taste first, because the smoked meat adds saltiness. Collards are done when they are tender but not mushy. Set bottles of hot sauce and pepper vinegar beside the collards. Some Southerners stir in bacon drippings or a spoon of butter, but Pa didn't do this even before his heart attack. Don't discard extra liquid. It's called potlikker and is delicious. Some folks actually sip it out of a cup like hot tea or drink it like a tonic. We like it poured over chunks of cornbread in a soup bowl.

*The degree of smokiness in smoked meat varies. Try to get meat that is heavily smoked. Pa prefers smoked neck bones. Some cooks leave the bones in. Pa removes the bones and chops the meat back into the broth before adding the collard leaves.

**Some Southerners chop the stems up into the pot. Pa wouldn't be caught dead with a stem in his collards.

Personally, I love the scent of collards cooking because it means there's gonna be a whole mess of something good to eat, but some people don't like the smell. Rizzie told Pa that putting a whole washed, unshelled pecan in the pot will make the smell less noticeable. I don't know if that's true because Pa won't try it. He likes the odor, too.

HOPPIN' JOHN

No self-respecting Southerner would let New Year's Day pass without eating Hoppin' John. A common saying is, "Eat poor that day, eat rich the rest of the year. Rice for riches and peas for peace," but Pa always says, "Eat peas for coins and collards for folding money during the coming year." So far as eating poor, I guess if Hoppin' John was the entire meal, it might be poor in price, but not in taste. Around our house, Hoppin' John is only a small part of the New Year's Day feast that includes lots of collards, sweet potatoes, other winter vegetables, and some kind of pork. When he was younger, Pa sometimes roasted a whole pig outdoors for New Year's Day. Now he usually cooks pork chops or a big fresh ham. Pa calls fresh ham "green ham." All that means is that it's not cured. When I was a little boy, I thought he was talking about the meat in my favorite book, Green Eggs and Ham *by Dr. Seuss.*

PA'S HOPPIN' JOHN*

Ingredients

2 cups dried black-eyed peas
1 pound meaty smoked ham hocks (or leftover Christmas ham)
1 medium chopped onion
4 cups chicken stock
2 cups long-grain uncooked white rice
Salt and pepper
¼ teaspoon red pepper flakes or a splash of hot sauce

Directions

Wash the peas in a colander and pick through them for stems, shells, or pebbles. Cover the peas with cold water in a pot and soak them overnight or, if you're in a hurry, put the pot with cold water and peas on the stove and bring the water to a boil. Cover the pot, remove from heat, and let it sit for 1 hour. Drain the peas and discard the soak water. Add onion and chicken stock to peas. Bring to a boil over medium high heat; reduce heat to medium low and cook covered for 1½ to 2 hours until peas are tender. Do not boil to cook because the peas will bust if you do. Remove meat from the pot. Take out the bones and cut the meat into small pieces. Add the meat, rice, and chicken broth to the peas. Put a lid on the pot and cook on low until the broth is absorbed and the rice is tender. Remove the Hoppin' John from the heat, taste, and add salt, pepper, and pepper flakes or hot sauce to suit yourself.

*Some cooks prefer to cook the black-eyed peas and rice separately. They serve the peas on top of the rice. Also, some Southerners put a washed dime in the peas. Superstition is that whoever gets the dime will be lucky all year. With the current inflation, a quarter might be better.

The stories behind names in the South are frequently interesting, so I looked up the origin of the name "Hoppin' John." Among other legends, the name is said to come from children hopping around the table in eagerness before eating peas and rice, from a man named John who was so excited that he hopped to the table for peas and rice, or from someone who invited a visitor to "Hop in, John," and stay for a supper of peas and rice. The one I like best is that back in the 1840s a man named John sold peas and rice cooked together. Because he was crippled, they called him "Hoppin' John."

CORNBREAD

Cornbread is perfect with many Southern dishes including Brunswick Stew, Collards, and Hoppin' John. Although there are many excellent cornbread mixes on the market, Pa refuses to use a mix. In the South, we like a slight sweetness in our cornbread. If you don't, just leave out the sugar.

PA'S CORN BREAD

(Not from a box or bag)

Ingredients

½ cup butter or margarine
1 cup self-rising cornmeal
1 cup self-rising flour
1 teaspoon baking powder
1 tablespoon sugar
2 large or 3 medium eggs
3 tablespoons vegetable oil

½ cup buttermilk*
½ cup whole milk

Directions

Preheat the oven to 400° F. Put butter or margarine in the bottom of a dark, heavy iron skillet and set it into the oven just long enough to melt, then remove and put it on a trivet or hot pad. Mix the first four ingredients together. Beat eggs, oil, and both kinds of milk together in a separate bowl, then add the mixture to the dry ingredients. Pour the cornbread batter into the skillet on top of the melted butter or margarine. Bake 30 minutes or until the top is golden brown and a toothpick inserted in the center comes out clean. This is good with lots of stews and vegetables, and hot or cold covered with butter.

*If you don't have buttermilk, make a substitute by putting 1½ teaspoons white vinegar or lemon juice in a measuring cup. Add regular milk to bring to ½ cup. Let sit for 5 minutes, then use just like buttermilk.

PA'S FAVORITE BANANA NUT BREAD

MS. GLORIA WISE'S PINEAPPLE BANANA NUT BREAD

Pa got this recipe from Miss Ellen who had copied it from her cousin Gloria Wise's cookbook.

Ingredients

1 cup self-rising flour
¼ teaspoon cinnamon
1 egg
⅓ cup vegetable oil
⅔ cup granulated sugar
⅔ cup mashed banana (about 1 medium)
½ teaspoon vanilla extract
8 ounces crushed pineapple, drained

¼ to ½ cup chopped pecans or walnuts

Directions

Preheat the oven to 350° F. Combine flour and cinnamon in a medium size mixing bowl. Stir egg, oil, sugar, banana, and vanilla in a separate bowl. When mixed well, add to the dry ingredients and stir until moistened. Fold in the pineapple and nuts with a spatula. Pour bread batter into two greased and floured 5¾x3x2-inch loaf pans to make mini loaves or into a regular loaf pan for one loaf. Bake for 40 to 45 minutes. Stick a toothpick in the center of one of the loaves. If it comes out clean, it's done. Remove from the oven and cool in the pans for 5 minutes and then on wire racks.

RIZZIE'S GULLAH RECIPES

Callie met Rizzie Profit and her brother Tyrone when she and Jane went to a bluegrass festival on the recently developed part of Surcie Island in *Hey, Diddle, Diddle, THE CORPSE AND THE FIDDLE*. Since then, Jane and the Parrish family have become close friends with the Profit family, and Rizzie has opened the Gastric Gullah Grill where folks on the coast of South Carolina eat some of the finest Gullah food around.

The word "Gullah" refers to a Carolina Low Country African-American culture—a language, a cuisine, a people, and their customs. Some authorities believe that the culture survived from days of slavery because of their long-time isolation on the coastal islands. Much of their knowledge and talents—everything from food gathering and preparation, use of herbal medicines, songs and stories in Gullah dialect, worship customs, and the intricate art of basket-weaving—is still seen on the coast.

Gullah food is based on cooking what was available to them way back when they came from Africa. Since they lived on the coast and its islands, their dishes include a lot of seafood. Recipes are characterized by one-pot dishes with seafood or game meats as well as staples of African cuisine—rice, sweet potatoes, okra, and peanuts.

To sum up Rizzie, she's Gullah and gorgeous as well as being a fantastic cook. After she learned I was writing out some of Pa's recipes, she offered to share some of hers if I would include *her* recipe for what's known around St. Mary by three different names —Beaufort Stew or Frogmore Stew or Low Country Stew—and made by dozens of different recipes though the basic ingredients are the same. I jumped at the chance. Rizzie says *bittle* is the Gullah word for food, so here are recipes for some of my favorite *bittle* I eat at Gastric Gullah Grill.

LOW COUNTRY OR BEAUFORT OR FROGMORE STEW

All three of these stews are basically shrimp, smoked sausage, potatoes, corn on the cob, and onion cooked in water seasoned with commercial crab and shrimp boil seasoning. The trick is to add the ingredients in a timed sequence that makes everything prepared exactly right with nothing overcooked.

Are there frogs in Frogmore Stew? None that I know of. The name Frogmore, like Beaufort, refers to a town on the coast of South Carolina. Rizzie cooks this in a humongous pot at the restaurant, but you can reduce the quantity by dividing the amounts in halves or quarters.

RIZZIE'S LOW COUNTRY BEAUFORT FROGMORE STEW

Ingredients

Water to fill large pot half full
3 cans of your favorite beer
1 bag of Old Bay Seafood Seasoning or ¼ cup other commercial seafood boil seasoning
4 or 5 pounds small red potatoes or quartered larger potatoes, not peeled, but scrubbed clean
2 pounds smoked sausage, cut into 2-inch pieces (use Andouille if you have it)
6 ears corn, cut into halves
4 pounds medium or large shrimp with heads removed, but not peeled

Optional: 4 pounds whole crabs, cleaned and broken into quarters. (Soft shell crabs are fantastic when in season.)

Directions

Bring the water to low boil, add beer and seafood seasoning. Add potatoes and cook 10 minutes. Add sausage and cook 5 more minutes. Add corn and crab and cook another 5 minutes. Remove one potato, one piece of sausage, one ear of corn, and one piece of crab. Check each for doneness. Return them to the pot. When everything else is almost done, drop in the shrimp and cook for 3 more minutes. Drain the water and discard it. Pour the food onto a picnic table covered with paper or into large restaurant pans. Serve on paper plates with seafood cocktail sauce. Most folks want sweet ice tea or cold beer with this stew.

Rizzie's stew is different from lots of others because she uses beer in the water and she likes to add crab. Some people use shrimp with the heads on while others prefer cleaned and deveined shrimp. Rizzie removes the heads because sometimes tourists don't like seeing them in their stew, but she prefers for her guests to shell the shrimp so they won't become tough while cooking. This is the way she makes the stew for Gastric Gullah Grill, but at her house, she sometimes adds whole crawfish. She also jokes that the next time someone asks her about Frogmore Stew, she's going to add some frog legs to the pot.

RIZZIE'S GULLAH SEASONING

The distinctive taste of many Gullah foods comes from a combination of salt, pepper, garlic, onion, and sometimes coriander or fresh cilantro. When frying, broiling, or grilling, Rizzie sprinkles her own homemade seasoning on meat. It's made of equal parts of salt, pepper, minced or powdered garlic, and minced or powdered onion. To that, she sometimes adds 1 tablespoon of paprika per cup and ½ tablespoon of coriander.

RIZZIE'S GULLAH OKRA RICE

Ingredients

2 cups frozen cut okra or fresh okra sliced about ½ inch thick with stalk ends discarded
2 tablespoons Rizzie's Gullah seasoning
1 pound skinless chicken pieces or ½ skinned chicken
½ cup vegetable oil
1 medium onion, chopped
2 small to medium tomatoes, diced
1 bell pepper, diced
¼ pound Andouille or other smoked sausage, diced
Another two tablespoons of vegetable oil
4 cups chicken broth
2 cups uncooked white rice (preferably long-grain)

Directions

Thaw the okra if it's frozen. Slice it if it's fresh. Set it aside. Sprinkle the chicken with Rizzie's Gullah seasoning and cook it in a heavy or stick-free skillet, covered, on medium heat in ½ cup vegetable oil until cooked through and browned. Bring the chicken broth to a boil in a medium-size sauce pan. Add rice, cover, and cook on medium low for 10 minutes without looking or stirring. (Cooks who just have to look can use a tight-fitting glass lid on the sauce pan.) Remove the chicken from the skillet and set it aside to cool. After 10 minutes, turn off the heat beneath the rice pan. Do not move the pot, uncover, or stir for 10 more minutes. While rice cooks, if there is oil remaining in the frying pan, continue. If not, add 2 tablespoons of oil to the skillet, and then stir in the sausage pieces, onion, and okra. Stir fry over medium heat about 5 minutes until onion is barely translucent and okra is no longer stiff, but not soggy. Add tomatoes, and bell pepper to the skillet and remove it from the heat. Remove the bones and chop the chicken into bite size pieces. Stir the chicken and vegetable-sausage mixture into the rice. Fluff with a fork.

Rizzie likes to use okra in one-pot meals, but she says her favorite way to prepare and eat okra is the way her Maum made it when Rizzie was a little girl. She told me, *Maum would go out to our garden in the morning and cut a basket full of okra. She wore gloves because okra kind of stings your fingers. She brought it into the house and washed the okra and laid it out on a clean towel, but now you could use paper towels.*

After the okra had dried from its bath, she cut the stalk ends off and sliced each pod into pieces about ½-inch long. She poured just a little bacon grease or oil in a cast iron skillet and turned the heat to medium high. Then she stirred the okra around until the edges turned brown. If she had a lot of okra, she'd fry it in more than one batch. You don't want to overcrowd the skillet.

You can eat deep-fried, breaded okra, but it won't touch Maum's okra. She'd sprinkle a little salt on the cooked okra just before she served it.

RIZZIE'S FRESH TOMATO GULLAH PIE

Ingredients

1 unbaked pie shell (homemade, frozen, or refrigerated roll-out)
2 tablespoons evaporated milk
4 cups firm ripe tomatoes, sliced (peeling is optional)
1½ teaspoons salt
⅛ teaspoon pepper
¼ to ½ teaspoon dried tarragon
⅓ cup mayonnaise*
⅓ cup grated Parmesan cheese

Directions

Preheat the oven to 450° F. Line the pie plate with the shell unless the shell is already in a tin-foil pie dish. Crimp the edges and brush the pastry with evaporated milk. Bake the shell for 5 minutes at 450° and remove from oven. Reduce oven temperature to 350°. Lay the sliced tomatoes in the pie shell, sprinkling each layer with salt, pepper, and tarragon. Stir the cheese and mayonnaise together and spoon the mixture over the tomatoes, spreading it out as much as possible. Bake 35 to 45 minutes at 350° or until the tomatoes are cooked and the top is light brown.

*After several phone calls and e-mails, I am giving in and

stating officially that the mayonnaise should be Duke's even though I'm not being paid for the promotion. Many Southerners don't consider anything but Duke's as "real" mayonnaise, while northerners praise Hellman's, and those of us on budgets buy whatever is on sale that weekend.

At a McCormick, SC, Friends of the Library book-signing, they served refreshments made from recipes on the website. They made tiny tomato pies in miniature tart pans creating a tasty as well as beautiful appetizer.

OLA BELLE'S SWEET POTATO PONE

Pone is a cross between bread and pudding. It's a Gullah dish, but Rizzie got this version from a lady named Ola Belle who had nine children who loved Potato Pone.

Ingredients

3 cups peeled, grated raw sweet potatoes
2 cups granulated sugar
½ cup soft margarine or butter
2 eggs
¼ cup cream or evaporated milk
3 tablespoons flour
1 teaspoon vanilla extract

Directions

Preheat the oven to 350° F. Cream the butter and sugar together. Add the eggs, vanilla, and cream or milk. Beat lightly. Add the sweet potatoes and flour. Do not beat, just blend. Spray a 9x13-inch baking dish with cooking oil. Spoon the mixture into the baking dish and bake at 350° until lightly browned on top and not squiggly in the middle (about an hour). It's done when a toothpick inserted in the middle comes out clean.) Cool before cutting into squares.

The McCormick Friends of the Library served Sweet Potato Pone as finger food by cutting it into 1-inch squares.

RIZZIE'S GULLAH SQUASH

Ingredients

3 slices bacon
1 medium onion, sliced
1 bell pepper, julienned
4 medium yellow squash or 2 medium yellow squash and 2 medium zucchini, sliced
1 teaspoon salt
¼ teaspoon black pepper
¼ teaspoon dried rosemary

Directions

Fry bacon in a non-stick skillet or cast-iron skillet. Remove the bacon and set aside to drain on paper towel. Sauté the onion and bell pepper in the bacon drippings. Put squash in medium saucepan. Sprinkle with salt, pepper, and rosemary. Pour onion, bell pepper, and bacon drippings over squash. Stir. Cover and cook on medium low heat for 15 minutes, stirring occasionally. At Christmas, Rizzie uses half a green bell pepper and half a red bell pepper in this dish. Crumble the reserved cooked bacon on top of the squash in the serving bowl.

RIZZIE'S SHRIMP SLIDERS

Ingredients

1 pound raw shrimp, medium or large
¾ cup fine cornmeal
¾ cup flour, plain or self-rising
1 tablespoon Gullah or Cajun seasoning
1 teaspoon salt
2 eggs, beaten
Peanut oil for frying
Remoulade sauce
½ head of iceberg or Romaine lettuce, shredded

2 - 3 tomatoes, peeled and sliced ¼ inch thick
1 medium onion, sliced as thin as possible
8 dinner rolls (Hawaiian rolls are great!)

Ingredients for Remoulade
¼ cup mustard, preferably Creole
1¼ cups mayonnaise
1 teaspoon pickle juice
1 teaspoon hot sauce
1 tablespoon sweet paprika
1 large clove of garlic, minced and smashed
1 teaspoon Gullah or Cajun seasoning
1 tablespoon prepared horseradish sauce

Directions for Remoulade

You may buy ready-made remoulade or make your own by mixing all the ingredients together in a bowl and setting it aside for flavors to blend while preparing the shrimp.

Directions for Shrimp

Peel and devein the shrimp. Remove their heads and tails. Wash and set aside. Mix cornmeal, flour, salt, and seasoning in a bowl. Pour peanut oil up to ½ inch in a large skillet. Set the pan over medium high heat until a small amount of flour dropped into the oil sizzles immediately. Dredge each shrimp into egg and then cornmeal mixture. Shake off excess and fry until golden brown on both sides. Set the fried shrimp aside on paper towels.

Directions for Assembling the Sliders

Slice the dinner rolls in half almost all the way through. Spread remoulade on both the top and bottom. Spread a layer of lettuce shreds on bottom. Arrange shrimp on lettuce and top with a slice of tomato and then a slice of onion. Press the top of the bread on top of the onion. Serve immediately.

This isn't a traditional Gullah recipe, but it's Gullah in two ways. The ingredients reflect Gullah influence, and it was created by Rizzie, a true Gullah lady who grew up on Surcie Island off the coast of South Carolina.

RECIPES FOR DISHES FROM CALLIE'S PREVIOUS BOOKS

I had so much fun putting together some of my favorite recipes from Pa and Rizzie that I decided to add some dishes from Callie's earlier mysteries.

Mother Hubbard Has A CORPSE IN THE CUPBOARD

CATFISH STEW

Pa's Uncle Pee Wee died before we kids were old enough to get to know him, but he was one of Pa's favorite relatives. Pa says, "Uncle Pee Wee was a man who always had a cigar in his mouth and a guitar in his hands. He made the best catfish stew around these parts." I've been lots of places and tasted lots of stews. Some have tomatoes and are redder, and some are chunkier with cubed potatoes, but Pa's is best, and his is made like his Uncle Pee Wee taught him.

UNCLE PEE WEE'S CATFISH STEW

The way Pa makes it from the recipe Uncle Pee Wee wrote on a brown paper sack for him.

Ingredients
6 slices fatback (can substitute bacon if necessary)
12 pounds whole catfish, skinned and gutted
5 pounds raw potatoes
5 pounds onions
2 jars ketchup, 28 ounce size
1 small can tomato paste
1 small bottle Lea & Perrins Worcestershire Sauce
Salt, pepper, and hot sauce to taste

Directions
Boil the catfish in enough water to cover them. Cool and

debone the fish. Peel *and* grate the potatoes. Peel and finely chop onions. Fry fatback or bacon. Eat fatback or bacon. Pour grease from fatback or bacon into the water the catfish were boiled in. Add onions and potatoes to fish stock and return deboned fish to pot. Add other ingredients except salt, pepper. Simmer covered for several hours or all day, stirring often. Add salt and pepper to taste. Finished stew should be more orange than red and because of long, slow cooking will have fantastic flavor. If stew seems too watery, remove the lid for part of the cooking time. Pa cooks this in a 30-gallon pot, preferably over a gas burner in the yard but it can be done on the kitchen stove.

If you want to try an easier version that makes about enough for 6 to 8 people, try mine:

LAZY MAN'S CATFISH STEW

Ingredients

2 pounds catfish fillets
1½ quarts water
1 20-ounce refrigerated bag grated potatoes*
1 10-ounce bag frozen chopped onions
1 8-ounce cup ketchup
2 tablespoons tomato paste
¼ cup Worcestershire Sauce**
1½ tablespoons salt
¾ tablespoon pepper
¾ tablespoon hot sauce

Directions

Place catfish fillets in water in big soup pot or Dutch oven and put a lid on it. Bring the fillets to a low boil, then reduce heat and let the water simmer until the fish flakes easily. Add the potatoes and onions. Simmer another 30 minutes. Add all other ingredients. Cover and cook on low heat for several hours. Taste and adjust seasoning if needed. Simmer until dinnertime.

*I use Simply Potatoes Shredded Hash Browns from the refrigerated section of the grocery store.

**Pa uses Lea & Perrins Worcestershire Sauce since Uncle Pee Wee insisted on that brand. I use whatever brand I have on hand.

Twinkle, Twinkle, Little Star, THERE'S A BODY IN THE CAR

Here's Jane's recipe for lemon bars. She was given this recipe by a wonderful lady in Columbia, South Carolina—Mrs. Nina Long.

JANE'S LUSCIOUS LEMON SQUARES

Ingredients

1 cup butter, softened
2 cups plain flour
½ cup confectioners' sugar
4 eggs
2 cups granulated sugar
6 tablespoons fresh lemon juice
1 tablespoon. plain flour
½ teaspoon baking powder

Directions

Preheat the oven to 325° F. Mix butter, 2 cups flour and ½ cup confectioners' sugar and press into 13x9-inch lightly greased or sprayed baking pan. Bake at 325° for 15 minutes—no longer. The pastry will be pale in color. Beat eggs, add granulated sugar, lemon juice, 1 tablespoon flour and baking powder. Mix well. Pour over the baked pastry. Return to the oven and bake at 325° for 40 to 50 minutes. Sprinkle with confectioners' sugar as it cools. Allow to cool completely before cutting into squares. Yields 24 to 36 depending upon size of squares.

CALLIE'S LEMON BAR RECIPES

Ingredients and Directions

1. Go to grocery store. Buy Betty Crocker or other brand box of Lemon Bar Mix. Follow directions.

2. Go to bakery. Buy lemon squares. Take them home. Remove lemon squares from bakery box and arrange attractively on your best cake platter. Throw away the bakery box. A sprinkle of confectioners' sugar makes them look more homemade.

PIMIENTO CHICKEN

There are many recipes on the Internet for Pimento Chicken. Note that some of them spell pimiento with the second "i" and some don't. I do because that's how I want to do it. Most include cheese and some kind of canned soup. The recipe that Jane uses has neither, but it's much older, yet simple, easy, and delicious. She got this recipe from Maum, who got it from Ms. Linda Derrick, who got it from Mrs. Jessie Grooms Jones.

JANE'S PIMIENTO CHICKEN

Ingredients

6 tablespoons butter or margarine
6 tablespoons flour (plain or self-rising)
1½ cups chicken broth
1 cup half and half (or low fat milk for lighter sauce)
1 cup diced cooked chicken
½ cup (4-ounce jar) diced pimiento
Salt and pepper

Directions

Melt the butter and brown the flour in it. Cook the flour and butter over low heat till it bubbles. Stir in the chicken broth and milk or cream and increase heat to medium. Boil gently for 1 minute stirring constantly. Reduce heat to low. Add the diced chicken and pimiento. Stir and heat throughout. Taste and add salt and pepper as you like. Be sure to taste before adding salt because chicken broth may have salt in it, especially if you make the broth from bouillon. Serve over toast. To fancy it up, cut the toast into triangles. Pimiento Chicken may also be served in small pastry cups.

CALLIE'S PIMIENTO CHICKEN POT PIE

Ingredients

1 recipe of Jane's Pimiento Chicken (Use recipe above or get Jane to cook it for you.)
1 frozen pie shell or refrigerated rolled crust and pie dish
2 cups mixed vegetables (drained if canned, pre-cooked by directions on bag and drained if frozen)

Directions

Preheat the oven to 400° F. Set frozen or rolled piecrust out to come to room temperature. Warm Jane's Pimiento Chicken on medium heat to slow bubble and then turn off the heat. If using a frozen piecrust, empty it from the aluminum pie dish onto a plate. If using refrigerated rolled crust, nothing is needed at this time. Stir the drained vegetables into Jane's Pimiento Chicken and pour the mixture into a pie dish. Spread your pie shell over the top of the Pimiento Chicken, crinkling the crust at the edges. With a fork or knife, pierce crust in several places. Bake at 400° about twenty minutes until the crust is light brown.

Winning Cookie Recipes from
Rub, a Dub, Dub, DEAD MAN IN A TUB
(Previously published as *CASKET CASE*)

PHYLLIS COUNTS'S WEDDING COOKIES

She borrowed this recipe from Mrs. Hillis Lundin.

Ingredients
1 cup butter
½ cup white sugar
2 teaspoons vanilla
2 teaspoons water
2 cups all-purpose flour
1 cup chopped pecans
½ cup confectioners' sugar

Directions

Preheat the oven to 325° F. Cream the butter and non-confectioners' sugar together. Stir in the vanilla and water. Mix in the flour and nuts until they're well blended. Cover and chill for 3 hours or more. Shape dough into balls about ¾-inch in diameter (about the size of an ordinary strawberry). Place on an ungreased cookie sheet. Bake 15 to 20 minutes. Place cookies on wire rack to cool. Roll in confectioners' sugar and store in an airtight container at room temperature with an extra helping of confectioners' sugar, which some cooks claim extends their longevity though these cookies are too good to stay in the container very long!

BENNE WAFERS

Benne is the Bantu word for sesame and was brought to America from East Africa in the seventeenth century during the slave trade era. The herb was planted throughout the South, and benne wafers are still sold in the Low Country. There are many slight variations to this recipe, but this is the one Jane entered in the cookie contest.

JANE BAKER'S BENNE WAFERS

Ingredients
1 cup benne (sesame) seeds
¾ cup softened butter
1½ cups brown sugar (packed firmly)

2 eggs
1 teaspoon vanilla extract
1½ cup all-purpose flour
¼ teaspoon salt
¼ teaspoon baking powder

Directions

Preheat the oven to 325° F. Spread benne (sesame) seeds on ungreased baking sheet and toast 12 minutes until light brown. (You may also buy toasted sesame seeds in some Asian food stores.) Mix all ingredients until combined in a large bowl. Cream brown sugar and butter. Add all other ingredients in the order listed and mix well. Drop dough by ½ teaspoonfuls about 1½ inches apart on lightly greased baking sheet. Bake 7 to 10 minutes until light brown. Remove from oven and let cookies cool 2 or 3 minutes before placing on wire racks to cool completely. Store in airtight container.

Hey, Diddle, Diddle
THE CORPSE AND THE FIDDLE

Surprise recipes from Callie of all people!

As everyone knows, Callie is not a great cook like Jane and Rizzie, so she looks for easy, foolproof recipes. This one has been around for ages and goes by different names, but this is the only pie Callie makes, and she calls it:

MY PIE

Ingredients

3 egg whites at room temperature
1 cup granulated sugar or Splenda
20 Ritz crackers
½ cup pecans or walnuts, chopped coarsely
½ teaspoon vanilla
1 pint Cool Whip or real whipped cream*

Directions

Preheat the oven to 350° F. Spray an 8-inch pie plate very lightly with Pam or similar spray. Put Ritz crackers in a plastic zippered bag and mash with a rolling pin until finely crushed. Beat the egg whites in a medium size bowl until they peak. Gently fold the crushed crackers, chopped nuts, and vanilla into the stiff egg whites. Spread the mixture in the pie pan and bake 25 to 30 minutes. Let the pie cool in the pan. Refrigerate, preferably overnight. Spread with Cool Whip or whipped cream before slicing and serving.

Note: Callie sometimes doubles this recipe and bakes it in a 9x13-inch pan.

*Callie likes the whipped cream that comes in a can because she likes to squirt it onto the pie in concentric circles. At times, she puts chopped nuts and/or cherries on top of the whipped cream.

BETTER MOONPIES

Just when you think something can't get any better, you find out it can!!! Sheriff Harmon says he loves MoonPies just as much as Callie does. He suggests that barely warming the MoonPie makes it even more delish. He recommends 8 seconds in the microwave for one regular sized MoonPie. Callie likes minis and 5 to 6 seconds makes a MiniMoon Pie a perfect delight! (They both remove the plastic and wrap their MoonPies loosely in paper towels before putting them in the microwave.)

EVEN BETTER MOONPIES

A very dear, sweet lady named Colleen Robinson Baker died young, way too young. Her daughter told me she thinks of her mom every time the advertisement comes on about the people bumping into each other while one's eating peanut butter and the other has chocolate. Years before that commercial, Mrs. Baker liked to spread peanut butter on top of her MoonPies. Callie tried it—absolutely yummy!

BEST EVER MOONPIES

Mrs. Baker's early death came before microwaves became commonplace in homes. After hearing how Mrs. Baker liked her MoonPies, Callie went one step beyond. She spread peanut butter on top of her MoonPie before she put it in the microwave. The peanut butter came out too drippy. She found perfection when she smeared peanut butter across the MoonPie as soon as she took it from the microwave. Warm graham crackers, chocolate, gooey marshmallow cream, and slightly melted peanut butter. It doesn't get any better than that!

Jane's Recipes from *A Tisket, a Tasket, A FANCY STOLEN CASKET*

JANE'S KILLER MEATBALL STEW

Ingredients

1 pound prepared cocktail-sized meatballs (frozen are fine)
1½ cups diced onions, preferably red
3 or 4 chopped large cloves of garlic
2 tablespoons olive oil
2 cups zucchini, sliced and halved into crescents
½ cup thinly sliced carrots
3 cups canned diced tomatoes in juice
4 cups meat broth (Jane uses 2 cups ham and 2 cups chicken)
5 tablespoons tomato paste (may use Italian seasoned)

1 teaspoon Italian seasoning
1 tablespoon parsley flakes
3 tablespoons dried sweet basil
1 teaspoon salt
2 teaspoons pepper
Optional:
1 teaspoon sugar, shredded mozzarella and/or grated Parmesan cheese and/or fresh chopped parsley

Directions

In a large soup pot with a lid, put the olive oil, onions, and garlic. Sauté them on low to medium low heat until soft—about 15 to 20 minutes. Be careful not to burn. Add the canned tomatoes, broth, and seasonings to the pot and bring to a low boil. Add the carrots and zucchini. Stir in the tomato paste. Taste and add 1 teaspoon of sugar if desired. Cut the heat to low or medium low and add the meatballs. Cover and simmer 20 minutes or more. Taste. Salt and pepper quantities are suggested, but adjust these to your own taste. Spoon the stew into soup bowls or cups. Sprinkle shredded mozzarella, grated Parmesan cheese, and fresh parsley over the soup if desired. Killer!

*Make or buy the meatballs. If using homemade meatballs, cook per recipe. Jane uses bought frozen Italian meatballs directly from the freezer.

JANE'S TO DIE FOR LASAGNA

Ingredients

8 ounces lasagna noodles
1 pound sweet or hot Italian sausage*
1 cup chopped onion
1 teaspoon garlic, chopped
1 jar 26-ounce prepared spaghetti sauce**
1 cup ricotta cheese
1 cup small-curd cottage cheese

2 eggs, beaten
1 teaspoon salt
½ teaspoon pepper
1 cup Parmesan cheese, grated
2 cups mozzarella cheese, shredded

Directions

Preheat oven to 375° F. Prepare the lasagna noodles by the directions on package. Cook the sausage with onions and garlic over medium heat, stirring to mix as it cooks. When meat is done, drain off fat and discard, then stir in spaghetti sauce, cover, and simmer 10 minutes. Drain with colander, saving juice. Pour enough sauce juice to cover bottom of 9x13-inch baking dish. Layer lasagna noodles to cover. Layer half of the drained sauce mix on top of the noodles. This will be thick. In a separate bowl, mix the Ricotta cheese, cottage cheese, beaten eggs, salt and pepper. Spoon half of the cheese mixture over the sauce. Sprinkle with one-half of Parmesan cheese, then one-half of the mozzarella cheese over the Parmesan. Repeat layers beginning with noodles. Bake 30 minutes covered with aluminum foil. Remove foil and bake 15 more minutes. Allow to stand 10 to 15 minutes to set before serving.

*Callie and Jane like hot Italian sausage removed from casings or you may use swet Italian sausage or substitute ham-burger, ground turkey, spinach, or zucchini.

**Jane prefers a 3 to 6 cheese prepared spaghetti sauce straight from the grocer's shelf.

THE BOYS' FRIED FISH

Ingredients

Fish—as many as you caught or froze and defrosted to feed your crowd. Pan fish about the size of a man's hand are fried whole. Great big, bragging-sized fish are filleted.

Oil—enough to just about fill up approximately ¾ depth of black, cast-iron Dutch oven. The Boys prefer peanut oil.

Brown paper grocery bags—what you get if you say, "Paper" when the grocery attendant asks, "Paper or plastic?"

Cornmeal—a little for a few fish, a lot for many fish—The Boys use self-rising yellow cornmeal. You might start with a cup of cornmeal in a paper bag and add more as needed. Cornmeal that has been used in the bag must be thrown out after all fish are ready.

Salt and pepper

Directions

Step 1. Catch or thaw the fish

Step 2. Scale, gut, decapitate and cut the fish, then wash. (If these are catfish, skin instead of scaling.)

Step 3. Heat oil to HOT. (To test heat, drop a big pinch of cornmeal in the oil. If hot enough, the oil will bubble around it immediately.)

Step 4. Dump a cup of cornmeal into a paper sack. To cornmeal, add salt and pepper to taste.

Step 5. Drop two or three fish into sack of cornmeal. Hold top closed and shake.

Step 6. Remove fish from sack and drop carefully into hot oil so the oil doesn't splatter onto the cook. Oil should be hot enough to bubble around the fish. Remove the fish from the oil and spread them out on paper bags (or paper towels if you're fussy) when the fish are golden brown. Repeat until enough fish are fried.

Serve with hush puppies and hot grits with butter.

About the Author

Fran Rizer is the author of the Callie Parrish Mysteries. She lives in Columbia, South Carolina, near her sons and grandson. To learn more or correspond with her, visit her website: www.franrizer.com.

CPSIA information can be obtained at www.ICGtesting.com
Printed in the USA
LVOW11s2013151214

418956LV00001B/48/P